W9-BCL-689

# CUTTLEFISH

# CUTTLEFISH

## Dave Freer

an imprint of Prometheus Books
Amherst, NY

Published 2012 by Pyr®, an imprint of Prometheus Books

Cover illustration © Paul Young
Jacket design by Nicole Sommer Lecht

Inquiries should be addressed to
Pyr
59 John Glenn Drive
Amherst, New York 14228–2119
VOICE: 716–691–0133
FAX: 716–691–0137
WWW.PYRSF.COM

16 15 14 13 12    5 4 3 2 1

Library of Congress Cataloging-in-Publication Data

Freer, Dave.
    Cuttlefish / by Dave Freer.
        p. cm. — (Drowning empire ; bk. 1)
    Summary: In an alternate 1976 dominated by coal power and the British Empire, Clara Calland and her mother, an important scientist, embark on a treacherous journey toward freedom in Westralia aboard a smugglers' submarine, the Cuttlefish, pursued by Menshevik spies and Imperial soldiers.
    ISBN 978–1–61614–625–2 (cloth)
    ISBN 978–1–61614–626–9 (ebook)
    [1. Science fiction. 2. Submarines (Ships)—Fiction. 3. Mothers and daughters—Fiction. 4. Voyages and travels—Fiction.] I. Title.

PZ7.F8788Cut 2012
    [Fic]—dc23

                                                                    2012000417

Printed in the United States of America

*To my beloved Goddaughters, Emily and Teagan.*
*May your stars always burn bright and cast a wide and beautiful light.*

# ACKNOWLEDGMENTS

No book is ever just poured out of an author. *Cuttlefish* is no different in that respect anyway. It owes its existence to my agent, Mike Kabongo, and to my editor, Lou Anders. Lou is the kind of editor most new authors dream they'll get when they venture into being published, and I'm glad it's happened to me at last.

The *Cuttlefish* is the submarine you get when a scientist spends too much time talking to an inventor about ways to do things in a coal-powered universe. I love talking to a guy who doesn't say "You can't do that," but helps me think of ways that allow me to do it plausibly. Thank you, Peter.

And always, this book would not be without Barbara.

# CHAPTER 1

It was after midnight, and London's lights shimmered on the waters that had once been her streets. Something dark moved down there, in the murky depths. Bubbles of smoke belched up in its wake. No one was likely to notice. The still, warm air already reeked of coal smoke, and the rotting ooze lying down on the drowned street that had once been Landsdown Way bubbled anyway.

The dark shadow crept onwards into Wandsworth Canal, and down into Nine Elms Waterway, and then slipped through the rotting concrete teeth into the deep channel.

Like the rest of the crew of the *Cuttlefish*, Tim Barnabas let out a sigh of relief. He knew all about the dangers of the Stockwell tube run—dead trees, fallen masonry, and, of course, the chance of detection in the relatively shallow waters of London's street-canals. Even though the submarines of the Underpeople did this run often, it was still the most risky part of their journey.

"Up snuiver, Seaman," said Captain Malkis. "Let's breathe before we head down-channel."

Tim worked the brass crank with a will, sending the breathing pipe to the surface of the Thames.

He swallowed hard to sort out the effect of the pressure change on his ears.

And then an explosion rocked the *Cuttlefish*. Rang the sub like a bell. Tim could hear nothing. But he saw Captain Malkis push the dive levers to full.

A blast of water sprayed out of the snuiver outlet, soaking them all, before the cutoff valve closed it off. The *Cuttlefish* settled onto the bottom of the dredged channel. No one moved or spoke. Tim's ears still rang, but he could hear sounds again, and saw the captain signal to the Marconi man hunched protectively over the dials and valves of his wireless set. The Marconi operator nodded, wound his spooler, and sent an aerial wire up to the surface.

Tim watched the man's face in the dim glow of the battery lights. His expression grew increasingly bleak. He flicked the dial expertly to another frequency. Then the Marconi operator pulled the headphones off. "I got the Clapham Common sender first. Transmission cut out after an SOS. I picked up Parson's Green. They weren't even sending coded messages. Just reports that Stockwell's been blown, and Clapham had reported that they were under attack by men of the Royal Inniskillen Fusiliers, before they went off air, Captain. And I picked up a signal on the Royal Navy calling channel. The HMS *Mornington* and the HMS *Torquay* are ordered to start laying dropping mines in the Thames Channel from Blackfriars Point to Rotherhithe Bay. The captain of the *Mornington* was getting mighty shirty about the operation not running according to orders, and him still being below Plumstead Shoal and not on station."

Captain Malkis's face showed no trace of expression. They all knew that the Inniskillens were Duke Malcolm's special troops. As the chief of Imperial Intelligence, the duke had made them into a regiment to be feared. "Get the aerial and the snuiver down, crewmen." He turned to the engine-room speaker tube. "Chief Engineer. I'll have all the power that you can give us. Mr. Mate." He turned to First Mate Werner. "You work out our time to the mouth of the Lea. We'll see how they like risking their ships in the Canningtown shallows."

"Captain . . . should we not go back?" asked the first mate, his voice cracking, his heavy Dutch accent even thicker than usual.

"No, Mr. Mate," said Malkis. "It's us . . . or rather our passenger, that they're after. It's just as well that we set our departure forward as soon as the Callands arrived."

Tim cranked the snuiver in. He could feel the heavy, slow thump of the *Cuttlefish*'s engines picking up speed. The breathing pipe clicked home. "Snuiver down, Captain," he said, trying to keep his voice as controlled as the ship's master. It quavered slightly. But he didn't scream. He didn't say, "My mam. I need to go back to the tunnels to see if she's all right," although those were the words that wanted out, and his fear dried his mouth and made it hard to speak.

"Good lad, Barnabas," said the captain, as if this was something that happened every day. "Get down to Chief Barstone in the engine room. He'll have work for an extra greaser if he's going to keep the engines running at this speed."

"Aye, aye, sir." Tim did his best to salute without bumping any of the brass instruments that protruded into the small bridge space.

He turned to leave. "Barnabas." The captain's voice halted him.

"Sir." Tim halted.

"The Underpeople have more tunnels, and locks, and secret ways than the king's men know about, boy," the captain said, reaching out to squeeze his shoulder gently but firmly. "It's our home, our territory; we know it. It's not the first time Duke Malcolm's had a go at us. And it won't be the last. Now get along with you."

Tim swallowed. Nodded. He couldn't actually say anything, because his voice was too choked up. He turned away before the captain could see the tears starting, and hurried along the narrow gangway, and then down the ladder to the lower deck. At the base of it he nearly ran smash into something that had no place on a submarine.

A girl. A girl in a flouncy dress with silly little puff sleeves. Honestly! Where did she think she was? On a pleasure barge cruising along Pall Mall Canal?

"Hi, hold on," she said, grabbing his arm as he tried to squirm past. Her blue eyes were bright and wide with excitement, and one of her pale blonde plaits had come undone. She brushed the fine hair away from her eyes, "What's going on?" she asked, smiling at him.

"I'm busy," he said gruffly, hoping that he'd wiped all trace of the tears away. "Got to get to the engine room."

"Oh, it's so important that you are," she said, teasingly. "Just tell me what the bang was?"

"The Inniskillens blowing up my home," he said fiercely as he pulled his arm free and blundered on, blinded by the tears again, down the passage.

Clara Calland stared after him. She nearly ran after him too, to ask him what he meant. But . . . horrible snotty London boy. He'd looked nice, with a bit of a grin on his brownish face, when she'd seen him earlier, bringing their two small valises to the cabin. And he'd helped to carry Mother's book trunk. When you considered the size of the cabin, maybe it was just as well they'd had to leave everything behind.

She considered going up the ladder to find someone else to ask. But . . . it sounded like trouble. More trouble. She'd been so relieved when they had finally got out of the smelly, wet tunnels under London, and into this strange submarine. The whole idea just fascinated her. Of course, submarines were something she'd heard stories about, and hadn't ever expected to really experience. They were illegal, banned in all civilized countries. Yet . . . everyone knew they existed. One of the girls from school, one of the Cashel sisters, claimed that she'd once seen one in Tralee Bay. Which was possible . . . anything could happen down in Kerry. It was crock full of rebels, down there, like Cork used to be before most of the city got drowned. She swallowed. Daddy had once let slip that his trips away had taken him to Kerry. She'd said that she hoped he was safe from those rebel scum. He'd just tousled her hair and laughed. That was before the men from Scotland Yard had come and taken him to the New East Barracks military prison, to be detained indefinitely at His Majesty's pleasure.

She stared blindly down the narrow little passage. She didn't want to be here. She wanted her old, familiar life back again. Mother and Dad together again, home and school and . . .

That was where it broke down. Clara, who always tried to be honest with herself, had to admit that she did not want her school life back. Nor did she want to go back to the tall, cold house on Redmond Street that they'd been living in when her life had suddenly turned upside down.

So, instead, she went back through the narrow little steel door and climbed up onto her bunk in their broom-cupboard-sized cabin. On the bed below, her mother was asleep, the deep sleep of absolute exhaustion, and, Clara realised, of relief.

Clara lay down on the thin horse-hair mattress and thought back about just how they'd ended up here. Parts of it cut at her like a knife.

# CHAPTER 2

On the day it had all started, Clara had not wanted to leave school. It was not that St. Margaret's School for the Children of Officers and Gentlemen in Fermoy, Cork, Ireland, was a place that she loved. She detested every inch of it, from the courtyard with its limp Union Jack, surrounded by three stories of clattering corridors and class-rooms, to the coal cellar that Ellen—helped by the three terrors—had pushed her into last week. Clara knew that she should keep quiet, keep her head down . . . but she wasn't good at that. And the girls on the top of the pile were bigger than her, better at sports, popular with boys and with the teachers . . . but stupid, too.

Well, the library—with its tall stacks of slightly musty leather-bound books—mostly fifty years old, and, often as not, from parts of the Empire that had vanished beneath the waves in the Big Melt—was the all right part of the school. It had books and protection, in the shape of a librarian on duty. Besides, going in there was some-thing the popular girls wouldn't be caught dead doing. So Clara had been lurking in between the stacks. She'd been looking at a book on the Australian Colonies, complete with pictures of funny-looking black men with painted throwing sticks and very few clothes.

No decent Englishman would be seen like that! Not even at New Brighton! The other girls would at least pretend to be shocked. That, and the angry expression on the man's face, made Clara curious enough to start reading. She'd read all the fiction in the place years ago, and besides, it was about a place that was a long way away, a place where she was unlikely to meet other St. Margaret's girls and be jeered at or, worse, sniffed at and turned away from. Books like this were good for dreams. She'd like to go there. . . . It would be far enough away from home so she would not have to explain to her mother that she had got a B for chemistry in the latest set of tests. It didn't matter that she'd got 98% for mathematics, no.

She looked at the leather cover: *Queensland, the Dominion of Australia. Its People and the Quaint Customs of the Native Inhabitants.* A place on the other side of the world . . . it would be far away from anyone who knew that her father was in prison. Clara wasn't sure if they regarded that as any better than her mother being divorced, but she knew that when you added the two together it made her life in Fermoy, and at St. Margaret's, barely worth living.

Then, to her utter horror, she'd heard her mother's voice. "Is my daughter Clara here?"

Did she *have* to come here?

"Yes, Dr. Calland." The librarian sniffed. "I believe Miss Calland is in the geography section." Disapproval was written clearly in the librarian's tone. Parents, even the daughters of an original founding lady-governor, were not welcome on the school grounds. They should hand over their child at the gate, and their money at the front office, and that was it. A divorced mother, wandering around unaccompanied, would be as welcome at St. Margaret's as leprosy.

What was her mother doing here? Clara wondered, caught between irritation and sudden fear. Something must be wrong. She should be at work, in her laboratory at Imperial Chemicals and Dyes.

Clara's mother was tall, elegant, and all the other things Clara had decided she wasn't ever going to grow up to be: womanly, and a research chemist. Her mother's hair was always so precisely pinned up, especially when she went out . . . but it definitely was not in perfect order right now. And she was very pale. The moment her mother stepped around the stack, Clara knew that something was very wrong.

The fact that she put her finger to her lips was also somewhat of a clue. "Ah, Clara," said her mother, a little too loudly and cheerfully, quite unlike herself. "You must come with me right now. I have a motoring car waiting out front."

A car? Almost no one had one of those. The trams ran well and to time. Fuel for motoring cars was ruinously expensive too. Well, in the British Empire. It was said that in America even a lot of ordinary people owned cars. The idea of going in one was rather exciting. "Yes, Mother," she said, doing her best to sound like a good St. Margaret's girl. "I must just take out my library books and collect my satchel."

"You can do that tomorrow, Clara. I am going to Belfast now, and I need to make certain arrangements," her mother said, firmly, while shaking her head and beckoning, a pleading expression on her face.

Clara got the message. She still wasn't sure what it meant. But she was perfectly happy to leave her satchel, and the chemistry test inside it—which had to be signed by her mother—behind. The library books were a bit more of a wrench. She put the book back in its place on the shelf and took her mother's outstretched hand.

Really. Holding hands. As if she were a little girl or something. But the look on her mother's face made her take it. Mother's hand was cold and damp.

Dr. Calland smiled politely at the sour-faced librarian, and led her out. Down the corridor. And then . . . away from the front gate.

"It's the other way," said Clara.

Her mother shook her head. "I'll explain when I have a chance. Come with me, Clara. Just come along without arguing, just this once, please."

That had been enough to get Clara to follow her into the junior teachers' common room. It was empty right now. They were all away taking luncheon at the dining hall.

On the far side of the room was a little fire escape door next to the class racks. Clara's mother reached over the top of the cast iron fretwork on the edge of the rack of workbooks waiting to be marked.

She felt about . . . and took down a key. She breathed a sigh of relief. "I was worried someone might have dusted and found it. Oh well. It's only been sixteen years."

She fitted the key into the lock of a door marked FIRE ESCAPE, DO NOT LOCK. Clara noticed that her mother's hands were trembling slightly. The little door creaked open. "They removed the key of the fire escape door because the headmistress found out that we'd been using it to sneak in when we were late for chapel and assembly," said her mother, with almost a hint of a smile. "I had had two spare keys cut, because I knew someone was bound to tumble to our using it. It'll serve them right if the place catches fire and they all roast."

Clara knew that her mother had taught here at St. Margaret's, back while she'd been a student. The idea of her being late for anything, or even doing something as . . . well, as underhand as that was quite strange, though. Parents didn't, did they? At least, not her mother. She was always so . . . proper.

They went through the doorway and out onto the landing, and her mother carefully locked the door behind them. That was more like her mother, than sneaking in late for assembly! The steep, rusty steel fire escape led down the outside of the old brick back wall facing the camogie fields, with the canal path beyond them.

"It's to be hoped that they keep watching the gate. I told them it could take a little time to get you out of there," said Clara's mother. "Here." She dug into her handbag and pulled out a pair of kerchiefs. Handed one to Clara. "Put one over your hair," she said hastily, shaking the other out. "We're too obvious with our blonde heads."

Clara was shocked. "We'll look like gypsies, Mother!" Being blonde in Ireland announced that you were possibly English or German. No one would hide that! Otherwise you might be thought to be merely Irish.

"Good. They're not looking for gypsies," her mother answered, tying the kerchief in place. "I wish I'd thought of shawls."

They made their way down the narrow stair and along the weedy edge of the third-team camogie field. There was a gap in the privet hedge at the far end of the field that girls who wanted to avoid camogie practice used to slip away through.

Clara knew it well.

It appeared that her mother must have known it too. It had proved to be quite a day for ruining the ideas she'd had about her parent.

They were squeezing through the gap when someone yelled behind them. It didn't sound like the King's English. "They're onto us," said Mother, pushing her forward. Clara had been trying to avoid ripping her school skirt, up to that point. It was obvious that her mother, who normally would have had words with her about tears or stains, didn't care right now.

There was a coal barge heading away from the Blackwater toward Factory Town, with its smokestack dribbling dirty smoke from the cheap brown coal.

"Thank heavens," said her mother. "Run Clara. Jump onto her. Tell Padraig to hide you. I'll try and head them off. I'll find you later."

"But—"

"Just go!" Clara saw, to her horror, that her mother, a lifelong pacifist, was taking a gun out of her purse.

Clara recognised it. It was her father's. She remembered the fight between her parents—because he'd dared to bring such a thing into the house—far too well to ever forget it. But surely he'd . . . he'd had it with him when he'd been arrested?

Mother's hands were shaking. "Go, Clara. Please!"

Biting her lip, Clara backed away. But she did not run. She wasn't sure why she didn't. Her mother had obviously gone mad, and was aiming the gun back through the scraggly privet. There was a bang. Her mother turned—even whiter in the face than before. "I thought I told you to run. Go. *Now!*"

"Come with me. Please. Please!"

Then there was the sound of several shots from back near the school, and a sudden crack of branches and a scattering of leaves.

And then a shrill whistle sounded, and someone shouted, "Stand! In the name of the King. Hold your fire!"

More shots were fired in answer to that, as her mother snatched her hand. "Hopefully they'll keep each other busy. Let's run. Next time please do what I tell you, Clara. This is not the time or place to argue."

They ran. The unfamiliar barge was already picking up speed, running barely a yard off the canal margin. A black-faced bargee beckoned furiously, and they jumped aboard. "Get down among the coal, like. Be quick about it," he said hastily. "Mad girl. Shooting! There be trouble about this."

Following her mother's lead, Clara burrowed down into the small lumps of coal, trying to dig her way into it.

It was black, dirty coal, and then the bargee took a shovel and poured it over them. And then more. And more. He was not that gentle about it. "Black your face," said the mother who normally told her to wash it.

The canal was a busy place, with barges pushing along both ways, as they slowly moved further from the school. "Squirm down as much as you can. And then keep still," hissed her mother.

The thumping of the engine's pistons slowed. "Face down. Keep dead still," said the bargee quietly.

Clara heard an angry English-accented voice, panting. "Why didn't you stop immediately?"

"Well, I'd like to have stopped immediately for you, sorr," said the bargee, in a slow drawl, his accent so thick as to make him hard to understand. "But t'irty-foive tons of coal keeps moving for a while, like. So, it's sorry that I am. But a barge isn't like your motorbicycle, Lieutenant. Can't start fast, can't stop fast. Can't do anything fast."

"Pah. Mind your cheek, you Irish scum," said the young officer, "or I'll have you locked up for disrespecting an officer. Now, I'm to search your vessel for a woman and a young girl."

"Be my guest, sorr," said the bargee. "No one in my cabin, as you can see, eh? T'eyre not here, unless t'ey're lying on my coal. But look for yerself, sorr. Maybe t'ey're buried in it. Here's a shovel if you'd like to dig t'rough it all."

There was the meaty sound of a slap. "I warned you not to give me any more of your lip. I'll take you with me . . ."

"And what'll you do with t' barge, sorr? Nowt to tie her to here. She'll drift. Likely to block the canal. Colonel'll have t'at shiny pip off of your shoulder for t'at, I'm t'inking," said the bargee, calmly.

There was a pause. An exasperated sigh. "Get on your way, then."

"Why t'ank you, sorr," said the bargee with mocking politeness. "I'll be doing t'at if you'd get off of my barge, like."

A few moments later the big pistons began clanking again and the vessel shuddered and pushed on through the water.

"Stay down," said the bargee quietly. So they did. The journey seemed endless.

"We're coming up to Mag's crib. Get yourselves off. And good luck," said the bargee.

They scrambled up out of the coal and leapt out onto the muddy bank, which was here overhung by willow trees. There was a half-tumbled-down thatched cottage just beyond the trees, and her mother, as coal-black now as the angry-looking man from Queensland in the book had been, led them through the tangle of mallows and bramble towards it.

Someone must have been watching, because the door opened before they got to it. "Get inside wit' you," said the old woman in the doorway, hastily, peering around for any watchers. They scrambled in and she closed the door and bolted it behind them. There was not much light inside, with what little there was coming from a fire and two very small deep-inset windows, and it was hard to see much. But the poverty was obvious.

The old woman pointed at a wooden settle. "Sit you down. Padraig will be along soon."

"Mother, what's going on?" Clara asked, as soon as they'd sat down.

Her mother was silent for a while, and Clara was about to ask again when she said, quietly, "I . . . I made a mistake. I've got into a situation where they're going to kidnap me, or if they can't do that, kill me. And they want to take you to use as a lever on me, darling. They told me I should cooperate or you'd be hurt."

"Who?" asked Clara.

"The Mensheviks. And now it seems as if the agents of Imperial Intelligence are after us too. The Russians brought me to the school to fetch you. But of course, the school porters won't allow men inside the gates of an all-girls school. I told the Russians you were doing some extra lessons, and it would take me a few minutes to get you out. They told me I'd have to hurry because Imperial Intelligence had just raided our house."

"Oh." Clara swallowed. She barely knew who the Mensheviks were, other than Russians. But she certainly knew who Imperial Intelligence were. They had arrested her father. "Who . . . who are these people? The bargee . . . this old woman? And what are we going to do?"

"Friends of your father's," said mother, in that grim, defensive tone she always used when she mentioned him. "Friends of my mother's—your grandmother—too."

"She was a fine lady," said the old woman, nodding, smiling, showing missing teeth. "Had her heart in the right place. And don't you worry, dearie. Padraig will sort it all out."

Her mother said nothing. But Clara felt her mother's hand tense in hers.

The old lady went back to peering out of the small window. "If the polis come you'll be away through the back." She pointed to a small door. "There's a crawlway under the briars."

But all that came for them was the bargee, Padraig. He'd cleaned his hands and face, and changed his clothes. And by the way he spoke, he was no bargee after all. The thick Irish accent had all but vanished. He grinned at them. "You're a sight, the pair of you. Well, you'd better stay that way. I've organised transport to a safe house for you. But it's in a tink's cart, so you may as well look the part. Although you're even a bit dirty for it."

"And then, Padraig?" asked her mother. There was a real edge to her voice.

"We're arranging things. You've caused quite a stir, Dr. Calland. Fortunately, it seems that there are still people keen to give you shelter. And not just, like me, because of Jack."

Mother said nothing. But her hand tensed again.

Jack was Clara's father's name.

Lying on her narrow bunk in the submarine Clara could hear the boom of explosions echoing through the steel walls. She wished that she knew what they were and what was happening. But, as with much of this journey, she didn't. And she didn't know who to ask, since that boy had plainly not been going to talk to her. It was hard with no one her own age to ask, she thought, suddenly irritated all over again by how adults tended to fob you off, telling you that you were too young. Not too young for the problems and consequences of things, just too young to be told exactly what was going on. She'd badly wanted to know more about Padraig the not-really-a-bargee, and about her father. She'd wanted to know about why Padraig being mentioned had upset her mother so much. And she really wanted to know just what her mother had done to get all of them following her like a pack of blood-crazy foxhounds.

Clara looked around the little cabin with its dim battery-powered light in its simple Bakelite fitting, and its plain riveted steel walls. It was very different from the elegant colonnaded mansion they'd been hidden in outside Fermoy. Very different from the way they'd got from Ireland to London too. Not so very long ago she'd wondered what it must be like to travel underwater, or through the air, instead of clickety-clack by tram. On the whole, the air part had been scarier—because mother was so very afraid—but it was also a lot more exciting and comfortable.

# CHAPTER 3

The Most Noble Malcolm Woldemar Adolf Windsor-Schaumburg-Lippe, Duke of Leinster, Margrave of Waldeck, Earl of Northhampton, and Baron of a dozen lesser estates, English, German, Canadian, African, and Australian, wore, as always, his full regimental dress. He had, after finishing his schooling at Harrow, gone to Sandhurst, and thence joined the Inniskillen Fusiliers. He'd moved on in the Imperial Hierarchy since then, but even as the chief of Imperial Intelligence he had not forgotten them. He'd shaped the Inniskillen Fusiliers from an ordinary regiment into the enforcement arm of the secret service he headed. He let the Inniskillens know that he was one of them, and they in turn were his. He was the Duke of Leinster, and they deluded themselves that he cared about them.

Duke Malcolm didn't care what uniform he wore. He had little interest in clothing. His half-brother Ernest made a spectacle of himself in tasselled boots and mulberry half-pantaloons. One could do that . . . if one were the king. Duke Malcolm's only personal affectation was his long ivory cigarette holder. He liked it, for reasons that were his to know, and for others to fail to guess at.

As usual, at this time of day, his staff were bringing him the morning summary of reports. "Your Grace," said Colonel Wexford, of the Irish Interest section, "we've picked up on the movement of several senior Menshevik agents entering our operations area. The Russians are up to something."

"I assume you're tailing them," said the duke, listening very carefully, to what was said, and to the tone of it. There was a wariness in Wexford's voice. If nothing was going wrong, the staff tended to tell him about it afterwards. Something plainly wasn't going to plan.

The duke's guess was right. "Yes, of course, Your Grace," said the colonel, nervously. "But I have to admit that we've lost track of two of them. We assumed they were there to interact with one of the rebel groups. But there has been no chatter from our informers about it." He cleared his throat. "I spoke to Major George, over at Russian Interests, and obtained some background on the men we've identified. One of them is . . . unusual. Count Alexander Pulshikoi is the science advisor to the Duma. Major George said he was once a very senior commander in their secret police. But what exactly he does now, and for quite what organ of state he works, we are less than sure. I can't see why he would be travelling to Cork. To Fermoy. There is nothing much there apart from a big dyeing works—Imperial Chemicals and Dyes."

Duke Malcolm tapped the end of the slim ivory cigarette holder against his teeth. He looked out of the window for a while, onto the soot-stained building reflected in the Pall Mall Canal, while the tension in the room grew. Then, without saying a word, he took up a pen, dipped it in the ink, and scrawled a note on his pad, ripped it off, and—after folding it neatly with slow precise folds—he dropped it into the vacuum-canister, sealed it very deliberately, and put the canister into the tube mouth next to his desk. He pulled the brass lever activating the system.

The canister whooshed away and rattled off down and along the tubes to the records and archives section. Duke Malcolm looked at his officers, tense and watchful. Little things could frighten them, and he played on that. "I will review the dossiers," he said, coolly. "Is there anything else?"

Just the sight of that note being sent had been enough to start the colonel sweating, little rivulets pouring down his florid face. "No, Your Grace. The usual low level of unrest among the Catholics. But we're monitoring it."

"You'd better be." It probably wasn't important. But Duke Malcolm believed firmly in keeping his officers just a little frightened. That meant sometimes taking a personal interest. They were afraid to tell him of their slips . . . like losing the Russians. But they were even more afraid not to.

# CHAPTER 4

The engine room of the *Cuttlefish* was steamy, and the air was thick with coal smoke and the smell of hot oil. Oh, and the smell of sweat from the engineers and the navvies. The air was not pleasant to breathe down here. They were using compressed air to run on, because it was too risky to put even the engine-snuiver up, and the batteries were strictly for short runs, and operating on them was slower too. So it was dim and smoky and busy.

Tim was grateful for both the busy and the dim part. He didn't want to think too much about Stockwell Tube Station, the explosions, and what might have happened to his home, but he couldn't really help doing that anyway. Not with the sound of the drop-mines that were exploding in the Thames Channel, echoing through the boat. Still, it was the silence between the explosions that was more worrying. The Royal Navy drop-miners would be listening with underwater microphones for the sound of the *Cuttlefish*'s engines, or—if those were silent—the sounds made by her crew. Tim kept a weather eye out for the "all quiet" light coming on. So far, so good.

They were running at a quarter speed at the moment, which meant the greasers had time to look at something other than the moving pistons. The slower speed meant that the *Cuttlefish* was back to edging her way about in the drowned streets of London. That was nearly as dangerous as the drop-mines were. The debris down in the streets, and especially the fallen wires, could trap the submarine or damage her hull. She'd have her catfish-feelers—long thin rods with touch-sensitive little plungers on them—out, and the captain and his bridge would be as nervous as tunnel rats now.

The thought of tunnel rats was enough to make him hungry. Above-people might regard them as vermin, but in the tunnels of drowned London, they were all the meat people could get, as often as not. One couldn't eat the fish out of the polluted water. In many stagnant areas the water was even corrosive, eating flesh and decaying even iron, and there was nothing alive near it.

Thinking about it was enough to bring the memories flooding back. It was hard enough to leave home. Was his mam still all right? Did the little dank Victorian-era rotting red-brick tunnel he'd grown up in, hunted in, played in, lived in, still exist? Who were this woman and her daughter anyway? Why had Duke Malcolm's men chased them so hard?

They were not good questions, and they gnawed at him as viciously as his hunger. Answers, like food, were not something that he'd get for a long while.

Clara had always found that uncertainty was far worse than knowing the worst could ever be. They'd hidden in the mansion in Deer Park for days. It'd been terrifying . . . and boring. Nothing much to read. Her mother not talking. So Clara made up stories in her head, and slept. It meant that she woke up at odd hours. Sometimes even in the middle of the night.

Clara hadn't even been sure what time of night it was in the mansion, when the quiet conversation in the next room had cut into her sleep. She lay dead still, listening, nervous. She heard a man's voice. "I'd like to wait longer, but . . . well, informers. We know we have a problem. That's how they caught Jack."

Her mother's voice was odd. A little shrill. "And you. Except that Jack took the fall for you. Made you out to be an innocent bystander, Padraig. And you let him."

"I've told you before. Jack's told you too, as much as he can," Padraig-the-not-really-a-bargee replied, his voice very even. "It was a case of him or me. And he chose that it should be him, Mary."

Her mother's silence spoke louder than words.

The next afternoon they'd been smuggled onto the train to New Dublin. There had been guards and checkpoints at the station checking the passengers getting onto the train.

They inspected documents carefully—especially those of women and girls. They even took some of the young men aside into specially set-up cubicles, where they were obviously making sure that they really were young men. Clara watched through a crack in the guard's van door. She and her mother had been smuggled into it while the guard's van and carriages were still sitting in the shunting yards, and missed the search altogether. Still, it was a relief when the whistle sounded and the *Royal Irish Mail* began to slowly gather steam, hissing and shuddering her way along the rails, away from Fermoy, along the great Southern and Western Railway's busiest track.

They'd got off the train at a small halt just before New Dublin itself. It was odd that the gleaming express train should even stop there. But it did, briefly, and the frightened little conductor shooed them off like hens.

They jumped down into the darkness, complete with their new valises and a little tin trunk. A mysterious someone had been shopping for them. The clothes were expensive, fashionable, and not at all what either of them would have chosen. But Mother had her own books in the tin trunk. Somehow they'd got those—but nothing for Clara to read. She'd had a go at *Chemical Principles* by Heydenbroek, but even peering out of the little window at the darkness had more to offer than that.

Her mother wasn't talking, lost in a private world of her own sorrows and worries. Clara wished she'd at least say where they were going, or why. When you were just little, a baby or at junior school, it was all very well being carried along by your parents' lives, she thought. But surely she was old enough now to know, to do something? To make decisions?

"They're supposed to meet us," said Mother, looking around into the darkness, fearfully.

"The train was early," said Clara. "I heard our little conductor man tell a passenger. Who is supposed to meet us?"

There was a pause. "I can't tell you, love." Her mother sounded . . . apologetic?

Clara twined her fingers in her mother's. "Can't or won't, Mummy?" She never called her that. It was . . . babyish. Her mother was too serious, too thoughtful. And always "Mother." Her father had been the jokester, always making both of them laugh. And he'd always been "Daddy." Yet . . . under the jokes, she'd always suspected that he was even more serious than her mother. It suddenly came to her that he must have been, and must have been hiding that side of himself from her. That hurt. And it worried her.

Her mother took a deep breath. "Won't. You see, if they catch us, you won't know. And people are risking their lives for us. The less you know, the safer they—and you—will be."

Clara had to admit that she'd always been the one to exasperate teachers with her curiosity and her quick tongue. They wanted her to learn just exactly what was put in front of her, and not to explain why or how. It had always made her irritated in class, because understanding why made learning so much easier. And now she felt just the same. Only with added fear, and too many hidden nasty things out there. She shivered. They were still standing in the middle of the tracks, staring after the departing train. She pointed to the little iron roof of the halt. "Well . . . let's go over there, and wait. And you can tell me what I can safely know, at least. Please."

"Very well . . . but over there. In the bushes. I think I hear another train." So they retreated with their valises and the trunk into what proved to be nettles, but the train was coming fast, so there was no time to move away from them.

It was only a green tank-engine spouting sparks from the stack, with its single headlight gleaming on the silver rails, racing towards them.

With a metallic screech, it came to halt, and four men leapt out of the cab. Their plumed shakos proclaimed them to be Duke Malcolm's own troops. That was enough to frighten Clara and her mother farther back into the nettles. "Search the station. And be quick. They might have got down at Clancree. That fool didn't know for sure," shouted the one who had remained in the cab with the driver.

Clara could see the gold of his epaulettes—a senior officer. Her mother pulled her down and they began crawling away from their belongings and deeper into the darkness as quietly as they could.

Along the road to their right a vehicle approached the station, coming fast, its powerful lights cutting through the drifts of smoke and the night-mist. "They'll be caught," whispered Mother.

But it didn't happen quite that way. The big touring car roared up to the station, followed closely by another. And a third. The five soldiers plainly weren't expecting them . . . or expecting any real trouble. Their rifles weren't at the ready.

The same could not be said of the men who tumbled out of the cars, and their weapons did not look like ordinary rifles either. They outnumbered the soldiers three to one, anyway. "Put down your weapons, and raise your hands," said the tall man from the first car. He had a slight foreign accent. "Now."

The first three soldiers did what they were told. The officer, in the cab of the tank-engine, tried to draw his pistol. And one of the newcomers shot him.

It was not a loud, dramatic bang like it was in those American Biograph shows. . . . It was just a stutter of noises no louder than a string of the smallest firecrackers on Guy Fawkes night. The weapon was plainly silenced in some way. But the officer fell out of the cab like a puppet whose strings had been cut. And there was blood. It was too horrific to be real. Clara knew she'd screamed. She couldn't help it.

The one soldier who hadn't surrendered threw his rifle at the nearest of the new arrivals and ran, straight towards Clara and her mother. He fell over the tin trunk—which might have saved his life. The guns might be silenced but they ripped into the undergrowth. "Don't shoot. Dr. Calland is in there," snapped the tall man. "Sergei, Ivan, Viktor. After him. He's unarmed now. Dr. Calland. You can come out. It is safe."

Some of the newly arrived men jumped down off the platform and walked into the nettles. Mother stayed dead still, and so did Clara. It didn't help. A beam of torchlight was fixed on them, and they had to get up.

"Count Alexander Pulshikoi," said her mother, to the tall man who had been giving orders, with a degree of coolness Clara had to admire. "What are you going to do with us?"

He clicked his heels and bowed. "Exactly what I said I would do, Doctor, before you were foolish enough to run away. You will be flown to Moscow. Our scientists are very keen to work with you. They are very excited about your work. It's a line that has not been pursued for some time."

"Flown? From here?" asked Mother.

He smiled. The smile was all teeth and no humour. "You will fly to London in a few hours' time on the regular shuttle-flight. There you can board a good Russian airship."

Her mother took a deep breath. "You'd better bring our bags and my trunk. I'll need that."

He nodded. "It will be done. I think we need to depart from here."

"What about those Inniskillens?" asked her mother. "They should not be hurt. Please."

He smiled his false smile again. "They will not be. Merely detained along with the train driver. We cannot afford to leave them here, that is all. And they would have killed you, you know."

Clara could feel her mother's hand squeeze hers. Her mother obviously didn't trust him either, but there was nothing they could really do.

They'd been whisked by car to the Dublin airship terminal, and from there—separately, to stop them doing anything rash in public, as Count Alexander had coolly explained—into a locked first-class cabin, part of a suite reserved for the Russian ambassador. The cabin had been about five times the size of the little cubby they would later share on the *Cuttlefish*. The other difference was that the door was open on the submarine. They could come and go as they pleased. . . .

On the airship Clara had had to crawl out along the ventilation shaft to go anywhere.

# CHAPTER 5

The Royal Navy commodore facing Duke Malcolm was doing his best to bluster and not to look very afraid.

Duke Malcolm felt the Royal Navy had . . . delusions. They liked to pretend they were the Senior Service. That the British Empire's existence and safety rested on the Royal Navy. But these days, with the Empire crumbling and unravelling on the edges, and buckling in the middle under the weight of people and the disastrous effects of the sudden melt, it was Imperial Intelligence that held the Empire together. The Royal Navy was still the world's greatest maritime force, and her fleets could sail anywhere in the world they wished to, as they had for more than fifty years since the 1914–1915 War. Well, they could sail anywhere, if they could get the coal, as his half-brother was inclined to say. The Americans and Russians had enough coal to get them anywhere. They just didn't have the fleet, and they didn't have the munitions for a long war either. The methane burst that had accompanied the Melt had killed off half the sailors in the Russian Navy, a problem that Duke Malcolm wished the Americans had too. But neither rival had the food for their guns for a sea war, or any other war, against the British Empire.

If Duke Malcolm had his way, they never would. This bungler would learn the hard way, that the navy, too, took orders from Duke Malcolm. And the navy saw that they were carried out. "Your ship was not on station, Commodore. You had your orders."

"We were waiting on the tide, Your Grace," said the commodore, stiffly. "We'd been told that the attack was scheduled for one hundred hours. . . ."

"Or on the receipt of our signal," interrupted Duke Malcolm. "Our informer let us know that submarine was due to depart earlier than scheduled. We needed you there and ready. Not three miles from where you were supposed to be."

The duke signed the order he had prepared. Folded it. Handed it to the naval officer. "Take that to Admiral Von Stael. You are dismissed."

The commodore opened his mouth to speak, changed his mind, saluted, and left.

Duke Malcolm wondered how far down the hall he would get before looking at the order for his own court-martial.

He tapped the brass communicator button set into the leather of his desktop.

"Your Grace," his secretary's tinny voice issued from the instrument's speaker. "Shall I send in the man from the Royal Academy of Sciences?"

"Indeed, Miss Farthing," said the duke. "I am waiting for him." He put another of his long black Turkish cigarettes into the cigarette holder and lit it with his desk lighter, which was amusingly crafted like a cannon. He inhaled the aromatic smoke and waited.

Professor Browne was rather different from the naval officer. For a start he was clever enough to be afraid, and to show it. And secondly, he actually did not need to be. He was a moderately competent scientist, according to the dossier, and he played the game of politics very well. That was unusual in a scientist.

He was sweating copiously, and it was not a warm day. "Sit down, Professor," said the duke with far more affability than he'd shown the Royal Navy officer. "Now, tell me, what do you have for Imperial Security about this Calland woman? So far we've only been responding to the Russians trying to remove her. The affair involves, plainly, science. Presumably something she knows about, that cannot merely be duplicated from a formula. What is it, Professor? If we know the answer to that, perhaps we can step ahead."

The scientist rubbed his forehead with a large brightly coloured handkerchief. "It's difficult to guess just what she has discovered, Your Grace. It must, as you say, be something complex, that she has a grasp of, which makes it more difficult to guess, as her specialty was apparently synthetic dyes. But by researching the two Russian scientists she's been in correspondence with, we think it may possibly be an alternative to the Birkeland-Eyde process."

"Enlighten me, Professor Browne," said the duke, sitting back and drawing deeply on the ivory mouthpiece of his cigarette holder, preparing to try to understand whatever scientific jargon the fellow came up with. Both the Russians, and now the Underpeople, the water rats that lived beneath London, had gone to great lengths for this Dr. Calland. She must know something very valuable, for the risks and effort and resources given to transporting her. Not just a new shade of maroon for King Ernest's pantaloons.

It was easier to understand than he thought it was going to be.

"It is the process by which we make nitric acid," explained the professor. "It's the feedstock for synthetic fertilizers and some explosives. As an alternative to naturally occurring nitrates like Chile saltpetre."

Now, a little too late, it all began to make sense, especially considering the slow bubbling war with Chile and Peru. No wonder the Russians wanted her! No wonder the Underpeople had helped her.

The British Empire controlled all the major natural sources of saltpetre. The source of nitrates that fed the army and navy's guns, as well as providing fertilizers . . . fighting a war without that, as the German Kaiser Wilhelm had found out, was a sure way to lose.

Duke Malcolm steepled his fingers and nodded. "Find out more about this woman, Professor, among your colleagues and her fellows. Try and find out more about the direction she's been working on too. Follow it up hard and fast. Expense is no object. In the meanwhile, if you'll excuse me, I need to authorize pursuit."

# CHAPTER 6

First Mate Werner came down to the engine room as Tim's stomach was about to start digesting itself. "Mr. Engineer, we need some labour for the tick-tock," he said.

Tim found himself "volunteered." He didn't really mind, even if he was rather wary of the first mate. The mate was supposed to be a great submariner, but he had quite a temper, Tim had been told. Still, it would be a change from greasing fast-moving brass shafts, thinking about food, and feeling guilty because he could think about food, when he was feeling so miserable and worried about his mam and his home. But his mam had said he'd better join a sub crew because at least they could afford to feed him. And she was only half joking when she said it. Food was always short, and always expensive, in the tunnels.

They used strong cotton-tape slings to carry the heavy tick-tock up from the storage hold to the escape hatch. The heavy iron oval's inner works had to be wound up and set before being sealed, and put into the escape lock. Tim watched in fascination as the first mate did the preparation. There were cogwheels and springs and wires and a bullhorn and a modified Victrola. The precisely machined brass setscrews were positioned, and the three clockwork motors wound.

First Mate Werner stood up. "Seal it and put in the lock," he said, dusting off his hands.

Tim had been standing reading the dials and labels on the device as the mate worked. "Um. Isn't the arming switch supposed to be down, sir?" he asked.

The first mate gave him a poisonous look, but one of the engineers standing next to Tim packed up laughing. "He's right, Mr. Mate. You nearly forgot to arm the thing."

"So I did," said the mate, and he leaned down and flipped the switch. "Seal it and launch it, boys. Well spotted, lad."

They screwed the seal-plate shut, loaded the device, and flushed the tick-tock out of the escape hatch to swim away behind them. The tick-tock's little fins would carry it off, and soon it would start its work, while they crept on their way and lay silent, waiting.

The first mate tapped him on the shoulder as they turned to go back to the engine room. Tim thought he was in trouble, but all the mate said was, "Boy. You better go and tell the passengers that we're going to be on utter silence soon. We don't want them undoing the tick-tock's good work, eh?"

So Tim made his way up to the cabin. It went with being the youngest and smallest on the sub. You got to run all the errands. Even ones to girls with flouncy dresses and puff sleeves. He didn't know that much about girls of any sort, not that he didn't want to, and nothing at all about the frilly ones, except that he did not like that kind.

He knocked, quietly. She—the girl he'd met in the gangway earlier—opened the door without leaving her bunk. She held a finger to her lips and pointed to the sleeping woman with the pale, tired face below her. *Great!* thought Tim sourly. *I might as well have left them alone.*

She swung down from her bunk and came out of the cabin and into the walkway. "What is it?" she asked in a whisper.

Tim looked at the girl with her lace-trimmed dress. Felt awkward, as he usually did with girls. "Message from First Mate Werner. We've launched a tick-tock. You're to keep dead quiet," he whispered back.

"Oh. A what?" she asked, eyes bright with curiosity.

"It's a kind of decoy," he explained quietly. "They're using underwater microphones to try to find us, see. So the tick-tock is a wind-up fake noisemaker. It's somewhere behind us. It's not going to help if you make a racket."

"A clockwork mouse to distract the ship-cat." She grinned, making her look both nicer and younger. "All right." She paused. "Mother is asleep. And I'm starving. And bored. Bored stiff. Can I come with you? I won't make a sound, I promise."

He shook his head and pointed back at her cabin. "No. You'd just be in the way," he said. Honestly! She thought this was a jolly good party or something. It wasn't a game.

Clara climbed back up onto her bunk, feeling more than slightly irritated. He wasn't that old. She was nearly fifteen . . . well, more than halfway to fifteen. She was as capable of doing anything as he was. After all, she'd got them off the airship.

The Mensheviks had obviously thought that being several hundred feet above the ground and having a locked door was enough to keep their prisoners trapped. She and her mother were prisoners, there was no doubt about it, but they were being treated well—as if they were needed, but not to be trusted.

The cabin, with its wood-panelled walls, deep leather armchairs, hunting scene prints, a little viewing bay window with a velvet-cushioned seat, heavy maroon-and-gold damask curtains, and a small roll top writing desk, wasn't what Clara had always thought of as a cell.

It was one, though.

Except that there was a polished brass gridded vent above the bed. The grid was held in place with two large screws. It wasn't a very big vent, but the truth of it was that Clara wasn't very large herself yet. Everyone said she'd grow. She spotted the grid right away. And pointed because . . . she was rather suspicious that someone might be listening.

Her mother's eyes widened slightly. They had taken the pistol from her mother's handbag. She had seemed almost relieved to lose it. But they hadn't taken her nail file. The big brass screws turned easily. The square duct behind it wasn't very much bigger than the vent. Mother wasn't going to fit down it. It was even going to be tight for Clara. Mother took a page out of her diary. She wrote: "I need to know if they're listening. If they are, keep crawling, and stay hidden. When you get a chance, get out and go to this address: 14 Brunel Close. Near the Strand. And ask to speak to your grandmother. By name." She paused, and then wrote and underlined: "If they are not listening, come back!"

Then she hugged Clara, very quickly, as if she was afraid to hold on for too long, and then made a stirrup with her hands for her daughter to get up and squeeze through the hole.

The next opening on the ventilator channel was onto the main suite. And Clara could hear, and even see, quite clearly, what was happening. Unfortunately she could not understand it. They were talking something foreign. She'd learned some German, French, and Portuguese at school, naturally, but not whatever language this was, presumably Russian. But she could count the men sitting there—the five who had brought them aboard, and the man that Mother had called Count Alexander. The count was talking to one of them, as they sat and drank some kind of wine. At this time of morning! The other four were playing cards and smoking. It made her want to sneeze. People weren't supposed to smoke just anywhere on an airship! Even she knew that, and she'd never been on one. There was a special room for it, as far from the gasbag and as insulated as possible. Trying to control her nose Clara began to wriggle her way back along the channel. It was nearly as difficult as not sneezing. She eventually could prevent the sneeze no more, and muffled the *hachoo* desperately into her arm. If they heard her, they gave no sign of it. The men just went right on talking.

And then came the next problem. Getting out of the hole backward. She eventually found it easier to go back past, and then forward and out. "Well?" asked her mother, quietly.

"I think," said Clara, taking a tasselled cushion from the window seat, and pushing it into the ventilation hole. "If we do this we could have a party in here and they would never know."

Mother smiled for the first time, Clara thought, in days. "We'll let them have the party."

"They are. They're drinking and smoking in there. Smoking, Mother. On an airship!?"

Mother nodded. "The smell carries. I wouldn't be surprised if the purser comes along to ask them to douse the butts. It's not quite as dangerous as it seems, as we're below the hydrogen and that is in sealed cells. It would take a leak to mix oxygen with it, and ignition in the main envelope for it to catch fire. But it gives me an idea. Let's see. I know I've got some potassium chlorate in here, and the trick will be to mix some bromine and some acetophenone without us being affected. "

"What?" asked Clara.

And now her mother's smile was more like that of a fox dreaming it had found a new way into a chicken farm. "The reason why they should not have picked on a chemist, and left her with a supply of chemicals. I'll give them an experience with lachrymals and a smoke candle that they won't forget in a hurry. And hopefully we'll be able to get off the airship in all the panic. We were heading for London anyway. But we were going via Mull-bridge and Glasgow. This is quicker and more comfortable."

It sounded . . . fun. Not like her mother at all. But a voice of caution sounded in Clara. Those were killers out there. She'd seen them do it. "Um. I could just crawl along and get help."

"Unfortunately, help would just arrest us. And not arrest the

Russian ambassador's military attaché," said her mother. "I suspect we are now wanted persons. And they enjoy diplomatic immunity. And I certainly don't want to be caught by the British any more than the Russians."

That was puzzling. Clara had always thought she was British. Even when Imperial security had arrested her father.

So her mother had set about mixing her potions. Very witchy business, thought Clara. Mother even looked like a witch when she was muttering formulas. A little later Clara had to squirm down the ventilator channel with the potions and their fuse and the little igniter.

Clara had to change her clothes, as the dress was a dusty wreck. Then they settled down in the bay window of the cabin to watch the coastline come closer, and then the countryside pass below. They could still see the drowned buildings, roofs and chimneys sticking up out of the water, or still visible through it.

And then, when London came in sight, with weak sunlight gleaming on the murky canals, the count's henchmen knocked on their door, with a steward accompanying him. "Take yer bags, ma'am?" asked the disinterested steward, unaware of the gun at his back. "We'll be landing in ten minutes."

So the trunk and the valises were taken from them. And there they sat, a prim young lady and her mother dear, Clara thought, keeping as straight a face as if she was in Algebra and the teacher had just sat on an ink-bomb and was not aware of it. Mother had a thin thread of silk tied to her wrist . . . leading up into the ventilator.

Count Alexander came in as soon as the steward had gone. "I have spoken with our man on the ground by coded heliograph. They are searching Dublin and the roads for you, Dr. Calland. We're still ahead. Now, we'll be landing shortly. You and your daughter will remain here. Viktor and his brother will remain here as well. We will come and fetch you one at a time, once we're certain that it's all clear."

Mother nodded stiffly. She wasn't very good at hiding her feelings, but fortunately the count wasn't very good at observing either.

The door closed and was locked again from the outside. That could be awkward, but not as awkward as Viktor and his brother getting into this side. As Clara crammed the seat cushion from the bay window back into the ventilator with the remains of her dress, Mother shoved the door wedge home and slid the bolt. She jammed the antimacassars from the chairs into the door crack.

Outside the thick hawser-laid hemp rope of the airship's bow line was snagged by the ground team down on the new levels of the raised part of Hyde Park. The ship was slowly hauled in to anchor it to the mooring mast. In their cabin-prison Clara and her mother wrestled the two heavy armchairs across and wedged them between the door and the bed, and then they tied makeshift masks over their eyes and noses. They couldn't see very well through the varnish, but the greasy stuff from Mother's vanity case did keep the masks stuck tightly to their faces. They tied wet rags over their mouths.

Mother used her shoe to break a windowpane.

Clara thought that was a bit feeble. She used both her shoes. They were twenty feet above the ground by now, and the winch platform was already lowering the bags onto the trolleys. The rolling-stairs were just about to be attached to the gondola.

And then there came the part they hadn't expected. The hooting, rising howl of Klaxon horns.

"Do you think it's the police?" asked Clara looking out.

"I think it's probably the fire alarms." The door lock opened and there was some shouting on the other side. Some heavy thumps.

Mother pulled Clara down on the far side of the bed. Just in time—because the men on the other side of the door had stopped kicking and began shooting. But that too didn't last long. Peering around the end of the bed Clara could see wisps of smoky stuff trickling through the holes in the door. Even through the wet rag—which had been torn from the dress they were abandoning—she

could taste the acridity of it. Mother got up and plugged the holes.
"We'll give it another two minutes and then run."

Clara risked a peep out of the window. "I think we could just go now.
Everyone is running away and we're higher off the ground, I think."

"Oh. They hadn't finished tethering. Then we'd better go fast."

They hauled the chair out of the way and pulled open the door.
The air in the stateroom was just about solid smoke and acrid stuff,
and they ran as fast as they could, out and down the empty corridor
to the first-class gangway. And that was fifteen feet above the stair
. . . and rising. "Grab the edge and drop," said Mother. "NOW!"

There are times to argue. This wasn't one of them, and so Clara
did it and dropped. She hit the top of the roll-stair and nearly got
knocked off it by her mother landing, petticoats and skirts bil-
lowing. They were caught and hauled upright by a gentleman with
a handlebar moustache. "Anyone else on board?" he asked hastily.

"Don't know," said Mother. "And we must run. If it burns . . ."

So they ran, tearing the masks off and joining in the throng that
blue-uniformed bobbies were already trying to hold back.

The crowds wanted to watch.

Clara and her mother merely wanted to leave. They made their
way to the Broadwalk Canal edge and found a boatman.

"Hit's going to burn up, hinnit," said the boatman cheerfully,
peering at the airship, slowly rising. "Did you come orf it, then?"

"No. But I'll give you five pounds to take us to Fleet Street.
Well, Somerset House."

"You one of them newspaper-reporter ladies? Not going to see
an hairship burn again in a hurry, marm," said the boatman, plainly
tempted by the money, but wanting to watch.

"It's not going to burn. It's not on fire. That's the story. I'll make
it ten pounds."

"'Cor Blimey. Ten quid! Right you are," said the boatman. "Will
yer mention me name in the story? I'm Ted Wilkins. I seen the
smoke and people runnin'."

"Can't promise what my editor will do. But the sooner I get there the more likely it would be," said Mother.

The boatie nodded. "'op in then," and he busied himself with his boiler.

So they did. The boat was narrow and rocked, but they sat down together on the holystoned slat-bench as the boatie fiddled with his steam levers and eyed the gauge, and shovelled on some more coal.

With a thump and clatter and hiss of steam, the stern paddle-wheel began to spin. The little vessel wasn't ever going to win any races, but they threaded skilfully along Piccadilly Canal and down St. James, and into Pall Mall. If it hadn't been for Mother's anxious glances back Clara would have been having the time of her life, looking at all the places she'd only ever read about, with business going on almost as if the lower floors of every building weren't underwater. They passed through the throngs of sightseers in boats throwing bread to the gulls in Trafalgar Square.

They paid off the boatie, who made sure—for the fifth time— that they knew his name (Clara felt bad about that—and maybe Mother did too, because she gave him a tip on top of the vast sum of ten pounds), and took to the duckboards and then the pavements. It was busy, dirty, and very crowded, to a girl from Fermoy, County Cork, Ireland. There were probably as many people on this one street as there had been in all of Fermoy before the flood.

Mother made it as hard as possible for anyone to follow them, by ducking into shops and going off down several alleys that really didn't smell too good. Eventually they made their way down a side alley off one of these, and back onto duckboards, and then along a raised walkway on piles. There were far fewer people here, and the houses showed more of signs of water, soot, and neglect. At last, when Clara's feet were killing her—she was still wearing her patent leather school shoes—Mother stopped and knocked at a black door. Number 14.

It seemed to take forever before someone opened the door a crack.

"We don't want any," said the little gray-haired woman from inside. "Can't you read? It says no pedlars on the door. Or Jehovah's Witnesses. Or even," she said, looking them up and down, "missionaries."

"I'm looking for Clara Immerwahr," said Mother, in what was barely a whisper.

The little woman's eyes opened wide. "Goodness. After all these years. Come in," she said. "Quickly. Did anyone follow you?"

"I don't know," said Mother tiredly as they entered the spartan little hallway with portraits of King Ernest at his coronation hung above the little scalloped half-moon table. "I think we had a tail, but lost them."

"Well, I'd best to get you underground as soon as possible," said the gray-haired woman.

That sounded threatening, especially after people had been shooting at them. But one couldn't get underground here. Underwater maybe.

The woman led them along her dark little hallway and into the kitchen. "Who are you, by the way?" she asked, waving them in. "I haven't heard the old lady mentioned in many years."

"She was my mother," said Mother, tiredly. "She said to come here if matters ever got out of hand. . . . Well, they are."

The little old woman's eyes twinkled. "Now that you say it, I can see the likeness. I met her when I was just a little girl. She was quite a woman."

"I never really knew what my mother was up to," said Mother.

That, thought Clara, as she watched the little woman reveal a dark opening by swinging a seemingly solid flagstone aside, made two of them. Maybe it ran in the family. If she ever had daughters, she'd tell them all about what she was doing. Maybe.

And, on that thought, she began her climb down the rusty iron staples into the dank-smelling blackness.

# CHAPTER 7

Once, before the sea levels started their rise, the tunnels of the Underpeople had been the London Underground railway. Well, that and everything from sewers to drains. Under London had been layer on layer of tunnels and crawl-ways, going back centuries.

Like the streets, most of them had flooded, and been closed. But of course not all of the tunnels had become flooded. The higher ones had just been closed-off holes. They'd made a good hiding place for people who really didn't want to be found. And over time, the flooded network had been pumped out and opened up by those hiding. They'd even added tunnels, linking the underways. There were airlocks, pressure doors, and dangerous areas, of course. It was dark, smoky, and perpetually damp. But to Tim Barnabas it had been his world. It was where he'd been born and where he'd lived.

In some ways the submarine wasn't that different. It was all of those things, but it was also like the tunnels, most of the time—relatively safe from those who hunted the Underpeople. For the tunnel dwellers, that was the police, the army, and, most feared of all, Imperial Security. The tunnels were the home territory of the Underpeople, and down there, they had the advantage. Their enemies knew that, and didn't try too hard. Likewise, the submarines generally had the edge on the Royal Navy, and as long as they kept out of sight, they weren't hunted relentlessly.

It was not like that right now. It was almost as if once those two women had boarded, the old rules had been suspended. The navy was hunting the submarine hard, and into places that were outside its normal run. Still, they'd bought time with the tick-tock. The sub had crept through the Canningtown Shallows on the electric motors. The big battery banks weren't going to last that long, but they were quiet. The Royal Navy ships were busy pounding the area of the tick-tock, and the explosions were at least some way off.

"New boy. You," said the chief engineer, pointing, after every last one of the now-still pistons were carefully greased, and the new-washed coal-dust hoppers filled.

"Tim Barnabas, sir."

"Barnabas. Leg it to the galley. See if Cookie has some food for us. We might as well give the lads a feed now, while things are quiet. Might not get a chance, later," said the chief.

"Sir!" Tim turned to go.

"And don't run and make a racket, and put yer shirt on. We've got ladies on board," said the chief with a half-smile.

Tim scowled in reply to that. Women had no place on a submarine. Except that these two were here already.

He made his way up to the galley. Cookie and his assistant were already hard at work in what was not enough space to swing a tunnel rat in, let alone a cat. Cookie had obviously anticipated the crew needing food. Heaped plates of sandwiches, and mugs of strong Himalaya tea were ready on pewter trays at the hatch. The cook looked Tim up and down, took in the grease on his face. "Engine room. That one. The chief's mug's the one with the teaspoon in. He don't take sugar," Cookie said in his odd, slightly nasal accent.

Tim could barely imagine the idea of not wanting to take sugar in your tea. It was such a treat! But he grabbed the tray.

"Thanks!"

Cookie waved at him with a butcher's knife. "No worries, mate. And if the chief can spare you, this tray needs to go to the bridge."

Tim nodded and sped off. His mam was right. They ate well on the submarines. And real tea too! Mind you, he could have stopped and eaten the whole lot right there, himself. And the chief could

spare him, he soon found. Worse, could spare him before he'd got a
sandwich.

The bridge got tea in a huge pot. Cups, not mugs, and thinner-
cut sandwiches.

Huh! thought Tim, looking at it. Not everything was better
about being on the bridge.

Captain Malkis was busy with his charts, while one of the submariners clicked the periscope through the quadrants. "One vessel,
south-southeast, seventeen. She's under way, sir. I can see sparks.
She's heading up-channel towards Greenwich. About six knots, I'd
say, Captain," said the man on the periscope.

You could still feel the tension up here on the bridge. In the
engine room there were a few jokes starting to be made. Not here. It
was still deadly serious, and they were all intent on their tasks.

No one noticed Tim, standing holding the tray. The periscope
clicked round one more sector. The submariner peered intently into
the eyepiece. Tim cleared his throat. He felt quite guilty doing that,
but the tray was heavy. He'd drop it any minute.

"Ah. Food." The captain smiled wryly. "Cookie thinks we're out
of the worst, and he's got more experience than most submarine cap-
tains. Put it here, boy. Fergal has one more sector to do with the
scope, and then you can relieve him on the periscope while he has a
cup of tea and a bite."

So Tim got to peer through their only window on the upper
world. The submarine was running, neutrally buoyant, and near
silent on her electric motors, using the tide to carry them away from
the half-drowned city of London. Tim looked back at the gaslights
of the city. He looked for running lights on other vessels, while the
others ate. He tried hard not to think about his home, under the
city's waters. He also tried hard not to think of his stomach. It wasn't
listening to him. The captain must have heard the gurgles.

"Back to work, Fergal," he said. "And Barnabas, we've eaten all
of this. Take the cups back and tell Cookie I said to feed you, and use

you. Unless we have more action we'll have breakfast at oh six hundred. We'll need him to send a message to our passengers. My compliments, if they would care to eat with us. Dr. Calland may not."

So Tim got to eat. And then to wash dishes. And to feel the coal-dust-fired engines begin their slow thumping vibration. They must be far enough from any Royal Navy ship for that to be considered safe. They were running north but still keeping below the waterline, using some of their precious stocks of washed and desulphured coal dust, instead of getting the gossamer sails up.

Hunger, added to fear, kept Clara awake. She hadn't realised how well water carried sound. And she'd always imagined that a submarine would have portholes, through which she could watch the fish swim past. Why didn't anyone come and tell them what was happening? The answer to that of course was "why should they?" but that didn't stop her wanting to know. Ever since they'd climbed down into the darkness under the little house in Brunel Close, her life seemed even more confined and confused. The staple ladder in the wall of the hole under the floor had led into a large, dark, reeking tunnel, wet underfoot.

Their guide had lit the little oil-burning Davy lamp that she took down from a hidden ledge just inside the tunnel, and led them on down, through several airlocks, down stairs, and another sequence of ladders, down, down, into the underwater bowels of London. The walls oozed and dribbled down between the bricks. The silence, except for their footsteps, was scarily not complete. Besides the sounds of dripping, there were distant scamperings and rustles. And they were not alone in their little pool of light, going down into the dark. At certain points along the way for no obvious reason that Clara could see, their guide had stopped and whistled a snatch of a tune. "I hope my memory isn't failing me," she said, turning back to smile secretively at them. "If I get it wrong, they'll flood the tunnel, and it would take hours to pump this out again, by which time we'd be long drowned."

Then they'd come to a place where the tunnel had been bricked up. Narrower pipes came in from the sides, dribbling red-brown slimy fluid down the glistening walls. Their guide counted bricks and then knocked on one. It looked just like any other brick. Then they waited.

A little later a platform slowly came down from the roof. It was nothing more than three planks with a brick facade underneath, and ropes at the corners.

"I'll go up first," said their guide, "to explain. Duke Malcolm's sappers have been a little problematic lately." She took her lamp with her, and left them standing in utter darkness, with nothing but dripping and the sound of their breathing.

"Mother. What's happening? Where is she taking us?" Clara had asked, trying in this pause to make sense of a world that kept turning upside down around her. A world that showed that there were more secrets all around her than she'd ever imagined.

"Hopefully to catch a submarine to America," said her mother. "My mother set up an escape route, oh, twenty years ago. Mind you in those days, the submarines had an easy passage. Half of London's tea came in by submarine, tax free. It's got harder."

America. Clara swallowed. That was a long way from Cork. "Will . . . will we be safe there?"

"I hope so. Hush. The platform is coming down again."

It did, with their little gray-haired guide and her lamp. She was smiling. "Arranged. Up you go, dears." She hugged them both and helped them onto the platform.

"My things. Our bags. My mother's notes . . . ," said Mother.

"They'll send someone for them. If they're not watched and can be brought safely, they will be. We have friends in very odd places. Don't you worry now," said the gray-haired woman.

Up they'd gone. The ragged, dark-haired, and white-skinned man waiting there looked as if he'd never seen the sun. He looked them over, coolly. "Come along then." There were a number of pipes, passages, and tunnel-mouths up there, and he led them into one of them—much narrower than anything they'd been along before, and this time made of iron, too low to walk upright along—leading down.

Stooped, they walked on. And eventually came to what was obviously another checkpoint, and an airlock. And that led out into a large underground space, the shadowy roof latticed with iron rafters. It was sparsely lit by gas flares, but busy with people and even a few donkeys, hauling carts. Somehow, that could only be a market there, by the voices touting wares. Coal, eels, and tea were being offered by the barkers. Set into the walls there were doors and even windows. It smelled of smoke and people, and was noisy with them, unlike the damp reek of the emptinesses they'd been led through.

"Welcome to Charing Cross," said their guide, dryly. "Passengers for Southwark or Temple Station should alight here."

"But we do not have a ticket," said her mother. "Where may we procure one?"

It was obviously the right thing to say, even if it sounded quite mad. "Old Madge vouched for you, but you never know," their guide said, putting back into his sleeve a narrow-bladed knife Clara had not even seen him draw. "Mick'll see you right, ma'am." He pointed to another broad man, standing in the shadows. "He's the Irish conductor."

Clara was not sure if the conductor was Irish or if they were supposed to be. Both, it turned out, were the case. Mick detached himself from the wall. "Word was you were using a very old code, ma'am," he said in a high, slightly lilting voice, at odds with his big square body. "I'd need to be knowing just who you are and what you'd be wanting. And there's a price."

"A price on ideals," said her mother, dryly. "My name is Dr. Mary Calland. This is my daughter Clara. My mother was Dr. Clara Immerwahr. She told me to say that she'd bought a season ticket for us."

Square solid Mick blinked. "Well now. Jack Calland's wife and the old dragon's daughter. It's believed she got money out of the Rothschilds for the first two submarines. Got the Hollanders in to help us and train us. I'll take you along to Southwark. What are you needing? A boat to Kerry?"

Her mother laughed bitterly. "A lot farther than that. We seem to have both Imperial Security and the Russians wanting to catch us. So, if you please, as I know the Underpeople do business with the Russians, and there are informers everywhere, even here, I'd rather not say."

Mick nodded slowly. "True enough. I'll take you to Southwark as quickly and quietly as possible, then. Come along, follow me." They'd gone down a metal stairway into yet another echoing hall lit with gas flares. Here men were off-loading long lidded barges that bobbed below the quay. Mick went over to a foreman who was over-seeing the line of pale-faced stevedores off-loading, by the smell of it, tea. "Tug. We'll need a bobber. These coves need to get to South-wark, sharpish."

"One over at platform seven. I'll get someone to hook it up to a dragline for you." Clara realised that the "dock" was actually the railway station, with the track area flooded so that the barges were floating in it. They crossed two little makeshift bridges and came to a hanging faded sign that read PLATFORM SEVEN EASTERN LINE.

Floating there was a little capsule sitting deep in the water—it looked rather like a barrel, made of wooden staves with iron bands, and a round manhole-like screw-opening. On either end there were metal staples and a cable drooping away into the water.

"It's a bit of a tight fit, ma'am," said Mick, who was easily twice Mother's size. "But it'll save you a few hours of tunnel walking and a lot of the risks."

So they'd squeezed into the barrel thing. Mick almost had to pour himself through the opening. It was dark inside, and the wooden walls were covered in quilted padding. "You and the gal better find a hanging strap, ma'am," said Mick. "Feel about on the roof."

Clara had found one, as someone outside closed the hatch and screwed it in place. It was dark and airless, and then they started to move.

"Why is it all closed up like this?" asked Clara, curious as they bumped and swayed. She was very grateful for the handle.

"Tunnel dips right underwater," said Mick. "We knock about a bit too, so hold tight."

They did, indeed. Clara was very glad to get out of the dark . . . into another gaslit drowned station, with the *thrub-thrub* of pumps underlying everything. Here Mick took them to what must have once been the ticket office. And to her disgust Clara got to kick her heels outside while her mother went into an office to talk to people. Time passed very slowly. She didn't even have Mick to ask questions about the clanking and hissing machinery in the distance, or the people who came and went, dropping parcels into a chute in the arch. It was all very mysterious, and very poorly lit, and damp smelling. Damp and coal smoke would always colour her memory of Under London. Eventually her mother came back, with as near to a smile as Clara had seen since they'd managed to give the count the slip. She squeezed Clara's hand, and her voice had some relief in it. "I've been able to send a Marconi message to a prominent scientist I know of in the United States of America. We have had a reply already. He obviously has more government connections than I knew of, and it seems that they also knew the Russians and Imperial Security were up to something. They've agreed to give us both asylum, darling."

"Does that mean we're safe?" asked Clara, wondering if she maybe was somehow in an asylum already, and all this was some kind of illusion.

Mother sighed. "Not yet. It means that we have somewhere to go. And the alternative was staying here, and that, I gather, would not be safe. It seems that they're still looking for us. The Underpeople say that collecting our bags for us may have been a mistake. Duke Malcolm's men are setting enquiries afoot in London. The leadership of the Liberty—as they call themselves—want us out of here, as soon as possible. So nice to be welcome. Well, I suppose at least they're not just tossing us out."

Looking around the station, Clara felt that "out" might have nicer air to breathe. But obviously her mother didn't think so. Soon they were in another bobber, heading for Stockwell Tube and that thing Clara had no real image of: a submarine.

The level of flooding in Stockwell was deeper, and the station's domed roof barely penetrated the murky water. Nobody on the surface would have guessed there were new tunnels down there, and that the generating station branch line led to the deep caverns, which was where the bobber took them—to the Underpeople's main submarine nest. Mick helped them out—it had been a long run and they were bruised and shaken. And there in the light of the methane-gas flares were three submarines being loaded . . . or unloaded. They were black, broad, and streamlined, the hull-metal bound with rivet-bands, the upper deck planked and tarred, but otherwise near feature-less except for their exhausts, and a low cowling. "Our gateway to the world, ma'am," said Mick, cheerfully. "The *Darter*, the *Plaice*, and the *Cuttlefish*. Over there is the *Garfish*, having her struts worked on." Clara looked where he pointed. A long sharp-nosed tube hung from several gantries, with the outrigger-like sides protruding outwards and downwards on rails. The sharp, actinic light of welding flashed and flickered from the workers there. "Pity she's not quite ready for sea. They've been working on the outrigger design. They work as hydrofoils when they're under sail. They're trying to adjust *Garfish* so she can run on her coal-fired Stirling on them."

He took in their expressions and said, "Greek to you, I'd be thinking. Well, let me take you to meet Captain Malkis. Looks like they got word, and *Cuttlefish* is readying for sea. He's a good skipper, and they've got a great navigator submariner in their first mate. He's one of the original Hollander trainers who showed us how to work underwater."

He took them to the third of the strange, forbidden craft, moored here, underground and underwater, deep in the heart of the British Empire's capital. And that was how they'd got here. It had only been minutes after they'd arrived that their valises and trunk had arrived, and the submarine had left Stockwell.

The submarine might be yet another new thing, but it was narrow and crushing to someone who had lived—well, at least walked to school and home again—under an open sky. And this cabin was smaller and more closed-in still.

Lying there, Clara finally decided she could take it no longer. She could smell food. She could hear the thump of the motors. When she got up she could even feel it through the soles of her feet. They couldn't still be on silence.

She followed her nose down the passage, and to the tiniest of tiny kitchens. That boy was there, scrubbing pots. So was a short man who was nearly as wide as he was high, stirring another large pot. "Ah, missy. Yer come for some tucker?" he asked with a gap-toothed beam.

She decided then and there she could like him, unlike the boy, who was scowling at her again. "What's tucker?" she asked.

"Vittles, missy. Food. That's what we call it where I come from. The new bread hasn't come out yet, and this porridge needs stirring or it'll stick, but if young Tim can get his hand out of the suds, he can cut you a bit of yesterday's baking."

Tim obviously got the message, and dried off his hands and fetched out a loaf while Clara asked the cook, "So where do you come from, mister? I've never heard your accent before."

The cook grinned. "Westralia, missy. God's own Republic, bless 'er. Dry as a . . . bone. But the finest place on Earth."

Westralia. She knew where that was. The rebel "Republic" of Western Australia that had declared itself independent when the

Crown abandoned the colony after the Swan River dried up. A desert no one wanted, full of runaways and criminals, so she'd been taught. Well, a lot of what she'd been taught wasn't quite as true as she'd thought it was. "What are you doing here, so far from home, Mr. Cook?"

He beamed at her. "You can call me Cookie; everyone does. It's a long story, missy. Submarines go everywhere, even if they's not supposed to. Westralia, they can sail on the surface and in the harbour too. I reckoned I'd see the world. So far all I seen is me kitchen." He didn't seem too unhappy about it. "Some butter for her in the icebox there, Tim-o. And there is jam here, see."

The boy said nothing. Just went back to washing up when he'd given her the butter. Clara had not had much to do with boys. Well, there were knots of them who would tease the girls and whistle at them as she made her way back from school. Of course the other girls told stories. And some of them had brothers. Clara ate. It was more interesting to watch them from the counter than to go back to the tiny cabin. She wondered if she should offer to help, even if Mother had told her to stay out of the way. The boy looked like he needed some lessons in washing up. And in washing himself. He had grease on his nose. And he'd been crying. She could tell.

But they seemed busy, so she ate, said her thank yous, and went back to her cabin. And now sleep came quickly.

She was awakened by someone knocking. Her mother sat up sleepily below her and bumped her head on the upper bunk. "Ouch. Who is it?" Mother asked, plainly trying to get herself orientated.

"Tim Barnabas, marm," said the odious boy from outside. "Captain's compliments, would you care to join him and the officers for breakfast?"

"Thank you. How long until you eat?" asked Mother.

"Officer's sitting in the mess in half an hour," said the boy.

"Half an hour. How like men," muttered her mother. "Very well. We'll be there. Can you come back and show us where to go?"

"Don't worry, I know the way," said Clara, then wished that she hadn't admitted it.

"Ah." It was an "Ah" that heralded a lecture later, Clara knew. "Now where is the light switch?"

Clara knew that too. And the way to what the submariner had called "the heads," all of which was necessary to get them to the tiny "mess" on time. It wasn't really a mess, in fact, a very square and neat dining area, with tablecloths and silver, Clara thought. Clean too. Even the boy Tim had washed his face before serving in.

It was a proper breakfast, with porridge—oats from Norway, and kippers from Greenland. Everyone seemed quite relaxed about their narrow escape from Stockwell Station. Well, there was sadness and worry, about what they'd left behind, but they were away now. Out in the open ocean submarines had little to fear.

And then a lieutenant—the one who was so proud of his moustache—came down from the bridge and saluted. "Sorry to interrupt, sir. We've picked up sign of two armoured cruisers on our track. And Sparks is monitoring a Marconi message. He thinks they're talking to a dreadnought. They were being asked about depths."

The captain got to his feet. "Excuse me, ladies," he said, as he left in a hurry.

A few minutes later a bell chimed and the captain's voice—odd-sounding through a speaker tube—said, "Crew to action stations. We're going to run into the Wash Fens."

"What's that?" asked Clara.

"It's the old flooded fen lands in around Lincolnshire, Cambridgeshire, and Norfolk," said the other lieutenant, getting to his feet. "It's shallow, but our charts are better than the Admiralty ones. We land a lot of cargoes there. And those armoured cruisers have a deep draught, missy. They need about twenty-six feet of water. If we flush our ballast and put out the outriggers we can run on the surface in six feet of water. And at twenty-five we're below water level."

"Not by much," said the first mate, heavily. "They could see us from the air."

"But they'd have to come hunting us in shallower draught ships, and the skipper is a canny old bird," said the lieutenant, taking his hat and leaving them with a sketch of a salute.

So they were left to go back to their tiny cabin again and to worry and to fret.

The submarine touched sand with an odd sugary grating sound a few times, but they kept moving.

And then they stopped.

A little later, the "all quiet" light came on.

# CHAPTER 8

Tim was off-watch and asleep when the submarine stopped. It was enough to wake him. "Wazzup?" he asked sleepily of the other sailor in the locker below the bed. It was Big Eddie, who used the bunk Tim was sleeping in during alter-shift. Eddie was one of the two divers aboard, as well as a junior steersman.

"I've got to go out and pull the camo-sheet over her. So if you're feeling like getting wet, you can come for a swim, lad," said Eddie, with a laugh.

Tim shuddered. He could swim. Sort of. You had to as a tunneller. But Under London water was likely to digest your clothes, or the eels might get you. There was supposed to be a giant killer pike up near Wandle. There'd even been a crocodile from Africa in a flooded tunnel once, he'd heard tell.

"And then?" Tim asked.

"And then we lie still until dark and I take it off again," said Big Eddie, setting off for the escape hatch in the bow, in a thick Arran pullover and heavy woollen breeches and thick socks.

He came back a little later, to get back into his normal clothes, before Tim had properly got back to sleep. "Not too bad out there for this time of year. Mind you, the Fens are fairly buzzing with boats. They're hunting this woman hard."

"Why?" asked Tim. She looked like, well, an ordinary top-side modern lady in a flouncy skirt. He'd seen a few when he'd been out with the bloods top-side London at night, before his mam had found out and put a stop to it. The woman didn't say much, not like Miss

Prisms-and-Prunes-snippy, the daughter. That girl had even cheeked the captain. And he'd laughed.

"I dunno," said Eddie. "Go back to sleep."

So Tim had done so. But his dreams had been full of the explosions and his mam.

He woke up when they got under way again. Obviously Big Eddie had come and gone again. The camouflage sheet had been taken in, and they were feeling their way through the sandbar waters before heading out into the deeper water. Tim went and had breakfast and reported for duty. This morning that duty was cleaning officers' cabins and making beds. He was in Lieutenant Ambrose's cabin when they struck. It wasn't so much of an impact, as a slowing . . . and then a stop. And then a twang that reverberated through the boat. And then all was still. Then the engines fired again, and they pulled backwards briefly. Another twang, and they stopped again.

Tim could guess what that meant. Submarine fouling nets were laid in London's drowned streets too. Divers cut them, or made panels that could be opened.

Big Eddie and his mate Albert would have to go out in the cold dark water, in their waterproof canvas diving suits and helmets again, and cut them free.

Only, a few minutes later Tim found it wasn't them that would be doing that.

It was him.

And there would be no diving suit either.

He was called to the bridge. That was alarming enough. "Barnabas," said Captain Malkis with no further finesse. "You're the smallest of the crew. The escape hatch is tangled in the net and can't open. We can see it with the periscope. There is a whole mass of net tangled over it. The hatch opens a crack, but the divers couldn't even get a hand out in their suits. It's a lot to ask of you, boy, but someone needs to go in there, in their skin, with small hands and some shears. There's a diver's breather pipe there. You'll have air, but you'll be underwater. If you

cut it clear enough you'll probably have to squeeze out and cut the
tangle away, so the divers can get out properly."

Tim swallowed. Looked around at all of them. That girl was
standing looking at him from the doorway, eyes wide. Captain
Malkis continued. "We've fouled the propellers too. If we try to pull
free—we'll wind the propellers right off. If we don't pull free, we're
only at ten feet down, and the tide is going out. By morning we'll
be visible to the observation dirigibles."

What could Tim do, except to nod?

A few minutes later Eddie was showing him how to breathe
with the hookah mouthpiece. "We're lucky to have these mouthpieces. They dive without helmets in Westralia, and that's where the
compressor comes from. The pipe usually screws onto the back of the
helmet, see."

The two air hoses were neatly coiled and still wet, as was the
chamber. It must be very tight in here with two of them in their
diving suits.

Standing, shivering slightly in his canvas knee-breeches and
nothing else, Tim could see just how attractive the brass helmet with
its windows, and the thick waterproof canvas suit could be too. But
all he had was a knife and a set of wire-cutters. The netting out there
had some strands cored with braided steel.

They closed the hatch on him. There was a waterproof light on
the wall, but Tim still felt very alone and very scared. He took a deep
breath, put the mouthpiece in his mouth, and cracked the outer
hatch. They could do that from inside too—to launch tick-tocks and
the escape pod, but now it was up to him. . . . The seawater came
spraying in. It was like being in an icy shower. And then a chilly
bath, the water in the narrow chamber climbing steadily around his
thighs and then up his body. Tim forced himself to duck down.
Breathe underwater, through the mouthpiece, while he could still
stand up and breathe, just as Eddie had told him to. Then he stood
up and opened the hatch some more. Eddie had said do it little by

little—it had a brass screw with a big butterfly nut letting you do so slowly.

Only it wouldn't open much. The water flooded in still. And soon the only air in the escape chamber was from the bubbles from the mouthpiece. Tim tried to force the hatch open more. Not with all his strength would it move. So he tried to get his hand out of the gap. He could. Just. Not holding the knife. He had to hand it through to himself and try to feel to cut. A thread snapped. And another two. But his arm just couldn't go any farther. His forearms were too thick. He tried the other hand. It was no better.

He had to close the hatch again and push and twist the purge knob, as Eddie had shown him.

They were waiting. Shivering, Tim had to shake his head as someone handed him a towel. "It's no good, sir. My arm is too thick . . . it needs to bend here. In the middle of my forearm."

"My arms and hands are smaller," said the girl, in the silence.

Clara never quite knew what made her say that. But it was true. She was a bit smaller than the boy was, and her forearms were nothing like as muscular.

"I can't ask you to do that, miss," said the captain with finality. "Your mother would never permit it."

"I cut some of the strands," said the boy, shivering. "I'll try again, sir. Just . . . just let me warm up for a minute."

"Get the boy something warm to drink from Cookie, Willis," said the captain.

"If we don't get free of the net, they'll sink us and we'll drown and be killed anyway," said Clara. "And I can swim."

The captain took a deep breath. "Let us go and speak to your mother."

So they did. And her mother said no just as firmly.

"Mother. I was the one who could fit through the ventilation shaft. This isn't any different," said Clara.

"You could drown, dear," said her mother.

"And if we're here by daylight, they could bomb us. Never mind could. Will. And then we'll all die." She had a moment of an almost satisfyingly gloomy image of their bodies washing in the tide.

"You're too young," said Mother.

"They let that boy who served us breakfast try. He's bigger than me, but I don't think he's much older. But he's a boy, right?" said Clara, knowing she was playing her mother's own sore points, but also knowing that it was true.

Her mother bit her lip. Nodded. "All right. How safe is it, Captain?"

The captain shrugged. "Not safe. But no worse risk than sitting here while they drop drop-mines onto us. It'll be cold and wet, but she can practice using the hookah before the chamber floods. We can close it when it is half-full, and she can check that she can do it."

Her mother closed her eyes, briefly, then said, "Very well. Can we do a trial?"

The captain nodded. "I'll get the boy to talk her through it too, as well as the divers. She's a very brave lass, ma'am," said the captain.

"She's her father's daughter," said Mother, looking as if she might start crying.

Clara didn't know what to say. So she hugged her mother instead. "We'd better find you some clothes fit for getting wet in. I don't think you have a bathing costume. Could you arrange some boy's breeches for her?"

"Of course, ma'am," said the captain.

The water was cold, so cold that it hurt and wanted to take her breath away, but at least it was really not that difficult to breathe through the hookah. All the trial did was to get her wet and cold before the real thing started.

So they closed the hatch again, and she opened the outer one herself. The icy water filled the chamber again, and soon she had to breathe through the hookah. Having to do it was actually better than having a choice about putting your head underwater and breathing.

The gap between the hatch and the hull was very narrow, but with a bit of wiggling she managed to get her elbow out. It was tight and awkward. It was also so cold it was hard to think. Ah. The boy had said you had to pass the knife out. So she did. And cut. She tried to move the screw for opening the hatch with numb fingers. It turned, it was wider now—she pushed herself up and out towards it.

Tim watched as the girl's mother stood there, wringing her hands. Looking at her watch. And Captain Malkis surreptitiously looked at his timepiece, and obviously reached a decision. "Seal the outer hatch. We need to open the inner airlock."

A submariner began turning the polished crank-wheel. Two turns . . . "It's not sealing, sir. Something in the way."

"Lieutenant Willis. Go up to the bridge. Put the forward spotlight on, and see if you can see the hatch."

Barely a minute later Willis came running, yelling, "Open the hatch! She's outside."

It was so cold. Cold cold cold. So hard to think. Once her head was out it had been easier to go out to try and snip with the cutters at the steel wires—which needed both hands, than to try and reach out. Opening her eyes underwater had been hard, but she could see a little in the water-filtered moonlight.

And then . . . the hatch began to close on her foot. She pulled it out. Tried to grab the hatch to stop it. It went on closing. It was too strong for her to resist. In a panic, she pushed the cutters in, and they slipped from her numb hands. The knife. She pulled it from the sheath, and got the hilt in, just in time to stop her air hose being crushed. But she could not even get a hand in to try and open it.

And in her frantic thrashing she'd got her legs tangled into the folds of net. The hatch had at least stopped closing now. Cold and desperately afraid, Clara tried to pull her legs free. Then the hatch that she had her hand on began to open again. And the knife tumbled slowly down into it, after the shears.

"It looks like she's trapped in the net. There is still net over the hatch. She's still breathing."

Malkis nodded. Tugged his beard. Then said, "Empty the forward ballast tank. See if we can raise the bow as much as we can to reduce the water pressure. We should get to within a foot or so of the surface—the tide is going out. We'll close the hatch as much as we dare. Then we'll seal the forward bulkhead and pump air into the escape hatch. Then we're going to open it—with water coming in. And against the water, boy, we're going to have to push you in and close it. You'll have to take the second hookah pipe and cut her free and bring her in. Can you do that?"

Tim nodded. "Sir."

"Don't try to do anything else. Just get her in," said the captain.

As they opened the hatch, the water sprayed in like a fire hose, bruising hard. Fortunately, it mostly hit the far wall of the escape chamber first. Albert and Big Eddie pushed Tim through, and he grabbed the wall-staple to stop himself washing straight back, as the hatch closed. Then, in the surge of icy water he had to grab the second hookah pipe, and start breathing. He ducked under the surface to stop the cold water beating at him. Air, precious air, came in through the mouthpiece.

The chamber filled quickly, and he followed her air-line up. Twisting the screw, he opened the outer hatch as much as it would go. He could barely squeeze out of the gap.

In the light of the spotlight from the bridge, he could see her in the water. She was trying to pull her legs free of the net, obviously not managing much with numb hands.

And then she saw him, too. She nearly spat her air hose, with her relief. She clutched onto his arm with hands that were only just warmer than the cold water.

Tim tried to keep calm, and simply concentrate on cutting the strands of the netting. He got her foot loose, and pushed her ahead of him, to the hatch. She tried to pull herself in, but obviously just couldn't do it.

Tim pushed her from behind. Got her arms in. Pushed more, grabbed the edge of the hatch and shoved her in with his other hand with all his strength. She kept floating up, of course. So, he realised, was he. If it hadn't been for the net she'd have floated to the surface.

Pulling down hard with his arms he got his head into the escape chamber. She was bobbing up at him, terribly in the way, trying to move herself, and in danger of floating out again. Tim pushed her away hard, so that he could get in. He jammed his legs across the opening and reached down and started winding the lever to close the hatch. He only realised their hoses were still in the way when the air stopped coming. In a panic he managed to open it a little. He hauled at the hoses with her trying to help, with hands that didn't obey either of them properly. Eventually, they got the hoses in. It seemed to take forever. Then . . . a turn more and he got the outer hatch closed.

Tim managed to dive down and hit and twist the purge knob.

Air began to bubble in, and water drain out.

The girl, from half-leaning against the wall, sat down suddenly in the water. Well, either sat down or collapsed. Tim sat down next to her. Put his arm around her to keep her upright. He spat out the hookah mouthpiece. Their heads were above water now. "You all right?" he asked through chattering teeth.

She nodded, weakly.

The inner hatch opened and they were both hauled out.

# CHAPTER 9

"Well done, boy!" said Captain Malkis, as someone wrapped Tim in a blanket. "Get them somewhere warm. Hot drinks."

Tim shook his head. He was shivering. It was even harder to do this than to go out the first time, but it needed to be done. "Need to go back. More cutting."

"The divers . . ."

"Too small still." He kept it short. It was easier to talk through his chattering teeth. "Two minutes."

The captain looked at him. "You need to recover, boy."

"Sooner. Best. And I need a weight . . . to keep down." Tim shivered. "We were floating away.

Albert slapped his head. "Of course. We've got lead boots."

A submarine captain had to make fast decisions. "Give him your boots," said Captain Malkis.

"Part of the suit, sir."

"Oh. Get a bunch of pry-bars from the engine room. Jump to it, man. And I'll want another man to go in with him. Not you, divers. You two get suited up. If the net can be cleared from the hatch, you'll be working on the rest as soon as they get in."

So, each with a belt with four heavy pry-bars hooked onto it, Tim and Submariner Smith, the bosun, had gone in to the escape hatch again.

It was no less cold, and still dark outside in the watery moon-light. But it was only six wire strands, and then a dozen cord ones, with hands that were clumsy and stupid with cold, and then the hatch could finally open properly. As it did that, the bosun reached up and pulled Tim back in.

They closed the hatch and purged. This time Tim was the one who sat down, before he fell down.

Smith helped him up, and soon he was out, stripped out of his wet breeches, bundled into a dry blanket, and half pushed, half carried down to the engine room. "Warmest place on the ship, boy," said someone with rough kindness, pushing a steaming mug at him as they sat him against the big firebox. "Get that into you."

Tim's hands shook and his teeth chattered against the cup as he tried to drink. It was sweet tea, full of condensed milk and rum. "Albert says you'll be bone cold. Takes it out of you, and you weren't wearing all their layers."

It took him a full half mug of the brew before he realised that he was sharing the warm firebox backrest with someone else. The girl was there. As was her mother, holding her hand.

The mother smiled at him. Took Tim's hand too. Felt it. "You're still very cold. You're a very brave young man. Thank you."

Tim nodded. It was almost all that he felt he could do. The rum was making his head muzzy, and it was spinning a bit. But fair was fair, he knew. "She did it. She got it open," he managed to say.

The woman stood up. "You both did well. Now, I am going to see if I can get you some bottles of hot water. Your core temperatures are very low. I don't think that the alcohol was a good idea."

"You got me back inside," said the girl, in a whispery voice. "Thanks."

"It was . . . nothing," said Tim awkwardly, cold and feeling remarkably stupid. He'd often dreamed of being a hero to some beautiful woman. Only the dream was a bit vague as to what happened afterwards. . . . Hopeful, but vague. And the damsels-in-distress hadn't been skinny ghost-pale girls who had already done what he could not. He hadn't set off to be a hero, either. Just been the smallest member of the crew. She was the one who had volunteered to do it.

He wondered what came next. It would probably not be much like the dream either.

It wasn't. Just as the girl's mother got back, the chief came along. "Going to have to move you two. The good news is we're starting the Stirlings again. The divers have cut us clear, but we're racing the tide, now. Just take you to back against the wall over there. It's still the warmest place on the ship, in here."

Tim was glad of it. Glad too when the chief decided that the two of them had been cluttering up his engine room for long enough, and should go and lie in their own bunks. It had been too busy with all the noise—greasers scampering to the rods with their buckets, and coal-monkeys filling the feed-hoppers—to fall asleep in the engine room, but Tim had come close.

"But this is much more interesting," said the girl with a little mischievous smile, the first smile that Tim had seen since she'd been hauled in from the sea.

"Now, Clara Calland! Behave," said her mother. But she was smiling too.

The *Cuttlefish* made it out of the Wash before daylight, and lay, safe and hidden, out on the Dogger banks while the hunters prowled vainly above.

But Tim didn't know this. He slept the deep sleep of the very exhausted instead. Who would have thought a few minutes in cold water could make you that tired? He slept clean through Eddie's watch too. The good-natured diver had to bunk on the floor.

He only woke up because his stomach told him it thought his throat might have been cut.

He dressed, and made his way to the galley. "G'day, diver-boy," said Cookie cheerfully. "I missed yer smiling face yesterday. But the skipper said you was to be allowed to sleep."

"We got clear all right?" Tim asked, feeling guilty.

"We're still alive, so me opinion is we must have somehow," said the cook. "You're a bit early for your watch. I got tea, and ship-biscuits, if yer need a feed?"

"Please!" Never had rock-hard tooth-breaker biscuits sounded so good.

So Tim went and sat in the mess and corrected the state of his stomach. Tea—made submarine style, with condensed milk—and the biscuits, which had to be soaked to begin to be chewable, were a solid foundation. He took the mug back. "Thanks, Cookie. That should just about hold me to porridge time."

"Funny, that's just about what the young miss said too," said Cookie. "She was here about an hour ago."

Tim found that he was actually rather sorry to have missed her. Two hours later, full of that second breakfast, he reported for duty. "Cabins first, and then at twenty hundred you're on with the sail-crew, then back to cleaning, and then at twenty-four hundred deck-watch, sonny. You're back with Cookie for the last hour. Get your sou'wester and oilskin and sea boots on, before you go out," said Lieutenant Willis, grinning. "Even if you have showed us all that you don't mind getting wet."

Tim found that he'd gone from being the new boy to being a part of the crew, at least as far as this officer was concerned, all in one day. It pleased him.

It obviously didn't please one or two of the others who were on the deck that night, changing the submarine from a sleek under-water craft to a sailing racer, but that was their problem. Standard, one of the other cabin boys, punched his shoulder. Too hard to be the friendly gesture he was pretending it was. Tim winced. "What's up, Darkie?" Standard said. "Got all soft in the cold water? Or was you soft before, and that hardened you up, but not enough?"

"I wish you'd go swimming, Standard. It'd do you good," said Tim. They were busy pushing out the spars that clipped onto the narrow deck and gave the sail-crews some space to work. It was noisy wet work, as the big rubber pontoons in the hydrofoil outriggers in the second hull would not be filled for this task That would lift the submarine mostly clear of the water, make her much faster, but easier to see.

"Uh-huh. Didn't wash you any cleaner. You still look like you could use a bath." He shoved Tim toward the dark water.

"Shut up, Standy," said one of the other ratings. "The kid did well. Get that net spar clipped in, and get a move on."

Tim shut up too. There was no point in getting into a fight with Standard, who was bigger than Tim, and knew exactly how to make the most of it. Besides, the mate dealt with fights, and he was supposed to be pretty tough on anyone who was involved, no matter what the reason was. Anyway, he was kind of used to it. It came with having darker skin in a place where most of the people didn't see the sun much. He didn't have to like it, but he knew he'd have to live with it. He'd had enough fights to find that out.

When they finished on deck Tim went back to clean his last cabin and then clean the heads, then kitted up again and went to the deck-shaft, up the spiral stair and out onto the deck to do his turn on watch. The *Cuttlefish*, out here in the North Sea, sailed on the surface at night, her mainmast erected, the big transparent sails catching the wind. In the dark, with the submarine running low in the water, with no funnels and no superstructure, and nothing to be seen against the sky but the thin mast, they were very hard to spot. It saved a great deal of fuel, but it did mean that someone on the masthead had to have sharp eyes. There were bow and stern watchmen too, with safety harnesses and a strong likelihood of getting wet. Tim was on stern watch. He was grateful that he was not up in the swaying crow's nest. The North Sea was not as bad as the mighty Atlantic, the other submariners told him. Then he'd be lucky to stay aloft. "It's why you got a berth," Banks had told him, when he'd come aboard. Banks was the biggest of the three cabin boys, due to move to being a submariner soon—well, as soon as he could pass the exam. He'd failed twice, and only had one more crack at it left. He liked to tell horror stories to the newest of the crew. "The last boy, he was moving his line and we hit a wave. He catapulted out into the sea. They saw him swimming after the sub, but we don't stop, see."

Tim had asked one of the senior ratings if it was true. The man grimaced, and said, "Partly. See, when the boat's under sail, she can't stop or turn fast. And at night, they'll never find you. So keep your line clipped in."

After that warning, Tim kept the broad leather belt with its riveted steel hasp tight, with its braided rope to the brass snap-link hooked on to the recessed running pipe, and then quickly, unhooked and reclipped to the hasp.

"Scared you're gonna be washed off, Darkie?" said Standard, who was on the stern, waiting to be relieved. "I thought you said you could swim, new-pup. Not much of a sea today to be scared of," he said scornfully before he ran back to the deck-shaft cowling without bothering to clip his line in.

Tim wondered if he should also not clip in. Just to show he wasn't scared. But the truth was, he was scared. And it was very . . . open, out here for a tunnel boy.

So he stayed clipped on firmly and scanned the dark water, and, as he'd been told to, looked at the line where the starry sky met the dark of the sea.

Clara found, after her diving exploit, that the submarine was a great deal more friendly a place than St. Margaret's School for the Children of Officers and Gentlemen had ever been.

Well, mostly anyway. A few of the boys seemed to want to be a little too friendly. That was . . . something she'd never really had to deal with before. It was interesting but a little scary too. There were girls who'd been involved with boys at St. Margaret's, of course. And they all talked about it. And one of the fifth-form girls had left very suddenly, after doing more than just kissing, if the whispers were to be believed. Clara was curious, but not that curious. And her mother was watching her.

She'd asked some question about spotting the anti-submarine nets at dinner.

"Just what were you doing out of our cabin when we tangled in the net anyway?" asked her mother.

"Oh, I'd, um, gone to the heads," said Clara. "And then the ship stopped, so I went to find out what was happening."

"You really ought not to be out without me," said mother, sternly.

"Well, ma'am, she's your daughter," said the captain. "And you set the limits and rules for her. But we're a small, closed community, and I've had a word with the crew about your status here. There is absolutely no harm that could come to her on the boat. It's a boat, by the way, Miss Clara. Submarines are always called boats. I'd say let her roam, so long as she stays out of the way and clear of the engines, and out of the cabins. And she's been sensible about it so far. It must be a little dull for her in your cabin."

Mother had smiled, wanly. "I must admit that we didn't plan ahead for entertainment for her, Captain Malkis. We were glad to escape with our lives. She should be resuming her schooling . . . but I am not the best of teachers. I'll set her some work too. But thank you. It's very confining for her."

So Clara found herself with her mother's idea of schoolwork, and a fair amount of free time. Mother was so absorbed in her own work, whatever it was. She seemed very frustrated by the lack of a laboratory. "I am convinced osmium is not necessary," said her mother, in the midst of setting her some mathematical problems.

Clara blinked. Osmium? It was on the table of elements . . . she was almost sure. "Er. For what?"

"Oh. Sorry. Your grandmother's work with her almost-husband, before she left Germany." Mother kicked the trunk. "Your great-aunt Irmengarde in Breslau had some of her things, still. When she died, I inherited part of the estate from her, remember. This trunk is full of my mother's notes and letters. A solid quartz pressure vessel . . . some chemicals. It's . . . interesting."

Almost-husband. It was a story that Clara had grown up with, how *Oma* Clara had fought with the man she was about to marry and broken off the engagement. And how the family had felt it better to send her away to stay with the cousins in England—where she'd fallen in love with and married an Irish engineer, and had never gone back to Prussia.

Her mother shook her head, as if trying to clear it. Then she said, "Why don't you go and ask if you can get some air? We are on the surface at night anyway. I'm sorry. I need to think about this."

*Oma* had been a chemist too. The first woman to gain her doctorate from the University of Breslau. Clara knew that she was supposed to follow the tradition set by her grandmother. Only she really didn't like chemistry all that much. She went up to the bridge to ask Captain Malkis if she could go out on the deck.

He rubbed his chin. "It's a bit risky, young lady. We run very low in the water. Waves break right over the top of the ship, sometimes. It's not exactly a pleasure promenade." He looked at her thoughtfully. "Mind you, you have shown us you're not afraid of getting wet. Go to the quartermaster, get him to issue you with wet-weather gear, and a deck harness. There'll be no malarkying about without it, mind. Lieutenant Willis here, will be doing a deck-round at oh one hundred, and you can go out with him, but not to the masthead! You're not to distract the watch. When we get to safer waters you can spend a bit more time on deck. It's rougher out in the Atlantic, but quieter there away from the shipping lanes."

The heavy Shetlands cabled jumper, oilskin, sea boots, and a sou'wester were all a little bit large for her—at the smallest size the quartermaster had. She felt a bit like a scarecrow, clumping back to the bridge. She obviously looked it too. The captain and lieutenant smiled. "Breeches are called for too, I think," said Captain Malkis.

So she had to go back to the quartermaster again. She changed in the heads so as to avoid explaining all of it to her mother, who might object, and went back up, and was taken to the inner door to the deck well.

She shivered. "It's a bit like the escape hatch." It still made her feel cold, looking at it.

"A bit. But the pit doesn't seal off on top, and the outer door can't open if there is pressure on it. We have to pump it out before we can exit this way," explained the lieutenant, leading her out and up the spiral stair, up onto the deck cowling and out under the dark star-spattered open sky, with the wind and the scent of fresh salt-laden air filling her lungs.

"You clip on here." He pointed to a brass rail recessed into a groove on the deck. "There's a second snap-link on your leash too, see. You never clip off the first until you've clipped on the second. Got me?"

She nodded, clipped in, and followed him down the deck to the bow. Out in the darkness spray splashed at them, and the wind bit into her face. And she revelled in it. In the feeling of space, and the fact it didn't smell like the inside of the submarine—of coal, rust, oil, and mostly people. This air didn't feel shared.

The submariner on the bow heard them coming, and turned and saluted. He had water dripping off his nose and forelock, and on his oilskins. It was amazing how well you could make out things just by a sliver of moonlight. "T'sea's picking up a bit, sir. Evening, miss," he said.

"It is. No more ship-sign?" asked the lieutenant.

"Not since just after I come on watch, sir. Lost sight of him, quick enough," said the watchman.

"Well, keep them peeled, Nicholl," said the lieutenant.

"Aye, sir."

They went back, past the low cowl of the deck shaft, and to the stern. That watchman didn't hear them coming. He was peering intently into the dark. The lieutenant cleared his throat. The poor submariner nearly jumped into the sea with fright—the lieutenant had to catch his leash.

It was the cabin boy, Tim. "Sorry, sir. I think I see something, sir." He stared at the sea again, intently. "On the skyline, sir."

They all stared into the dark, to where he'd pointed.

On the up-roll Tim pointed again. "There."

"Didn't see anything. But I'm going up to the crow's nest," said the lieutenant. "You stay here, Miss Calland. Clipped on. Don't move."

So Clara did, staring into the dark too. "What did you see?" she asked, not seeing anything.

"Square black edges," explained Tim. "I think . . . a ship's super-structure, and maybe funnels. But she doesn't have any lights on. But the sea doesn't have any square things about it."

"It's eyes like a cat you must have! I can barely see anything!" she said, staring again.

Tim was feeling a little foolish about not having heard them coming. But the belief and, well, trust in her voice set his prickles at ease a bit. "It's from living in the tunnels. You spend a lot of time looking into the dark. Get used to it, I guess," he said gruffly, not stopping looking at the sea. "There it is again. See. On the upswing. Just there."

"I . . . think I might have," said Clara, doubtfully.

Lieutenant Willis came back as they stared out into the night together. "Good spotting, youngster. The masthead watch had just signalled the bridge about seeing something when I got there. I got a sighting of it through the masthead night-glasses. It's a four-stack destroyer, Margot-class. Running without lights, she's hunting."

"So what do we do now, sir?" asked Tim.

"Pretty much what we were doing, son. Watch her. We'll reset the sails a bit and run slightly more easterly, I'd guess. She's maybe eight knots off, and probably won't pick up our sails or mast in the dark. She might hear our engines, so we're unlikely to use those until we've added a bit of distance between us. Come, miss. I'd better get you belowdecks. We'll have a sail-crew up here in a few minutes."

So Tim was left to look out alone again until the sail-crew came up to reset the sails, and then he went off watch.

# CHAPTER 10

**D**uke Malcolm was doing his best to remain patient with the Lord High Admiral. Visiting the admiral in the Admiralty irritated him. Duke Malcolm liked people to come to his offices, but the admiral had asked the duke first. "It's uncertain how the Russians knew that we had planned an intercept when the airship docked in London. The point is, they did and organised a very effective distraction. It was obviously decided that it would be safer to send her by submarine, something they were quite correct about," said Duke Malcolm.

Lord Admiral Lesseps nodded. "You've told me before, Your Grace, how allowing these submarines to survive serves our purposes. But they're underhand and unfair and un-English."

Not for the first time Duke Malcolm wondered if the Lord Admiral had quite understood that the submarine traders weren't particularly concerned about being "un-English." Unfortunately the Lord Admiral was far too well connected for Duke Malcolm to be rid of him easily. His family had influence that was of value even to the house of Windsor-Schaumburg-Lippe. They owned vast steelworks and collieries in the colonies as well as here and in Germany. The duke therefore chose to ignore this idiocy. "The question now is just where we anticipate them going to port, as it appears the Royal Navy can't find them at sea."

The admiral looked mildly offended, but not quite ready to start a fight with the head of Imperial Intelligence about it. "The new equipment we're fitting does mean we can triangulate on them when they use their engines, provided we have two ships with the new gear, within a ten-mile radius of the submarine. We can detect them at twenty miles, but not work out where they are. But when they run under sail, not. And there is a lot of ocean out there." The admiral pointed at the large wall-map stuck with varicoloured pins. "It seems unlikely that they will try to run the Baltic Sea, so that leaves the North Atlantic route to Romanov-on-the-Murman."

"Which means they have to re-coal at either their nest on the Shetlands or Trondheim's Fiord," said Duke Malcolm, tired of being told what he already knew.

The admiral bowed. "Quite so, Your Grace. My aide, Captain Margolis, has the disposition of the fleet elements ready to deal with these nests," said the admiral, with a small smile of satisfaction.

The aide got up and indicated on the map with his long wooden pointer. "Because of the possibility of trouble with the Norwegians, the dreadnought *Invincible George* and her group will be steaming here. They will be on station from the twelfth. The armoured cruiser *Martinique*, and the Margot-class destroyer *Camberwell*, and their coaling support vessel are already in Scapa Flow. If we fail to detect them, or receive information from you, Your Grace, they are scheduled to sail to join the *Invincible George* on the morning of the thirteenth. We have the submarine access channels mapped, and those will be mined."

The duke didn't listen to the admiral's aide droning on about coaling and the plans on how to raid the nests. Instead he was thinking about the report from Professor Browne. It appeared that Dr. Calland was a Cambridge graduate. She had worked on azoic dye isomers—whatever that meant. There had been an explanation. Nitrogen came into it somewhere. Browne had some of his men checking her work at Imperial Chemicals and Dyes.

In the meantime he had better get the Irish Interest section to compile a complete dossier on this woman. She had a child. That presumably meant that it had a father.

And that might be a lever.

The duke did not understand familial love at a personal level. But he knew it worked on lesser persons.

# CHAPTER 11

The submarine ran on its coal-fired Stirling engines, just below the surface, all day, diving on a couple of occasions to avoid spotter airships. Once they heard the distant sound of drop-mines. Tim knew this was unusual—once the subs had got out to sea, they seldom used their engines, as the coal dust was heavy and took up cargo space, and besides, the blowers had to be re-ceramic-coated after they'd done a certain number of hours. The boat would have to be laid up in a safe port, not working, while that happened. And usually, once away from the cities and the coast, the submarines had a peaceful enough time of it.

Usually.

Not this time.

"Looks like we'll be running for the Faroes instead of the Shetlands. They're hunting us hard," said one of the senior ratings.

Tim had to wonder just why they wanted this submarine so badly. It had to be the woman. But why on earth was she so important? She seemed quite ordinary, if rather bookish. She was a doctor. But not a people-doctor, as some of the crew had found out. "I asked her for something for my chilblains," said Smitty, the bosun. "She said she might be able to help if I had chemical problems, not medical ones. Dyeing clothes was more her line than curing the dying, she said. Used to work in that big industrial dye-works in Ireland, she did."

"So why are they looking for her?" asked Tim. Maybe everyone else knew?

Smitty shrugged. "Maybe she made King Ernest's new weskit the wrong colour."

That got a chuckle from the mess-crew. The king was famous for setting the fashion, and his bright cravats, waistcoats, and odd-coloured knee-breeches were as much privately laughed at as publicly imitated. He was most unlike Duke Malcolm, who only appeared to wear military uniform. They said the duke even wore his shako to bed. And everyone knew that the duke really ran the British Empire. . . .

Tim decided to ask Clara the next time he met her, which happened while he was cleaning cabins. She was becoming quite friendly with all of them, although Tim didn't quite know what to make of the way she treated him. He wasn't really used to girls, and knew nothing about the way top-siders behaved.

"Oh, you're talking to me now," she said, smiling to take at least some of the sting out of the words when he asked. "I don't really know. Mother won't tell me. And to be honest I don't know if I would understand. Or really want to."

Tim was taken aback by that. "But why don't you want to?"

She sniffed. Pulled a face. "You didn't have to grow up being expected to also be a chemist. I want to do something else, thank you. And you? What do you want to be?"

Tim blinked. "I guess I never thought about it much back home. It was always about getting enough for dinner, really. My mam"—he swallowed, wishing he knew exactly what had happened in the tubes under London—"she said I should be a submariner, because they ate well." He looked down at his feet. "I worry about her. I used to look out for her. She . . . she should get some of my wages. If . . . if she's all right."

She squeezed his arm. "She will be, I'm sure. I worry about my dad, too."

"Oh. Where is he?" he asked.

It was her turn to swallow, and pause. "In jail in Ireland," she said quietly. "He's a rebel."

She didn't know why she'd told him that. She'd lied about it often enough before. Been found out and been teased and bullied mercilessly. But here they would hardly know if she made something up.

"I'm sorry they caught him," he said sincerely, without a single trace of the mockery she was used to about it, on his broad face. "You must be very proud of him."

Clara blinked. For a moment she thought she was going to explode with fury and hit him. And then she realised he was not persecuting her. Not teasing. His brownish face really was earnest, and his voice showed no hint of the usual sneers she'd lived with. "Proud?" she asked, warily, almost tasting the word, attached to her father.

He looked rather confused at her response. "Well, um, yes. Aren't you? I mean, my mam said that Duke Malcolm's men would as soon shoot a rebel as look at him in Ireland. He must be very brave."

Clara thoroughly embarrassed herself by bursting into tears.

Tim gaped. Then hastily said, "Here. I'm sorry. . . ." He reached a tentative hand out to her.

She shook her head. "Thank you," she somehow managed to say, and then retreated to the heads to cry . . . and think.

Tim wondered if he should go after her. Women. The older lads were right. There was no understanding them. He went back to work, still wondering just what he'd said wrong. Only that "thank you" seemed, well, grateful. But exactly what was going on inside her head he was not too sure. Cotton, hay, and rags in a woman's head, according to the other lads, but his mam was as sharp as a tin-tack. She'd been a teacher once upon a time, before she'd had to flee underground with him as an unborn baby. But the Irish girl had got him thinking about this "what do you want to be" business. Now that he was well fed, food didn't seem quite so much of all that there was to life. Maybe he could add "safe," he thought wryly as the "all quiet" light came on again.

They'd run hard and fast toward the Shetlands. They had days more running to get anywhere else that the boat could refuel. There were submarine lairs off Ireland, in the Hebrides, and several along the wild coasts of Norway. Of course the Royal Navy knew roughly where these were, if not their precise locations. It was just to be hoped that they didn't realise they were pushing on for the Faroe Islands. The weather helped in its own way, by getting worse. It kept the spotter airships at anchor and gave them lots of wind to run with. It also made using the engines during the day difficult, with the engine-snuiver catching too many waves, and the sub bouncing and pitching and rolling. So it took them three days to catch sight of the cliffs and mountains of the Faroe Islands. The weather chose to settle too, meaning near-windless conditions.

"It's shaping up for a big blow," said the old submariners as they packed the gossamer sails into the deck-hatch in the outer hull. At least the submarine could travel below the surface when the weather turned really bad. That helped a little, although they still rolled. Tim hoped it would hold off for a few more days. It would be wonderful to walk on land for a bit.

Clara had fought hard against the wait for nightfall, so that the *Cuttlefish* could come inshore, heading for the second largest island of the Faroes, Eysturoy. She'd done her best smiling at the officers on the bridge, and been granted a quick look through the periscope. In the moonlight it seemed entirely made up of cliffs, chasms, and peaks. There wasn't a light to be seen, but they still crept in, underwater, into one of the fiords. And then in a secluded bay, onto the surface. The submariners preferred marine caves, but this was so out of the way, and they needed to get alongside the coaling barge. The high walls of the fiord kept it still and dark and safe seeming.

Clara had even managed to slip out on deck—wishing she could go on land while the sacks of washed and desulphured coal dust were carried in. The high walls of the fiord cut down the light, and with scudding cloud blacking everything out intermittently, it was too dark to see much. By the race of the clouds across the moon, the weather, so steady before, was beginning to pick up.

The remoteness of the place nearly lulled the *Cuttlefish*'s crew into a false security. It was only the sharp eyes of a lookout that saved them. "Airship!" he shouted.

Everyone looked up, and there it was, high and distinct, and unlike the wispy clouds. Silhouetted against the moon, it was long, silent, and sharklike, closing on them. "Close hatches!" yelled one of the officers. "All below."

They scrambled and fell down the stair. Clara found herself under someone and hauled into the pit, as something made a ripping sound across the water, and a sharp metallic *spang!* sound. They all bundled through the hatchway. Then the captain said through the speaking tubes, "Secure the deck-shaft doors. Prepare to dive."

Already the electric motors were throbbing, and a few moments later the vibration of the Stirlings' feed compressors cut in too as the boat angled down into the fiord. In the meanwhile Clara, various submariners, and two of the Faroese from the coaling barge untangled themselves and hastened to where they were supposed to be. Well, except for the two Faroe Islanders—big, blond-bearded, scared-looking men who didn't seem to speak much English. They were confused and afraid. Clara tried with her few words of German to help. The last place they'd be welcome right now would be the bridge, but short of their cabin she couldn't think of where else to take them. Fortunately, Tim came hurrying by. "Where shall I take these people to?" she asked, grabbing his arm.

He blinked at them. "Oh. The mess, I reckon. I'll ask the mate. He speaks their lingo."

So Clara led them down to the mess. The sub was not diving anymore, but was plainly moving as fast as possible. There was a far-off boom of explosions, but they were some distance away. They waited. Clara tried to explain the "all quiet" light to the two Faroese. Quietly. It didn't stop her feeling guilty when the mate, Mr. Werner, came down as she was speaking.

"Sorry," she whispered. "Was trying to explain." She pointed.

"I think you should get back to your cabin, miss," he said sternly. "But it's not likely that the enemy are listening." He spoke to the two Faroese in their own language while Clara slunk off, feeling guilty. She met Tim again, this time carrying a tray and several empty cups. Whistling as usual.

"Shh!" She looked up pointing and saw that the "all quiet" light she was pointing at was off. "Oh. Sorry."

He grinned. "As Cookie says, no worries. Sparky got his aerial up and picked up their transmissions. The wind is getting up and they report that they can't keep their station. Probably halfway to Norway by now. Said they were going to try to drop some troops, and they were talking to a ship. A dreadnought yet!"

"However did they find us?" asked Clara.

"That's got the captain in fair sweat too," said Tim. "He thought we'd lost them at the Shetlands. And the *Invincible George*—the dreadnought—was steaming towards Bergen, so maybe we had. Anyway, I better run. Got to take those Faroes men up to the bridge, and bring more coffee. We've got a busy night ahead—got to get the rest of the coal dust on board and get gone."

Tim found himself assigned to the loading crews as the submarine slipped back to where they'd left the barge. The captain had out-thought the airship crew. In the narrow fiord, it seemed obvious that the submarine would flee for the open sea. So Captain Malkis had made it look like that . . . and then headed farther up the fiord, while the airship wasted its small stock of drop-mines on the mouth of the fiord.

Well . . . that had saved them. But the barge had no such options. And right now, when they surfaced, it wasn't there.

"Must have sunk her," said the lieutenant, waiting with them to start the reloading. "Hell's teeth. We need that fuel!"

"Loading crew to the deck to look for survivors," said the captain's voice through the speaker-tubes.

So Tim found himself up on deck scanning the dark water. The captain decided to even risk a spotlight, and that shone out across the water. Someone spied floating debris, towards the shoreline. The submarine turned in towards it. And someone flashed a light from the shore. The spotlight swung over, to show three men waving. They edged closer, with the two Faroese on the submarine calling out to the men onshore.

A small boat was pushed into the water, and they paddled out. The Faroese sailors hugged each other . . . well, two of them did. The third man was one of their own crew, who had been down on the barge, collecting the next sack. "They shot up the barge, Lieutenant. Holed her. The locals tried to run for the beach. They were still shooting at us, even if they were trying to chase the submarine down. They've killed one of the local lads and wounded another."

"And the barge?" asked Lieutenant Willis.

"Ach, we had to abandon her," explained Submariner Daniels. "Couldn't have been thirty yards from the beach, but the airship had tried to come back and was being blown over those mountains there. The airship dropped a few parachutes, up there."

"They'll be lucky to get broken legs if not necks, landing up there in the dark," said Lieutenant Willis.

The rescued submariner nodded. "From what Harald—he's their

captain, speaks a bit of English—says, they'll be lucky if the local fishermen don't get to them with gutting knives first."

"Still, with us on the surface, the skipper needs that light off, and to be told about this. Jump to it, Daniels. To the bridge. And take this Harald with you. The rest of you, below, except the deck watch."

Clara sneaked up to the bridge to find out just what was going on.

"She has a hole in her bow, ja. The fiord is steep sides, see. Even so close to the wall, it is deep water. Maybe . . . seven, eight fa'am," said the Faroese man with a grizzled beard—an even bigger beard than the two men who had been trapped on the submarine. He shrugged fatalistically. "We troll with a gaff, we find her. But she is too heavy to pull out. It's our life-blood down there, ja. And they killed Thorvald."

Captain Malkis sucked his teeth. "We've got divers aboard. We can try and patch her and refloat her. We need the coal."

"Divers is goot. Maybe just take the coal out. Then we pull her out, ja."

"The trouble is they have soldiers up there. And there is the garrison in Tórshavn," said the mate.

The Faroese captain spat. "Them. Ha. They won't put to sea in the wind, ja. Like babies. So if they come it is overland, then over the Kollafiord. And then over the mountain. It could take . . . a day, maybe more. And, it will be going to rain soon."

Captain Malkis nodded. "Very well. Can you take us as close as you can to where the vessel went down?" He looked up at the eavesdropping Clara. "And maybe our youngest diver can make herself useful by finding the divers for me, and telling them to report to the bridge." As she left she heard the captain say, "Lieutenant Willis, I'll need two armed patrols on shore. As lookouts. The bad news is if we have to run, they'll be left here, if they can't get back in time. So pick men we can somehow spare." Trapped and left behind here? That was quite a terrifying idea, thought Clara. Captain Malkis's next words rubbed it in. "Responsible and reliable men . . . but that we could still run the boat without."

Tim looked at the rifle and the issue cutlass. It was the first time he'd ever held one, so he practised a swing with it. "Easy. You'll cut your own fool head off," said Smitty. "Don't know why they bother. We're no match for the king's soldiers."

"Yes . . . but we have to be able to fight back!" said Tim.

"Stop waving that thing around, Barnabas. It's not a toy," said Lieutenant Willis, coming up to them. "And stop that perpetual whistling too. Right. Bosun. You're in charge of this lot. Here's the Very pistol. You're to use the green flare if, or when, you sight them, and retreat with all speed. Fire a few shots in their general direction and run. The red flare means you're in trouble. We probably won't be able to help you. You've got a local with you as a guide, but Olaf doesn't speak much English." The Faroe Islander grinned at them and waved a large hand. He was even bigger than Big Eddie.

They took the Faroes' men's small boat in to the shore. It was so small they needed to do it in two shifts. The other patrol, heading for the farther shore, took the submarine's own rubber inflated pontoon boat.

It was still before dawn, but the sky was definitely lighter, as Tim, Olaf, the bosun, and three other submariners walked away from the pebble beach and up towards a higher point. Olaf said there was something there, but he was not very good at explaining. It turned out to be the ruins of a house, just unmortared stone walls, half collapsed, and the last little corner of a sod roof. It was on the highest point, just before a little secondary valley, and the bigger mountain beyond. They had a good view of the fiord, and out to sea, and some view up the steep slope. It was after dawn by now, but the sun would not be coming up onto them. The sky was heavy with cloud already clinging to the tops of the mountains. There were plenty of those. There actually wasn't a lot of the place that wasn't mountain, Tim thought. He was fairly warm from the slog up here, but there was an icy wind blowing and a drift of cold rain hazed everything briefly as they got to the ruin.

The warmth of the walk up soon went away. The rain came and went, the clouds getting heavier and lower. Below, in the small cove off the fiord, the submarine crew was working like busy little ants. Tim actually saw the barge come up, like a sort of big whale. The crew dragged it closer inshore with ropes. Tim wished he was down there. It looked like hard work, but it had to be warmer, and drier, than up here.

"You're supposed to be watching the mountain and the sea, Barnabas," said the bosun.

"Someone is waving at us. Looks like Cookie," said Tim.

"Bless his Westralian heart," said the bosun, grinning. "Lieutenant said he'd organise some food for us. Run down, Tim. You can tuck that rifle into the dry here."

So Tim put the rifle under the remains of the eave outside the ruin, and ran down the steep slope to the cove. Cookie was standing on the black sand with a sack. "Tucker and some hot brew, boyo," he said with a grin. "They're coming on nicely here. I'm going to borrow the little boat and take some across to the other patrol.

So Tim set off up again, carrying the food sack. It was steep, and another of the waves of rain came hissing down on him, obscuring everything. Still, it wasn't complicated. Just up.

A few yards short of the ruin, Tim slipped on a muddy tussock and landed on his knees, dropping the canvas food sack.

He started to get up when he heard something that made him freeze. "You'll all keep dead still."

It wasn't a voice he knew. It took him a few seconds and a cautious look up to realize that it wasn't addressed at him, either. It was being said inside the ruin.

Tim's first instinct, once he'd got over freezing, was to run. His second thought was that he couldn't. Just couldn't.

He still had the cutlass.

# CHAPTER 12

Clara had quietly got herself up onto the deck at least. She knew well enough by now that they wouldn't let her help. Huh. She was as strong as . . . as Tim, anyway. She looked around to see if he was carrying sacks of dripping coal dust. The chief engineer was lamenting about how to get it dry, to get the salt out of it, and what the salt would do to his precious engines. She went on scanning the crew. No, he wasn't there. Could he be below? There were a few people not out working.

Then she realised: he must be one of the guards they'd posted. One of the ones that would be left behind if the submarine had to run. That made her mouth dry. She still had to talk to him, sometime, about what he'd said about her being proud of her dad. She was, now. Enormously. It was like some immense dam had broken inside her.

She wanted to talk about it. And she didn't dare talk to her mother about him. She was scared it would build the dam again. And, well, she didn't really know who else to talk to. She supposed . . . they were all rebels, trying to bring down the British Empire. Or at least outlaws. She and mother were that too, now. But she knew very little about it, about the struggle to be free, about the people who lived in hiding under London, about how it all fitted together, and she was too embarrassed to ask. They'd all know, and they would think her strange for not knowing. She'd had enough of being out, and being different. She wanted their acceptance, she realized.

She saw Tim come trotting down to the beach—a thin band of black sand—and collect the bag from Cookie and then begin running up the hill again. Then it came on to rain: big, heavy drops. Maybe that would wash the chief engineer's coal a bit. So she went below and collected her sou'wester and oilskin jacket. She'd just come back on the deck when she heard something up the slope.

It sounded like a distant gunshot.

Tim had started to draw the cutlass from his belt. Then the bosun's words came back to him, "We're no match for the king's soldiers." He knew, in his heart of hearts, that he couldn't fight anyone with it.

But his rifle was still under the eave. He crawled forward. He at least knew how to work the bolt and squeeze the trigger. He'd fired a whole three shots at the training range back in the tunnels. Even hit the target. He took the rifle down, carefully took the safety off, and crept to the door arch.

Inside were the submariners . . . and three Ulster Hussars, their red breeches and green pelisses no longer looking parade-ground smart.

Tim didn't notice their appearance. He was too scared. "Drop your weapons." His voice cracked.

The one, startled, did. The other two looked at him. And the bigger of the two, the one with the sergeant's stripes, snorted. "Wee kiddie. Put it down, or I'll kill you."

So Tim shot him.

Well, he tried to.

He'd only ever fired a rifle while lying down, as instructed. With the butt firmly pulled in against his shoulder. As instructed again. It had kicked him into bruises then. Standing up, not with an instructor making sure that the rifle was well against his shoulder, his shot never hit anything, but it knocked Tim half off his feet. He dropped the rifle in the process. The Hussar lunged at him—with a bayonetted rifle. Tim rolled, narrowly managing not to get impaled by the bayonet.

The moss-chinked wall was less lucky. The bayonet screeched on a piece of rock and slid its full length into the mossy crack . . . and a rock fell down onto the rifle. The Hussar tried to wrench it loose and failed. Frantically, Tim pulled at the cutlass in his belt as the man let go of his rifle and dived for Tim's dropped one. The cutlass came free, and Tim's desperate, wild swing got the Hussar across the hand. Tim had hit him with the back of the blade—not the sharp edge—in sheer panic. It didn't cut the Hussar's fingers off as it might have otherwise done. But it hit his hand hard enough to make him drop the rifle, as Tim staggered upright, pointing the cutlass at his chest, tip wavering. "Don't move."

"I wouldn't, or I might shoot you," said the bosun, pushing the muzzle of a rifle into the man's back. And the sergeant might have thought he could beat Tim, but the bosun's voice was grim and steady. The prisoner's hands came up slowly.

Tim looked at the rest of the scene now, feeling as if he might just faint. Olaf had the man who had dropped his weapon in a bear hug. The other Hussar was lying on the ground, his caubeen off and his head bleeding.

"See if there are any more of them, Tim-boy," said the bosun. "And pick up your rifle!" He prodded the man with the rifle he was holding. "How many of you are there?"

"Hundreds," said the Hussar sergeant sullenly. "If you surrender I'll be seeing you get fairly treated. And the boy too."

The bosun chuckled. "Likely. I reckon you'd have to kill him, and your mates, to stop the story getting out."

Tim peered into the rain. "Can't see anyone. Can't really see anything. It's bucketing down."

"I reckon it'd be no use firing a Very light in this, except to tell his friends—if he has any—where he is. How's that one?" He jerked his head at the bleeding man. The submariners were busy tying up the man who Olaf had squeezed.

"He's not dead. You hit him hard with that rock," said Jonas.

"Tie him up, and haul him under the roof," said the bosun.

"Why?" asked Jonas.

"Because he's wet through and he'll probably die otherwise," said the bosun.

"But, I mean, he would have killed us," protested the submariner.

"He might have, but I'm no Hussar," said the bosun. "Come on. I think we may as well leg it down until we can see the boat. No use signalling in this."

"And the other two?" asked the other submariner.

"Bring 'em. That's for the captain to decide. Give me some more of that cord of yours, Sam." He prodded the captive. "Roll over, you. I'll have nothing against shooting you if you try anything. Put a leash on that one's neck."

So they tied the man's hands behind his back, and, after taking a careful look outside the half-fallen walls, where all they could see was rain, they retreated down the hill.

"Was that a shot?" Clara asked the mate.

"I do not think so, no," he said in his guttural Dutch-accented voice.

Clara was sure that it had been, but wasn't sure what she could do next, except to listen. Listen really really hard, and stare into the rain.

She was sure it was a shot. But why just one?

Halfway down, Tim had to stop and be sick. The bosun stopped with him as he retched.

Tim stood up, wiping his mouth. "I made a proper mess of it, didn't I?"

The bosun chuckled. "Well, you saved our lives, and maybe the boat and probably the men on the barge. There were only three of them, but if they had got down, got into a good position, and started shooting, well, they'd have killed a few, and the skipper would have dived without us."

"Oh. Leave us here?" Tim asked, trying to deal with the idea.

"If he had to. So you did good, lad. How was the loading coming on?"

"Dunno. I just took the food from Cookie . . . Cookie. I left the food and his bag up there. I've got to go back." Tim turned.

The bosun grabbed him by shoulder, turned back him downhill. "No, you don't, you young chump."

"But it's food!" protested Tim. Food in the tunnels under London was always a little tight, even at the best of times.

"And we've got more, and chances are you wouldn't find it, and the skipper is going to leave. You want to stay here?" asked the bosun.

"Um, no," admitted Tim.

"Well, get a move along then," said the bosun.

When they could just see the barge and the submarine, the bosun picked out a tumble of rocks. "Right. Take cover here. Sam you run down and find the duty officer and tell them we've got prisoners and that the Hussars might be close. Judging by the state of these we can hold them off if we have to."

So they watched the hill. Tim made very sure to hold that rifle so that the butt was pulled in tight to his shoulder. He hoped that he wouldn't have to use it.

Clara spotted the man running down out of the rain. Too big for the cabin boy, and too pale-faced too. The lieutenant was over on the half-beached barge, helping load bags of coal dust. She couldn't quite hear what the man panted out, but the word "Hussar" carried. Lieutenant Willis ran across the planks they'd been using to carry the coal across and down into the submarine.

Minutes later three of the crew went off with the man who had run down, and the coal loading got an extra boost of haste added. Then the three came back . . . with two extra men in very dirty and battered Ulster Hussar uniforms. They were hustled across to the submarine—but not before Clara had been told very sternly to go to her cabin and stay there. "It's important that they don't see you," said Captain Malkis.

Up on the slope, Tim watched nervously. And his stomach, now that it was completely empty, gurgled and grumbled about the bag of food up there in the rain. He could see the coaling barge was riding a bit higher in the water. Some of her crew were fiddling with the engine powering their big stern-paddle. By the looks of the steam-cloud, not with much success.

"Sprung a seam, I reckon," said the bosun, knowledgably.

Then there was a green Very light flare, obviously fired low over the water. It whizzed over the barge and hit the bank they were on. "Must be troops from the garrison at Tórshavn," said the bosun. "I reckon that's our recall, boys. Yes. The barge has cast off. I hope the others make it. I wouldn't care to be on an inflatable boat when they're shooting at me."

"Look." One of the men pointed. "That was what they saw."

There were several small boats coming down the fiord—from the upper end. "They crossed over and got boats from the village at the top of the fiord!"

There was a crackle of gunfire . . . and the submarine—while Tim and his companions were nearly at the shore now—slipped away, underwater.

"They're leaving us!" screamed Tim, as the smoke trail from the engines bubbled up.

The bosun swore. Long and colourfully. Then said, "We'd better head back uphill. See if we can find the food bag, and see if Olaf's people will hide us. No point in your shooting at them, Mac," he said to the man who was carefully lying down and taking aim. "It'll just tell them we're here. You'll never hit them anyway. They must be half a mile off. And we might need those bullets."

"She's not running away, Smitty," said the submariner. "Look at the smoke."

Tim could do more than that, now that he knew what to look for. He could see the periscope, slicing through the water at speed towards the two small fishing boats. "They're going to ram them!"

The bosun shook his head. "Probably lift them."

As he said that, the two attacking boats turned as one, racing towards the shore, the troops in them firing down into the water.

"Fat lot of good that'll do them. Water's powerfully slowing stuff. Idiots are giving the skipper their tails. Bows are harder." As he said this one of the boats did a good imitation of a bucking horse, and nose-dived. It didn't quite sink, but there were uniformed men in the water. The other vessel . . . suddenly stopped. People fell off that too. Olaf laughed. "Hit Shteen for the vorter." He tapped a rock.

They looked at him in puzzlement. Sam was quickest on the uptake. "They've run aground. And look, the other patrol has the inflatable out. They're rowing down as fast as they can, away, towards the sea."

"They're thinking quicker than we are." The bosun spat. "There are too many of us for that little boat. Olaf, are you coming with us? We need to get to where we can get aboard the sub. And this water is too cold for swimming."

Olaf shook his head, pointed up into the cloud and the rain-shrouded mountainside. "You go. Me goot."

"She'll take three, not more. Mac, boy, and Jonas, onto her. And don't argue," said the bosun. "We'll run along the shore, and you can come back for us if you've got the chance."

So they paddled out, and sure enough, the *Cuttlefish* came up, water pouring off her flanks. "Jump. I'm going to fetch Smitty and Sam," yelled Mac. So they did. Nearly had the little boat over, and the water was icy, but someone on the deck flung a loop at them and they were hauled, gasping, over the curve of the deck and up. "Get below. We're after the inflatable," said the lieutenant.

"Sir, the bosun . . ."

"We'll be back if we have the chance." The sub was already accelerating toward the inflatable, which was paddling towards them as fast as the submariners could. Tim could hear small-arms fire in the distance. Tim, heart-sore and scared, almost fell down the spiral stair and was hauled in. Just behind him came the first of the other patrol. The *Cuttlefish* turned. Tim desperately wished he knew just what was happening.

"Get yourself dry," said someone roughly. It was the mate. "Sir. But I need to know—"

"That's an order. Move," he said with rough kindness.

So Tim moved to his tiny shared cabin and shed his very wet clothes. Put dry ones on and went back out to try to find out what had happened.

He walked smack into Clara. She looked ready to faint. "Oh. It's not you."

"What? What's not me?" he asked.

"Someone got shot," said Clara, uneasily. "Just as they were getting them off the boat, I heard."

Tim closed his eyes. "Are they . . . dead?"

"I don't know. I didn't even know if it was you or not," said Clara.

Just then Lieutenant Willis came along. "He's alive, before you ask. Boy, they could probably use you with the greasers in the engine room."

"Yessir. Uh. Who is alive, sir?" asked Tim.

"McConnell. We hauled him out of the water. Mac is not in a good way, but alive," said the lieutenant. "I'd like to have a good surgeon to treat him, but at the moment he's holding his own." The lieutenant was the submarine's medical officer.

"And the bosun, sir?" asked Tim. Ever since the net incident the bosun had looked out for him.

The lieutenant bit his lip. "He, Sam Jones, and the local, Olaf, fled up the mountainside. I didn't see them being pursued. It's possible that they got away. The local resistance is quite well organised. We'll be in touch with them by radio tonight."

"Any chance of picking them up, sir?" asked Tim, still hopeful.

The lieutenant shook his head. "Not much, lad. The Faroes see quite a few submarines, though. If they don't get caught, there is a good chance of them getting a berth on another boat."

It was not much comfort, but it was all he got. So he went to work in the engine room.

Clara could see how upset the boy was. She hadn't known either of the submariners that well, so it didn't hurt as much. Still, it felt like desertion. She smiled at the lieutenant. "I hope I am allowed out of our cabin again?"

"I didn't know you were confined to it. What did you get up to this time?" he asked, raising his eyebrows. The lieutenant was fast becoming one of her favourites.

"I didn't do anything. I got told to go into my cabin and stay there, when the Hussar prisoners were brought aboard."

"Ah. The skipper didn't want them confirming that you, and therefore your mother, were actually on board. They're down in the brig now. So long as you stay away from there, it will be fine."

"What are we going to do with them?" asked Clara.

"Probably drop them on one of the outer islands," said the lieutenant. "We're waiting to hear from the local resistance if they can use them for some kind of prisoner swap—if the Imperial forces caught our men, that's likely something we'll try, not that they usually agree. But at least the two of them talked. Gave us a bit more information."

"Oh? What did they tell us?" asked Clara.

"Us?" He smiled. "You're far too quizzy, young lady."

"Please?" she asked, giving him her very best smile. She'd found it worked quite well. She wasn't too sure why.

He laughed. "You'll just pester it out of someone else, if I don't. They didn't want to talk either, but when we separated them, we persuaded each of them that the other one would never know, and it was a case of whether we dropped them overboard . . . or dropped them back on the Faroes. It seems the skipper was right. We lost our tail at the Shetlands, but they got a tip-off that we were heading here. The nearest ship was a long way off, so they came from Aberdeen in the airship. There were only twenty of them and they had a terrible jump, in the dark, and in the wind, onto mountainous terrain. They failed to find the rest of their squad—they left two injured men behind on the mountain and came on, just the three of them. They hoped to keep us from loading fast, or at least from filling our coal bunker—because the dreadnought *Invincible George* is on its way here as fast as it can steam.

The lieutenant smiled. "And I hope she enjoys searching for us. The weather topside is really foul. I think we may have finally shaken them. Finding a submarine out in the Atlantic is not that easy."

Clara hoped that that at least was true.

# CHAPTER 13

Tim was in the mess, finally catching up on some of the food he hadn't seen much of, when Lieutenant Willis sought him out. He was a good sort, the lieutenant. "You'll be happy to know your friend the bosun and Jones are in good shape, and being hidden. They've been moved to another island—and now, too late, all of the Faroe Islands is under lockdown, so they can't move. Anyway, we can drop off the two Hussars."

"Drop them off?" asked Tim.

"It's that or feed them. And they eat even more than you do. We'll drop them off on a life-raft just off Fugloy. It's a little eastern-most island with some sheer cliffs. It'll take our Winged Hussars a little while to find their way to one of the villages on the other side, and still longer to get news off the island."

Tim found out, in his apology to Cookie about the bag and food, that oddly he had barely been at the fight with the Hussars. Well, he hadn't exactly been very good at fighting them. But it seemed that he'd turned up, given the others the distraction they needed, and they'd overpowered them. It was kind of . . . annoying. Not that he expected to be a hero or anything. Not after the mess he'd made of it. But he hadn't seen what Jonas had done in the fight either, so he couldn't say much. Cookie asked what had happened. "Dunno. I was too busy falling over my own feet and dropping my rifle to see."

Cookie laughed. "That sounds more like me sort of heroics."

Still, his adventure with the Hussars had its reward. Well . . . sort of. More like a punishment really. He got to clean the rifles. And the quartermaster, who was also the armourer, showed him how to hold and cross-draw the cutlass. "I tried to do it in the fight. I wasn't any good at it," explained Tim, when he asked for advice.

The quartermaster pulled a face. "It's really an outdated weapon. But I'll show you a few passes if you like. We should teach everyone. The Japanese still make a big thing of it." He patted Tim on the back. "At least you have the common sense to admit that you know nothing. That takes guts in a youngster. You come back when you knock off. I'll give you a few lessons."

Tim—as the junior cabin boy—also got the job of cleaning out the now-empty brig. It was not exactly something that looked as if it took a lot of cleaning. There were metal shelves for sleeping on, with folded-over edges, and the floor, walls, bars, and a metal roof. But the prisoners had been muddy, and had obviously collapsed onto those shelf-bunks. Tim got a bucket and set to cleaning it. One of the men had plainly rubbed the mud off his boots on the edge of the lower shelf-bunk. It had dried hard—as hard as cement, it seemed. Tim tried to rub it off, and then to chip it off with his fingers, and then, grabbing the folded edge, he tried his thumb.

Only there was something sharp under there. It cut his finger. He sucked it. It was a nasty cut, just on the thumb-tip. He bent down and felt—very cautiously—to see what on earth it could be that had cut him.

It was a knife. A long, thin-bladed, double-edged dagger, with a horn hilt. The blade must have been fully eight inches long, but it was narrow enough to be hidden on the inside lip of the shelf-bunk's fold.

"What are you doing with that, boy?" said the mate in his gruff Dutch accent, from behind him. Tim had trouble understanding him, sometimes. Even when he hadn't made him jump out of his skin.

"I just found it, sir. Under this shelf," he explained.

"Ah!" said Mate Werner. "I'd better take that to the captain. Well found! Those Hussars must have had it hidden about them."

The mate took the knife, slipped it into a pouch he was carrying.

"Well, get on with it, boy. And you do not mention this to anyone. We don't want to cause alarm."

Tim, without meaning to, did tell. His next job took him to the galley, to wash pots and dishes. Cookie liked his dishwater almost scalding hot. Tim stuck his hands into it. "Ouch!"

"What's wrong, Tim-o?" asked the cook.

"The water's just a bit hot on this cut," he said, holding it up.

Cookie inspected it. "Nasty! You was trying to shave your hands?" he asked, laughing.

"No, I was cleaning the brig, and I found this big knife under the bunk . . . um. I wasn't supposed to tell anyone."

"No worries. I don't dob in me mates," said the cook, giving him a cheerful slap on the back. "Wonder how long that's been in there for! Doing time for assault, maybe."

"Um. The mate reckoned it must have come off those Hussars."

Cookie shook his head. "Couldn't be. Mickey and me searched them. Stripped them right out of their boots. Must have been there a while."

"Oh," said Tim. He'd worked with Cookie. If Cookie did anything it was well done. Tim was sure Cookie wouldn't have missed a razor blade, let alone that knife.

Tim couldn't see any way of telling the mate without getting either himself or Cookie into trouble. So he didn't.

It was good to be away from the dangers they'd encountered. The submarine, out of sight of land, ran mostly on her sails—even during the daylight hours. The crow's nest had two watchers on duty then. Tim drew his first watch up there. Banks and Elman were aloft, and Tim had pulled his first duty with Jonas.

Still near the base of the rigging, barely thirty feet above the deck, Tim looked down. His hands clawed tight to the ratline. He froze. He wasn't used to being this high, and . . . and . . . and *open*.

Unfortunately, Jonas chose to look down just then. "Get a move on, you lazy little scut!"

"I . . . I'm scared." The moment he'd said it, Tim knew he shouldn't have.

"Oh poor likkle baby. Darkie, you should love going up here. You've nearly gone white."

Tim gritted his teeth and climbed another step. Standard, Jonas, and Banks had been at this for a while now. They caught it from each other.

"Want me to come hold your hand, diddums?" said Jonas, waving one at him. "Not so brave up here where the men are, are you?"

Tim climbed. Somehow he climbed. Not looking down. Sweating. Clinging to each ratline with all his strength. Eventually he got near the crow's nest. Banks came scrambling down past him. Gave him a shove—not hard enough to push him off. Tim screamed. Couldn't help it. He'd faithfully clipped and unclipped his safety all the way up, which most of the men didn't bother with, unless it was bad weather aloft.

"Scaredy-cat!" said Banks, not even bothering to clip in, descending with casual ease.

It was a four-hour stint of mockery. Tim barely noticed. He was just scared of the climb back down. He was not much of a watchman, but fortunately there was nothing to see.

When their relief came up, Tim was barely able to talk. It was Nicholl and Sampson come up to relieve, and Jonas greeted them with, "Nothing to see except that Darkie's gone white with fear."

"First time aloft?" asked the grizzled Sampson with a smile. "Used to frighten me witless when I first come on the boat."

"Seem to recall you had a bit of funk yourself, Jonas," said Nicholl. "Show you something, kid." He was clipped onto the safety loop on the edge of the nest. And he stepped backward. Hung on his belt, and then pulled himself in again. "You're relieved, Jonas. Get down. Kid. You stay here a minute. Sammy and I want to sort you out."

Tim did, nervously. But it was less terrifying than going down. There wasn't much room up there, so both of the new lookouts hung onto the outside of the basket. "Tim—that's your name, right?"

Tim nodded.

"Reach up as high as you can; there is a high loop for clipping in. Clip it. Do it in two stages so you're never unclipped."

Tim decided that no matter what they did to him, he was not going any higher. The flagpole terminated some fifteen feet above his head. Not going to do it! But he clipped in, cautiously.

"Right, young 'un," said Sampson. "Now if I ever sees you unclipped up here again, I'll clip both your earholes so your head will ring like a bell for a week."

"Jonas said we didn't up here," said Tim, gratefully.

"He's an idjit," said the older submariner. "Now, I wants you to lean your weight onto the belt. Then hold onto it, both hands. Then take your feet off the floor. You can't fall out of the nest, and me and Nicholl are blocking the gap."

Gritting his teeth, but reassured by the rough kindness, Tim did it. Hung by his waist, as the mast swayed.

"It'll hold you, see. You see you allus have one clip on a shroud line, not on the ratlines, and you can't fall."

"Take it slow going down. Don't look down. Follow a shroud line with your foot until you hit the ratline," said Nicholl. "You'll be fine."

It took him a long time to get down, but he got down, which for the last three hours he'd not been able to believe he could.

With the submarine up on her hydrofoil outriggers, and under as many of the gossamer sails as the sailing master could find space for, the *Cuttlefish* moved at a goodly speed across the water. There was a fair amount of sail-work to be done on some days. On others . . .

well, you had to be ready, but Tim found himself with—for the first time in his life—time when he wasn't out foraging for rats, or working at something. A lot of that time was spent on polishing the brass-work, and other make-work jobs that the officers invented to keep the crew busy and the ship looking polished.

It was also the time that cabin boys and junior submariners were supposed to put in extra work toward their certificates. Tim had never really thought about "what he wanted to be" until she had put the idea there. Now he thought about it quite a lot.

Clara went up on deck—many of the submariners were there, when they were off shift, and the ship was sailing on her outriggers, which fascinated her. They fitted flush against the submarine when she was diving or riding with her deck just on the surface, making the submarine more the shape of an ordinary ship. But for fast sailing the thin metal false hulls were pushed out and downward on curving arms, making hydrofoils filled with inflated rubber pontoons, and these allowed the sub to skim above the water. Submerged and on her electric motor the submarine was very slow, barely able to do five knots and only for a very short time. On the big coal-dust burning Stirling engines, she could, the chief engineer had proudly told her, do fourteen knots, on the snorkel. Running on the big gossamer sails, all the masts erected, "We don't rightly know, missy," said the sail-master. "It'd depend on the wind. But faster than his smelly coal-fired engines anyway. A good bit faster."

"Ah, but my engines don't need the wind to be blowing," said the engineer, cheerfully, leading two of his men out on a swinging plank-seat to check the thin metal of the false hull for damage.

"And the wind replenishes itself, not like your coal dust," said the sail-master, going forward to check on the stunsails. It was plainly a well-exercised argument between two old friends.

Clara spotted Tim, nearby, leaning against the cowling, nose in a book, forehead wrinkled in concentration.

"You've got books!" she exclaimed. She'd missed reading so badly that it hurt.

He looked up. Blinked. "Borrowed it. It's navigation. There is quite a lot maths in it, and I never learned that much."

"I was quite good at maths at school," said Clara, carefully not saying "top of the class." She'd learned that being good at maths came a close second to having a divorced mother and a father in prison, for making you unpopular with people who weren't.

"There's not that much formal schooling in the tunnels," he admitted. "I mean . . . um. Anyway. Could you show me how to do this equation? I don't understand it at all. And I need to be able to do it if I'm to pass my junior submariner's ticket. And I want to."

"Surely," said Clara. It was rather a novelty to be asked to explain maths. It was a novelty too to have someone who wanted to understand. "So: what's a submariner's ticket?" she asked, once she'd explained how to do the equation. He was quick enough to learn, even if he didn't know all the basics; but more importantly than being quick, he was trying hard. He desperately wanted to understand, and she could see it in the intense concentration on his face. "Like tram tickets, but only for underwater stations? Do you have conductors waiting to come and clip our tickets?"

He grinned. "Well, we use underwater stations in London Town." And that thought plainly stirred up worries. "Wish I knew about my mam."

"You haven't heard anything?" she asked.

He shook his head. "Not really easy to find out. Sparky says they're getting radio messages from the Underpeople again. But that's official stuff. I'd love to hear her voice."

She was silent for a bit, not knowing quite what to say. "Same with my dad," she said, eventually. "I . . . I haven't spoken to him for nearly a year." She felt as if she might burst into tears again.

"Let's talk about the ticket instead," he said, his voice a little gruff. "See, it's a certificate. You have to get them to stay on the boat, and to move up. I'm only a cabin boy now. And . . . and if I want to go on, um, you know, to be something more than just an ordinary ranker or submariner . . . I have to pass these."

"Oh. Really?"

"It's not like the top-side, where you get born to your situation," he said with an edge to his voice, and she realized that this too was dangerous ground for some reason. "Or that's what my mam told me. In the submarines, if you can learn, you can be anything. Mr. Amos says I have a chance to go for diver or bridge-hand. If I work hard."

Clara felt slightly guilty. "I didn't know. I thought you sort of learned it on the job," she said. She'd always known that she'd go to university. Not that everyone did. Lots of girls just grew up and got married. But her mother and her grandmother had. She was expected to, too. "But of course you can. You could do anything," she said, trying the smile that worked so well on Lieutenant Willis.

It was wasted on him, though. He was obviously seeing something else in his mind's eye, not her. He didn't even seem to notice. Instead, he answered, "I couldn't be a soldier. I thought . . . I might join one of the rebel companies and well, pay the Imperials back for blowing up my home," he said fiercely, as if his home hadn't been a pumped-out damp hole under London's canals. "But when I shot that man up that hill . . ." He shuddered.

"You shot someone? I heard the bang. But the mate said he didn't think it was a shot," said Clara.

Tim managed a bit of a smile. "Let's rather say I tried to shoot him. I had to. And I missed. He couldn't have been ten feet away. And then I tried to hit him with the cutlass. Only I messed that up too. But it all came out all right. Only the one Hussar that Smitty hit with a rock really got hurt. I didn't like the blood much. So I've thought about it and decided that I'd . . . I'd try and get my ticket, as a bridge-hand. See, we all have to study, and I had thought that

I'd try for something easier. Just get my basic submariner's ticket. But now I'm going to try for the bridge. If I can."

Clara blinked and realised that she hadn't really quite judged him right. She'd thought he was just not scared of anything. Brave. Now . . . she suddenly realised that he was scared. He really was alone too, far more so than she was. When she'd thought he was some kind of brave hero . . . he'd just been doing what he thought had to be done, even though he was terrified. And that was braver still than not being scared of anything. She'd have liked to hug him . . . but, well. No. Not right now. Encouragement and support though, yes. "Indeed, you're going to! Mr. Amos is quite right. Uh. Who is he?"

He seemed to find that funny. "The quartermaster. He's also the armourer. He's a good 'un. He gives some lessons, and he also is part of the examining board. They say he's very strict, though. Doesn't play favourites."

She placed the man he was talking about now. Except for the two divers, whose work took a lot of very heavy lifting, most of the submariners were not large, and Mr. Amos was smaller than most. He had a shiny bald head and sharp little blue eyes. "He gave me my deck kit. So when does he teach you?"

"There's a roster next to the mess door. He really was a teacher once, like my mam. But she taught little children, and he taught sixth form. Long ago. He got into trouble for teaching a part of history he wasn't supposed to . . . and well, he ended up underground, and he's been on the submarines for years. He's been everywhere. America. Japan. Australia."

Clara had not really realised just how far and wide the submarines travelled and traded. She said so.

"Oh yes," said Tim. "Mr. Amos says the British Empire would probably fall without them."

"What? I mean they're trying to sink and kill us," said Clara.

"Yes. I didn't understand it either. But he says all sorts of goods that come from countries the British Empire is at war with, but can't do without stuff from, arrive through us. He says we're keeping alive something we want to kill. But if we don't keep the Empire supplied we'll starve the Underpeople. He talks like that. I never really understand half of it. He says it's the real history we ought to learn. He likes history."

The quartermaster sounded just the person to ask about all the parts of her own life she couldn't really ask her mother about. Like just what her dad had been doing. And why.

So: later she looked at the roster, and . . . went to talk to the captain. She overheard what the other two cabin boys said about her looking at it. And she'd overheard the first mate earlier. That was life on the submarine. It was a small and crowded place. You couldn't help overhearing things. . . .

"Captain," she said, seriously. "I may be being a disruptive influence on the discipline of the crew."

Captain Malkis looked at her from under lowered brows, with a small smile hiding itself under his moustache. "Now who are you quoting at me, Miss Calland?"

"It'd be just something I heard," she said airily. The captain was rather like her dad had been. You could tease him. The mate was much more serious. "The younger men are not working towards their qualifying examinations. And I am missing my schooling."

"Ah." The captain nodded. "I see where this is leading. Mr. Amos is complaining about the lack of attendance again. Don't worry. . . ."

This was going in the opposite direction from which Clara had intended. "Oh no. It wasn't Mr. Amos. Never. I was thinking, though, would it be a good thing if you were to order that I attend the classes for the junior ratings? As an example."

Captain Malkis laughed and shook his head. "It would probably distract them even more. And make the mate even more sour about having women aboard. He'll get used to it. He's an old-style submariner. From Holland. They're very traditional over there."

Clara gave up on being tricky. The mate was always very polite to her. She'd thought at first he didn't like her, but he seemed to be going out of his way to be nice to her now. It showed you just never knew what people said behind your back. Or maybe it was the captain remembering an early part of the voyage. "Well, actually, Captain Malkis, I'd like to do it. I'm bored too. And we've at least a week before we get to America. That's a long time for me, but not long enough to disrupt anyone's studies. Please?"

Honesty obviously helped. "True. I can't really order you to do it, though. Those sort of orders need to come from your mother," said the captain.

"She's so busy, she won't notice," said Clara. "And I might learn something useful."

The captain shrugged. "It's barely another eight days. You may as well."

She gave him her best curtsey. It was a ladylike thing to do, and so her mother had insisted that she'd learn to do it gracefully. She'd been shocked to find that her mother, having made her learn, didn't actually approve of it. Parents were so hard to understand. "A woman can be anything she wants to be, but in this world you sometimes have to curtsey to get there. One day that'll change too." What was that supposed to mean?

They'd all thought it was a bit of a joke when the girl joined the class. Well, Tim had been less sure it was going to be as funny as they thought. She'd showed him how to calculate that angle. But he laughed with the others. He didn't want to stick out too much. It was hard enough with Banks and Standard picking on him all the time.

They didn't laugh for long. She was pretty smart. And she'd done things at school that they hadn't. "So if your current is running at 3.3 knots southeast, and the wind-speed is 4 knots northerly, at what minimum speed and on what heading do you have to travel to move due south?" said Mr. Amos. "Write it up on your slates."

Clara drew the vectors while the others were still scratching their heads. Mr. Amos stalked about. After a few minutes he took her slate. "It appears, Miss Calland, that you do not know what the minimum speed for steerage is."

The other juniors and cabin boys laughed.

"She does, however, know more than the rest of you. A submarine does need to be moving faster than a certain speed for its rudders to work effectively. Add the fact that the *Cuttlefish* needs to move at at least two knots to have reliable steerage and explain your method to the class."

It got quite competitive after that.

No one liked being beaten by a mere girl.

"No classes today. We're running silent in an hour," said Mr. Amos.

"What's happening?" asked Clara, ever curious.

"Just a migrant fleet heading for Greenland that's been sighted. But there might be ships with hydrophones."

So that day was a silent, still one. It was still very much better than the early days. Clara spent much of it reading a text on navigation, which, seeing as she was catching up and determined to be better at it than all of the rest of them were . . . was actually rather interesting. It was odd; they were only five days off the Boston Shoals. They'd be going ashore there. She and her mother would be out of the smelly narrow confines of the submarine and safe and comfortable again.

She wasn't looking forward to it.

"So have you kissed her yet, Darkie?" asked Banks, after they finished their cabins.

Tim blushed. At least it wasn't quite as obvious on him, but he could still feel his face getting hot. He really didn't like being called "Darkie" for starters, but as his mum said, taking any notice just made them stick it into you more. He didn't like Banks at all either, but he had to try to get along with the rest of the crew. He knew just exactly why he was being given a hard time too. Clara was a bit too smart for some of them. Him too, sometimes. But she didn't mock him when he got things wrong. She was fairly merciless otherwise. It was done in fun, but it surely got under some skins and itched. And she was obviously enjoying it. Nav was a game to her, and she was already better at it than Banks would be in ten years. "I don't know what you mean."

"Your little up-dweller girlfriend, Darkie. She must like 'em small and rough."

"She's not my girlfriend." Tim rushed off, his ears burning, before Banks went on. He wouldn't mind kissing her. He just had no idea how to even suggest the idea, or what to do about it. Or even how to make any kind of move at all. And he was scared if he did . . . he'd be in trouble and she'd stay away from him. And he really, really didn't want that.

Tim was quite glad to think Dr. Calland and her daughter would be getting off the sub soon. Glad, because it was mixing him up, making trouble between him and the others, but sad too. He'd like to have kissed her. At least once.

# CHAPTER 14

Duke Malcolm stood impassive while Prince Albert raged at him.

"You don't understand, Malcolm. You can't send our fleet into their waters. They're sitting on nearly a quarter of the world's coal. Their consumption is nothing like ours. Yes, I know it's been picking up, they're using more, but we really need access to their stocks. We need to stay on trading terms with them. That is why we are officially neutral in this war the United States is having with the Canadian Dominion. We can't afford to confront them right now. Why, the needs of the Greenland colonies . . ."

Malcolm had finally had enough of Prince Albert's going on. And on. "None of that will matter in the event that someone gives the Americans—because that is where it looks like she's going, Albert—a synthetic method of producing nitrates."

Prince Albert snorted. "They already have the nitric acid plants in Wyoming and Kentucky. Synthetics will take over, even if they are expensive. They've been getting efficiency of up to 5 percent now. And the best we can do in Manchester is 3.8 percent. I've been telling the Privy Council this for years, but no one listens."

Trust Albert to know about anything that smacked of science. To have the figures at his fingertips—figures that meant nothing to anyone but Albert. And yes, no one listened to him. If they did, the Empire would have collapsed long ago. It was a good thing that Ernest was the older, even if he was a vain little peacock. The British Empire under Albert would be Hyde Park. Duke Malcolm looked at him, staring in the way that he had long ago discovered totally discomforted his older half-brother. "This—if the fuss the Russians have made of it is any indication, is a much cheaper method," said Duke Malcolm. "And we have no idea of how efficient it is, except that the Russians and now the Americans are keen to have her. At a very large price. They do not do this because they think it unimportant or *they* would not risk our ire. They have. She has something that could change the nitrate problem, take it away from our control."

"Then you need to either capture her, or kill her before the Americans or Russians get her," said Albert.

Duke Malcolm was surprised. His older half-brother was developing sense. . . . And then Albert spoiled it all by adding, "But capture is first prize. You must focus on that, Malcolm. Imagine how many more of our people we could feed if we had a better supply of nitrates."

Malcolm knew Albert was a fool. It wasn't fertilizer that the Empire needed. It was munitions! They'd been badly wrong-footed on the Faroes having assumed that the submarine was headed east. The famous Winged Hussars had made such a bad landing that they might as well not have tried. But at least he did know, definitely, that they had the right submarine. Calland and her daughter were on that one. That much the freed prisoners had been able to tell them, having heard the voices, as well as being told by the spy on the boat. The folly of letting the prisoners go, instead of executing them, left Malcolm shaking his head. His informer had a hidden Marconi transmitter, but was very loath to use it. It had a relatively short range, and the man seemed terrified the submarine's Marconi man would pick it up. The duke's spy was a deep sleeper agent, supposed to maintain cover at all costs. Well, that status would have to change.

Malcolm thought about the dossier on their target. He'd have to shake up the Irish Interest section. Yes, she had divorced Jack Calland, and had been living apart from him when he had been arrested. But associating with rebels left its mark. He'd wondered why the man had escaped execution . . . but he could possibly be used as a lever. Not with the mother, but on the daughter. The dossier had included young Clara Calland's letters to her father. One a month, as permitted. Jack Calland might not have any leverage over his ex-wife. Probably the opposite, in fact. But Dr. Calland was obviously fond of the girl. And in turn, the father could be used as bait for the girl. And the girl as bait for the mother . . . If they failed to kill them, which Malcolm regarded as more practical.

It was a pity his informer balked at murder himself. Of course, it would be difficult on a small vessel with no way of escape, to get away with it. But Duke Malcolm was certain he could have done it. The duke had done so before.

In the meantime he would work on these submariners' American contacts. There'd be some unexplained deaths there. His men had penetrated that part of their organisation very effectively some years ago. Anything happening there . . . he would deal with, perhaps before the United States could take Dr. Calland into its official bosom, but while she was still in the hands of the submariner scum.

The only problem was that of course the American government spied on the submariners and their American sympathisers and contacts too.

# CHAPTER 15

The gossamer sails were checked and packed into their compartments on the outer hull. The masts were not just strapped down onto the deck, but actually taken apart and packed away in the outer hull. Before dawn tomorrow, the submarine would no longer run on the surface, but would start to creep toward the Boston Shoals underwater, sneaking deep into the complicated swamplands to make their rendezvous.

Clara heard them get under way. The clack of the compression bellows and the ozone smell of the massive warming coils permeated through the submarine, waking her. Now the fireboxes were ignited, and the smell of coal dust burning began to tickle her nose. Most of the smoke bubbled out onto the surface, but there was always a little scent of it inside the sub. The *Cuttlefish* hadn't run on her Stirling engines much, out in the Atlantic, and getting them going again, properly warm and effective, was quite a process. Gradually, the noise smoothed. Clara knew the greasers would be oiling the flicking shafts, and the coal-heavers filling the hoppers to the filters and pressure vats. The chief would be muttering and looking at dials and gauges in his smoky, noisy little kingdom.

She wondered if she should go down there. She'd probably never see it again. Her mother said that a woman should be able to be what she wanted to be, but Clara didn't see this door opening easily.

And then the sound died. The "all quiet" light glowed amber in its Bakelite fitting.

And someone came knocking at their door.

It was one of cabin boys. Not Tim. It was that smarmy Banks who had tried to stroke her hair. "Captain requests you come up to the bridge, ma'am."

Clara went along as well. Mother didn't notice. She was just too absorbed at the moment to notice anything much.

Captain Malkis was there, pacing, looking worried. He bowed. "We seem to have blundered into something, Dr. Calland."

"What?" asked her mother.

"Possibly a war," said Captain Malkis. "Sparks is monitoring the Marconi transmissions. But there is a fleet of Royal Navy warships between us and your destination. There appear to be American vessels about too. At this range it is hard to tell quite what they're up to. But the Boston shallows would be highly risky right now. We'll try sending a coded message to our contacts there at our prearranged time. But we are close to the maximum range for our transmission."

The steersman on periscope duty was making a series of notes on a pad, before moving the scope on to another notch.

Clara's mother looked stricken. "A war. A war with the British Empire?"

"There is no actual firing at the moment, Dr. Calland. The smoke from ten-inch guns is quite easy to spot. But there are a substantial number of ships. Certainly enough to make a very dangerous blockade for us to try and run. Of course if we can arrange another rendezvous elsewhere, things become much simpler. We will let you know, just as soon as we have some more definite information."

"Could . . . Could I have a look through the periscope?" asked Clara.

Captain Malkis tugged his neat little goatee. "I suppose you could, Miss Calland. Seeing as you have been learning navigation," he said, with a slight smile. He was plainly quite worried. "Nicholl, let her have the periscope. Turn it to quadrant four, first sector."

On the skyline in the grey of a cloudy morning with the haze of land behind them, Clara saw the smokestacks and sharp square outlines of ships. Ships spiky with guns.

"There are no less than three dreadnoughts there. That's . . . unusual," said Captain Malkis.

Sparks took his leather headphones off. "They're keeping radio silence, sir. I've only picked up one bit of chatter. American, sounding worried. Asking for orders. They got a station assigned. I also got a public broadcast, sir. About the war with the Canadian Dominion."

"So: the British Empire is at war with the United States of America," said her mother.

"Not according to the broadcast, ma'am," said Sparks. "There's some senator demanding the British ambassador be called on to explain what the Fleet is doing in American territorial waters."

"Canada is a Dominion of the British Empire," said her mother with a grim finality.

The captain shrugged. "I think you'll find the Crown calling it a local border dispute, ma'am. They did that in the Nyassaland–Congo conflict, when they did not want an open breach with King Leopold."

Clara's mother said nothing. But the set of her shoulders said a great deal.

It was several tense hours later that the captain came down to see them. The "all quiet" light was out, and you could feel the faint gentle vibration of the electric motors. "Good news, ma'am. Sparks received a coded message from our friends in the US. It was a bit broken up, but we have a fresh rendezvous off the Florida banks. We'll get the Stirling engines going as soon as we're sure we're well out of hydrophone range."

Mother nodded. But you could see the tension in her. "Thank you, Captain Malkis," was all she said, though.

When he'd gone, Clara asked what was wrong.

"I think the Americans lied to me. I want . . . I wanted this to make a better world. To help grow crops. To feed the hungry. Not for it to be used to make war with," she said, and sat down on her bunk and pointedly opened a book.

That didn't leave Clara any wiser. Or any happier herself. She went out looking for someone else to talk to. The best she could come up with was Cookie, as everyone else was asleep or busy, or in areas she'd been quietly but firmly told were off-limits.

The cook and his assistant were dicing onions—his two assistants did work in shifts, but Cookie seemed to be there about eighteen hours a day, anyway.

"You've come for a cry with us?" said Cookie.

"It'd be a good place for it," said Clara, blinking. "No, I was just getting away from my mother."

"A boat's a mighty close place. You can't escape anything down here. Not even the onions," said Cookie, crying with his work.

"What do you know about America, Cookie?" asked Clara, not even to be put off by the onions.

"Not much, missy," he said, not looking up from his cutting. It was just as well, at the speed he used a knife. "It was a pretty closed place for a good many years. There was a lot of bad feeling about the British Empire over the 1914 to 1915 War, a lot of German immigrants there too. It was all a bit iffy as to who they supported during the war, and then, when Germany surrendered, well after that they kind of turned inwards. Kept themselves to themselves. It's a big country, and it mostly came through the Big Melt all right. Grows its own food. Good tucker, even if it is a bit long on corn. It's feeling its oats now a bit. Got lots of coal, and the British Empire is getting short of it. Got oil and a fair number of what they call automobiles over there. I reckon you'll like it. There are a lot of other Irish people there."

It was on the tip of her tongue to say that she wasn't Irish. At St. Margaret's School no one would have ever admitted to being Irish. They were all British and proud of it! Only now it seemed that the British wanted to capture her and her mother. Maybe even kill them. And these "rebel scum" were a lot nicer to her than her school companions had ever been. And her father was an Irish rebel. A brave man, as Tim had finally let her acknowledge.

It was quite difficult to get used to all the changes in her life, in the way she had to see things now. Just as difficult as coping with mother not telling her anything. She said so, instead of telling Cookie she wasn't Irish.

"I reckon," said Cookie thoughtfully, "she thinks she's looking after you."

"Well, she's not," said Clara, crossly.

"Ah, well, you don't know that, missy. Also . . . what you don't know, you can't give away. There might be other people involved, see."

"I wish she'd tell me, anyway."

"In good time, I daresay she will," said Cookie, grinning. "My old man did, only by the time he did, I'd gone walkabout."

He pointed to the amber light that had just come on, and so Clara had to retreat in silence.

That was the story of the next few days. Constant ship alarms, and silences as they crept south.

The strain told on all of them. The sergeant-at-arms had to break up a fight between a repair-rating and an engine-room mechanic. The food was not quite what they'd got used to in the Atlantic crossing. Keeping low in the water the boat rolled a great deal too, which did not make life easy or pleasant.

"We've made contact with our friends in the US," said Captain Malkis on the third morning, which was really night. Time ran differently in the enclosed world of the submarine, with the main working "day" being night.

There was something of an edge to his voice. A wariness that made Clara ask, "What's wrong?"

"They've suggested a rendezvous off the Bahamian shoals. We've only met up in the Okeechobee lagoons before. The shoals are disputed waters, although the United States now claims them, as they took the refugees when most of the Islands were flooded. They were part of the British Empire before that, though. It's odd. It means your pickup will have to run the Straits of Florida. That's quite heavily patrolled. It would be quite a lot safer to run you in on the submarine. I've got Sparks trying to raise them again to change it."

"You take very good care of us, Captain," said Mother.

"We do our best," said the captain, with a small smile.

Sparks, however, got no reply. So they nudged toward Bimini anyway.

The captain came down to talk to them again, later that day. "It looks like we might be taking you into the Florida wetlands after all. We got a message that they've had engine trouble and are stuck on a sandbar off South Great Abaco, and are waiting for the tide. Tricky waters, those. So we've agreed to rendezvous closer to them, and if they're still stuck, pick them up, otherwise transfer you. We should be there in about four hours. If you can be packed up in case we can trans-ship you?"

Clara packed. She didn't have very much, and she decided that the breeches, sou'wester, and oilskin she'd been issued for the deck should maybe go back to the quartermaster. Well, it was a good excuse to visit Mr. Amos, anyway. And she'd stop by at the engine room and say good-bye. And thank you. The engine room was noisy and smelled of coal . . . but it was friendly. Then she'd visit the mess, before a final stop at the bridge. The captain was on duty now, so that was fine. When the mate was on, it was a little more awkward. He was stricter.

And then . . . as she got to the bridge, the "all quiet" light came on again. She was about to tiptoe away when the captain saw her. "Just being careful," he said, quietly. "One of the hydrophone men thought he picked up a ship's engine sound—a large vessel. The remains of the Islands make it possible to hide a ship's superstructure here. So we're going to send a tick-tock ahead. We've got one of the new long-range ones on board for testing."

"A tick-tock?" she said, pretending she didn't know. It gave her an excuse to remain there.

"A clockwork device that produces submarine engine noises. It's in a sort of torpedo. We use them as decoys, to fool the drop-miners."

Clara watched it being armed and then loaded into the escape hatch. She was still uncomfortable looking at the escape hatch. The mate came along, looking at his pocket watch. "Captain. We will be late for the rendezvous."

"I've had Sparks send them a coded signal that we're on our way," said the captain. "Better safe than sorry, Hans. We'll wait and watch for a little."

So they did. The little tick-tock had a swim range of nearly four miles, which would see it very close to the place they were due to meet the Americans.

"I've just heard engine sounds again, Captain," said the hydrophone operator, urgently. "Big steam turbines. Lots."

Sparks said, "They say we can surface and transfer the passengers, Captain."

"Prepare to dive, and complete silence," said the captain. "It's a trap."

# CHAPTER 16

"They must be blowing up half the ocean," muttered Tim to himself, just very glad that he—and the submarine—were some miles distant, and moving further away, on the electric motors.

The captain was very good at dealing with Mother when she was on the edge of panic. He didn't, like Daddy had, tell her to stop being hysterical. Clara could still remember that row, even if she had never known quite what it was about. She could guess, now. Instead the captain nodded sympathetically and said, "Quite so, Dr. Calland. That is why we're being careful. There is a blue hole—a deep limestone sinkhole where we will be invisible to aerial observers too—which we are going to lie up in."

"More waiting, while we don't know what is happening," said Mother.

"We'll send a wire to the surface, ma'am, and once we've anchored down there, it's possible we can put someone on the surface with a field telephone, as an observer. There is a little atoll attached to it," said the captain, calmly.

Soon the submarine settled, and even the electric motors were still. Clara went up to the bridge with her mother a little later. The captain didn't look pleased to see them. He pointed at the "all quiet" light. And wrote on his pad: "Ships searching. Find-and-destroy order. Return to cabin. Quiet."

He didn't quite write "And stay there," but he might as well have.

They'd been hunted before, but not by this number of warships. Tim knew that only the captain's wariness had saved them this time. And the agony of quiet waiting drew on and on. The boat could only stay down just so long. Sooner or later, they would have to breathe. It was hard to remain patient and remain calm, when waiting was all they could do. Each minute felt very long.

Eventually, the boat rose. Ballast and vanes only—a dangerous process, Tim knew. Forward movement helped stability a lot, but plainly the captain wasn't risking any engine noises at all. Still, he could soon feel the air quality improve as the ship hung at snuiver-depth. They must be confident enough about the distance of the nearest listener, because Tim could feel the faint *thrub-thrub* of the small compressors running off the batteries, filling the tanks. And Big Eddie came in to their cabin and changed into his diving gear. Not a word spoken, of course, but still, something was happening.

More hours passed. Eventually, Tim reported for duty again. He was assigned to the engine room, where the chief engineer and his mechanics were stripping out the liners and feed-pipes of one of the engines. It was not totally silent work, and Tim was slightly sur-prised to see it being done right now. Of course it was something of an ongoing process, with compressors or feeders being partially stripped, and having their ceramic liners replaced. Coal—even desulphured, washed, dried, and powdered—was still abrasive stuff, as the mechanics had told him.

And then Tim noticed that the "all quiet" light no longer burned. "What's happening?" he asked one of the mechs. The man was one of Big Eddie's friends, so Tim knew him slightly.

"The chief reckons we're going to need to run, and the engines are getting near rebuild. So the captain said we could use the waiting time to do what we can. This one's not running at more than seventy percent load right now."

"Oh. Where is Big Eddie? Do you know? He hasn't come back," asked Tim.

"Sitting under a palm tree up there with a field telephone. Swearing about the ants. And the scorpions. And the heat. And the flies," said the mechanic with a grin. "He's counted eighteen ships up there searching for us. And three airships, and a bunch of the ships have towed blimps too. Says he's seen a couple of American vessels too, off in the distance."

"Glad it's not me sitting out there." Tim knew, all too well, from the Faroes, that if they had to cut and run, they might have to leave the diver behind. That was almost more worrying than the eighteen ships.

The mechanic grinned and handed him a set of rods. "Polish those. It's a good thing they sent Eddie. Imagine if it been a little 'un like you. The ants would have eaten you all up by now."

"I taste horrible," said Tim, taking a rag and polishing. "Really. Ask any of the eels back in the tunnels."

They worked on. And the captain called the chief up to the bridge. A little later he was back. "All right. Get a move on there. The engines need to be back up and ready to run in an hour. We're picking up the diver and running just after dusk."

At least they'd be picking up Big Eddie first. Tim hadn't liked the idea of leaving him to the ants.

They used the electric motors to start their flight with, but within a few minutes had switched over to the Stirlings, running on the surface as fast as possible. The roll of the sub told Tim exactly what the captain was doing and why: the weather must have deteriorated. It would make the chase a little harder.

Tim found himself mopping the gangways. Work went on, despite the chase. Standard came bouncing from side to side down the passage and nearly knocked Tim into his own bucket. "Oi! Mind what you're doing!" yelled Tim.

The other cabin boy took a wild swing at him. "Need the heads, Darkie," he gasped, as Tim fended him off with a mop handle.

Tim let him go. There was something nastily satisfying in seeing that piece of work in such misery. He'd have kept him there for the "Darkie" if it hadn't been likely he'd have had to clean up the result. The rough sea would stop them being followed easily. "Got to be something good about it," he said, trying to control the bucket of slops. He'd be cleaning both it and his own sick up at this rate. The ship smelled of vomit, and by now, none of them were green hands that got seasick easily. It was that nasty. But he'd outlasted Standard.

"Good about what?" asked Clara, coming up behind him.

Unlike his earlier encounter, Tim was delighted to see her, even if he did, in his heart of hearts, know that the Royal Navy was hunting the submarine because of her and her mother. He'd . . . got used to seeing her every day. Now the pursuit had cancelled all thought of classes, and he had been working down in the officers' cabins mostly, where she was not supposed to go. "The roll. The weather. We can make a faster speed on the surface, so the captain is staying there. But I can hardly stay upright."

"I know about that, all right," she said feelingly, bracing herself on the walls. "Mother is feeling sick. So will this get us away?"

"Well, no," admitted Tim, armed with the answers to questions he himself had asked other submariners, not long before. "The trouble is, quite a lot of the ships chasing us are faster than us, underwater."

"Not much use running then, is there?" said Clara, pulling a face.

"Except we have a shallower draught and newer charts. The submariners go on updating and surveying all the time, and the last Admiralty survey here was 1928, before the Melt. If they chase us into the shallows they'll sink. We can move in less than ten foot of water if we have to, see. Lots and lots of reefs here that we can cross, they have to go around, and they have to feel their way around, carefully, because they have no charts showing depths for the areas that were flooded. So it's sort of like cat and mouse, I suppose. We're the mouse."

"I wish there was a dog to chase the cats," said Clara. "Maybe the American Navy."

"They'd probably eat mice like us too," said Tim.

The *Cuttlefish* ran and dived and hid in holes. And shuddered with drop-mines dropped near her, for the next three days and nights. The brief stormy weather had got her across to the bays and swamps of Cuba—which was even closer to trouble, as far as Clara could work out. The island was under British Imperial occupation to protect the nickel mines there.

But now the air in the submarine stank. A different stink to its usual smell that she'd got so used to. Clara said so to Lieutenant Willis.

"It's a good stink," the lieutenant told her with a grin through his moustache. "It's fresh air, even if it does smell a bit like rotten eggs and mud."

"I suppose my nose has got used to coal smoke and people smells. Swamp mud isn't my idea of perfume," said Clara, waving her hand in front of her nose.

The *Cuttlefish* had gone to ground in the Zapata swamps, and lay covered in camouflage—nets full of water lilies and reeds were draped over her, to hide her from the airships prowling the sky overhead. There were probably patrols of marines cursing and splashing around too, but the swamp was a vast network of thousands and thousands of channels, many of which had been scoured relatively deep by the floods that had come with the Great Melt and the hurricanes that had resulted from that. Now the swamps were the refuge of rebels . . . and mosquitoes and crocodiles.

The lieutenant chuckled. "We could bottle it and sell it back in Blighty. There is not so much coal smoke in it as back there. Just a lovely mud smell. And we should be well supplied with that by tonight."

"Oh? Why?" asked Clara, quick to catch the hint of excitement.

"Some of the crew are going with the locals to Australia," he said, trying to keep a straight face. "And it's quite muddy."

Clara could play this game. "I thought Australia was quite dry, and quite far from here," she said airily. "Did you find a shortcut through the middle of the earth?"

He grinned. "Well, actually we're going to raid the railway coaling depot at a little sugar mill called Australia, of all things. We're getting low on coal again. We've got a treadmill-crusher in the engine room, and we will just have to turn lumps of coal into fuel ourselves."

"I volunteer," said Clara.

He shook his head. "Not likely. Well, maybe for the treadmill!"

"I can speak Spanish," said Clara.

"Really?" He was impressed.

"Um. No. Well, a few words," admitted Clara, truthfully. She had—like her entire class—memorised the Spanish heroine's lines in the biorama they'd all seen, because their teacher wouldn't translate them. It had something to do with the romantic scene, and had made the teacher blush furiously.

"Like *sangria*, *paella*, and *toreador*?" the lieutenant said with a laugh. "Very useful I am sure those would be, but no."

Tim found watch duties in the swamp warm, and just as full of the insects Big Eddie had complained of on the little island. At least he didn't suffer from sunburn the way some of the crew did. There weren't many advantages to a West Indian father, growing up in the tunnels, but here a darker skin was an advantage. Not that he could blame his father for leaving the Caribbean, even if it had been slightly cooler back before the Melt. But someone had to do the job, so Tim stared intently out of his watch place. The little hide was made of dead branches draped with netting filled with a mixture of reed tops and green twigs—which all had to be replaced every night, so they looked like all the rest from the air. Not that he could see a lot from the observation post: a channel of dark water, clattering reeds, a corner of one of the little lagoons.

They were just farther inland from where the swamp changed from mangroves to an endless sea of reeds and patches of trees, and the water became mostly fresh. It would seem that the Royal Navy were sure that they'd be in the mangroves, which made sense really, as there was more cover, so it was just as well they weren't. The only other thing Tim could see from his little floating hide was the sky—in which an airship was slowly crisscrossing the swamps. It had flown right over the *Cuttlefish* earlier, but had only drifted on past. No drop-mines, no flares . . . which didn't mean it hadn't spotted her, and that boats weren't closing in on them.

"You're a dozy beggar, Barnabas," said Jonas, scornfully, coming up behind him. "If I'd been a Royal Navy marine I could have cut your throat."

Tim was developing an increasing dislike for Junior Submariner Jonas. But he kept his temper. And it was partly true—he'd been staring at the water, not concentrating on sounds. Nothing could come through the reeds without making a huge racket anyway. "Good thing you weren't, then. What's up? I'm not due for relief yet."

"All of the crew for tonight's coaling trip get to rest now. That means you. They're sending out the deadwood off with some local guides. If you're this dozy now, they'd better hope you sleep. Not that that's likely down in the tin can. It's noisy, hot, and airless down there," said Jonas, grumpily.

The sub was, except when the silent light shone, not the quietest place on earth. But by now it was home. Tim got a slightly more complete briefing from Lieutenant Willis. They needed manpower to load as much coal as possible onto a raft. He was to report at 2100 and have collected his small arms from the arms master before that. And he was to have eaten and slept. "And I'll be with you," said the lieutenant, "so no more heroics from you, Barnabas!" he said, smiling. "Mac told me about what a fine hand with a cutlass you are, taking on those Winged Hussars."

Tim felt eight feet tall, and felt himself stand that way. Mac was still invalided out and, once they got to a safe port, would probably go ashore and stay there until he recovered. But Lieutenant Willis was also their medical officer, so he'd obviously got the story. Huh. Deadwood. The lieutenant was the best officer on the boat, except maybe the captain. If he was going, it could be no easy mission.

Tim soon found it was a muddy one, and that the lieutenant was a wary officer who planned things carefully. They'd met the local rebels at an islet nearly a mile off, where they left the inflatable boat, and went with the locals in two large flat-bottomed punts. The men spoke very little English, but seemed to know their way around the dark waterways. They led the *Cuttlefish* crew, poling through a complex network of channels, along to a stand of swamp trees with buttress roots.

There was almost no way that Tim could have found his way back—but he had noticed that the lieutenant reached out and nicked a reed with his cutlass every now and again.

"Won't they be able to follow that, sir?" asked Tim, working out what it was for.

"Not unless they can read my mind," said the lieutenant. "Now shut up. I memorise the turnings. The cuts are a number pattern of turnings apart. We used to do it in the upper sewers of London, when I was with the Militia."

They rowed on. Occasionally a searchlight from an airship shone down across on the vast swamp, fortunately nowhere near them.

When they landed, the lieutenant ignored the local rebels who were all for charging in straightaway, and stationed a guard, and then went to scout the path. And then came back, motioned them to stay and stay quiet, and went off to scout another. He scouted with one other crewman and the only one of the locals who could speak more than two or three words of English, so Tim and the others had to wait. The other five local men liked it not at all.

Eventually, talking in Spanish, they got up and headed inland. Not a thing that the *Cuttlefish* crew could say to them would stop them.

"I reckon the lieutenant's going to be as mad as a cut snake," said Artificer Thorne, who was the next most senior submariner, and had a pair of very big muttonchop sideburns that Tim really envied. Tim didn't have any really decent chin hair yet, but one day . . .

The thought was disturbed by some shots in the distance. Some yells.

They all froze for a second. Then Thorne said, "Right boyos. Let's take cover. It might be all right, but if—"

Lieutenant Willis reappeared with the men who had gone along with him. "There was a trip-wire on that trail. Who the Hades went up it?" he demanded.

"Them foreigners, sir. Excitable lot," explained Thorne.

The lieutenant hissed his irritation. Spoke to the other local, whose eyes were the size of saucers in the moonlight. "Ees trap, *señor*! Only one guard always. We go!" In the distance, there were more shouts and shots. And then, from above, a searchlight came stabbing down onto the trees.

"Trap all right," said Lieutenant Willis, laconically, lifting his rifle. "No, hold your fire. No need to advertise with the muzzle flash of more than one rifle." He took careful aim at the questing searchlight. Fired.

It swung wildly about and began to rise, presumably with the airship. "Right," said the lieutenant. "Into the boats, gentlemen. We'll push off and watch—"

"Stand in the name of the King," yelled someone in the distance. And there was another yell, in Spanish, closer.

"Esteban! Is calling for help!" said the local guide, getting to his feet.

"Stay put," said the lieutenant, pushing him down. "You show them the way back if we don't make it. Tamworth and Gordon, with me. The rest of you, give us some covering fire. Aim for the tops of the trees; otherwise you'll probably hit us."

The three left at a run, and the rest of the crew fired their rifles. It was enough to draw a lot of fire into the night from some distance off. The other side weren't firing into the treetops though.

Minutes later the lieutenant and the other two submariners came back with three of the five men, carrying one, and half carrying another. They scrambled in to helping hands, and the punts pushed off. Just as they got there, several bright flares exploded into the sky, making the scene quite light, and the shadows stark. They could hear a motorboat suddenly, and the airship's searchlight began playing over the reeds again, from far higher up.

The *Cuttlefish*'s crew and the two unhurt locals poled the boat down the channel with such a will that Tim nearly fell overboard from holding on to the pole too long. The channel curved, and the local men wasted no time in getting them into a shallower, narrower inlet, where the reeds almost met overhead. High above more flares burned and the searchlight quested. Bullets ripped blindly through the reeds.

"Right. Barnabas. You're about the smallest. Pull your pole in the boat, and give me a hand." The lieutenant's voice sounded a little strained.

Tim did as he was told, expecting to have to help with the injured. What he hadn't realised was the lieutenant was one of them. In the flare-light crisscrossed with reed shadows, Tim could see that Lieutenant Willis's arm was dark with blood, and his hand was dripping it.

Tim had to cut away the cloth, trying to control his own breathing, and fright, and the feeling that he might just fall over. But it had to be done, so he did it, with the lieutenant telling him

what to do. In the meanwhile they fled deeper into the swamps—
avoiding going back towards deeper channels, where several patrol
boats were now to be heard, but keeping to the shallower water, and
the narrow channels. Getting out and pushing occasionally. Listening to the airship's machine-gunners strafing anything that they
thought might be a boat.

It did seem that the hunters had made the assumption that their
quarry would go for the main channels towards the sea. That was a
good thing, as the *Cuttlefish*'s crew were not in the area that was getting searched and strafed hard.

It was a bad thing in that they'd have to cross that area, later, to
get back to the sub.

"Wonder why they're so hot down that way, instead of searching
here?" said Thorne, listening to the distant gunfire.

The local shrugged. "I think they shoot at prawn fishermen, and
the fishermen, they shoot back. They have the guns for the crocodile."

"I suppose around here if you shoot at someone, they shoot back,
and the airship is a big target," said Lieutenant Willis.

It took them nearly eighteen hours to get back—incidentally with
quite a lot of coal, looted off a half-sunken river-gunboat that had
been abandoned on a mud bank.

Clara took the first chance she got to ask Tim all about it, not an
hour after they'd all returned to the submarine.

"I wish I'd been there," she said, eyes bright with the excitement
of the story.

Tim thought of the lieutenant's arm and the blood, and the fear.
Shuddered. "You could have had my place."

# CHAPTER 17

"Well, it appears we've got them cornered," said Duke Malcolm, looking at the map. "How long until they are captured or killed, gentlemen? This has gone on long enough."

The two naval officers looked at each other. Finally the older man spoke. "Well, Your Grace, the Zapata swamps are a very large area, actually. More than a million acres. And the area is a hotbed of resistance. We'd . . . we'd do better if they were in open water. We have several vessels fitted with the trackers that pick the high-frequency radio pulse of the submarine engines in the area. They were just lucky escaping in the Bahama shoals. Sooner or later they'll bolt for America again. Probably as soon as the weather turns bad. By travelling underwater—"

Duke Malcolm slapped his hand down on the desk. "I know we have more accuracy than that, gentlemen. You should have rounded it down to ten square miles by the information we have. Saturate it. And patrol the Florida channel with those tracking vessels!"

He had more on his mind than these bumblers. There was disturbing news out of the Australian territories, as well as trouble in Africa, and yet another rebellion in India. There were looming coal shortages, trouble with the Chinese in Tibet.

The Empire was short of food, short of coal, and being nibbled at by lesser peoples. Duke Malcolm knew that it was up to him to keep it alive.

He sighed. "Look. Saturation bomb the area from the airships. They're waiting for a patch of bad weather to try and sneak across to the United States. As I recall, this is the season for storms and hurricanes there. We cannot afford to pussyfoot about, gentlemen. And now I have work to do. Report back to me when you have something to report. I expect that to be within three days.

Duke Malcolm shook his head. They probably thought that he did not know that they'd had one gunboat run aground, and looted before it could be salvaged. Or of the sporadic resistance the marines had encountered from the locals who knew the swamp far better than the marines did.

He did not approve of the fact that they had not seen fit to tell him of these matters, though. He'd have to punish a few people.

# CHAPTER 18

The sky was the colour of slate, not its usual blue. It looked more like London than the Caribbean, but without the umber tinge the coal smoke gave to the light there. It seemed to be growing darker even as they watched, although it was only midmorning. There were still a few fires burning to the east, where the Royal Navy and the British Airship Force had been bombing and shelling the swamp to pieces. The rising winds had at least got rid of the airships. "The barometer's falling fast," said Nicholl, coming up to relieve Tim.

"Better catch it then," said Tim flippantly.

"You're a cheeky brat," said Submariner Nicholl, smiling, grabbing him by the collar and arm, shaking him out over water. "I ought feed you to crocodiles, only I don't want to poison them. Means we'll be moving, sonny. So you probably pulled the last full watch up here with the mosquitoes."

Tim liked Nicholl. He wouldn't have dared clever comments with some of the others, but submariners like him and Thorne, and some of the engine-room crowd . . . they made life on the submarine good. Of course there were a few lowlifes too. He met two of them as he went down the hatchway. Banks and one of the other ratings were polishing. And they weren't about to let Tim through. He stepped forward; they stepped back into his way. "What's the matter, Darkie?" said Banks, mockingly.

"Just let me pass."

"When you say please . . . nicely enough."

"Please," said Tim, stepping forward.

"That's not nicely enough," said Banks with a smirk, pushing him back. "There was no 'master.'"

Tim shoved the hand aside, pushed forward. Next thing they were grappling and fighting. And Tim was smaller and lighter than Banks. He'd just landed hard on decking, with Banks on top of him, when the other rating grabbed them. "Mate's coming!" he hissed.

Banks was already on his feet when the mate came down the passage. Tim staggered up and continued on his way, feeling his lip. But the mate had plainly seen or heard something. "What is going on here, ja?"

"I tripped over someone's feet, sir," said Tim.

"Just helped him up," said Banks.

Mate Werner obviously was not convinced. But he seemed to have other things on his mind rather than following it up. "I'm watching you two. You will not make trouble or I will put for you both into the lockup, ja. Now get on with your work."

Tim was glad to.

Clara found herself tagging along to listen in on her mother and Captain Malkis.

"One thing we do know, the Royal Navy have a belief that submarines aren't affected by surface storms—of course waves are not just a thing on the surface. Maybe if we could go deep enough we could escape the effects, but honestly we can't. The steel of our hulls can't take the pressure, but they don't know that. Instead they believe we can travel peacefully under stormy seas, while they get tossed about on the surface. They believe, or can be made to believe, that we're running. But to be honest with you, Dr. Calland, it's not so much a case of running, as where we run to. It would appear that our American contacts have been penetrated by Duke Malcolm's spies. . . ."

"If we have any choice, I don't want to go there anyway," said her mother, haltingly. "I . . . I think they lied to me. I need to talk to them first . . . if I can."

The captain nodded. "Well, my suggestion is that instead of trying for Florida or Texas, where the Royal Navy probably expect us to go, we let them think we're running to Florida, but instead wait out the storm here and then go across to Rivas."

"Where is that?"

Clara was glad her mother asked. She had no idea either.

"It's on Lake Nicaragua. Since the blocking of the Panama Canal, the Americans have gone back to running an overland track railway over the Rivas Isthmus to get people to vessels on the Pacific, just like they did before the Panama Canal was built. I believe they're working on a canal-link through there to San Juan del Sur. It's much more defensible than the Panama Canal was, and the Royal Navy's Pacific fleet is quite stretched, anyway. You can make contact with the American Legation in Rivas. There is not much government in Nicaragua these days, since the bombing of Managua, but what there is, is in Rivas."

"And where will you go, Captain?" Clara asked, forgetting she was keeping quiet and listening to something she wasn't strictly invited to listen to.

He smiled crookedly. "We were supposed to pick up cargo drogues off the Boston Shoals, due for Peru, around Cape Horn. And then, in exchange, take a cargo of Chile saltpetre in our drogues, and head for Westralia. The mines need it, and so do their hydroponics."

Her mother looked down. Closed her eyes briefly. Then said quietly, "Captain, that's why they're hunting me so hard. My mother and Fritz had got as far as a table-top way of producing ammonia. I think I can scale it up, and from ammonia . . . we can produce artificial nitrites . . . Chile saltpetre. At a tiny fraction of the cost of mining it and shipping it. The fertilisers can help to feed millions."

The captain looked puzzled. "Why don't you just give it to them, ma'am?"

Mother sighed. "Because the nitrites mean explosives too. Not just for mining, but for munitions. The British Empire controls access to the Atacama fields in what is now mostly Chile. The Ganges Delta saltpetre quarries in the Indies are of course under Imperial control. The other ways of making nitrates are all expensive, and the other mines are far smaller. They want my knowledge not for fertiliser, but for war. And the British Empire would rather let the world starve than let anyone else have it."

"I see," said Captain Malkis.

Clara got the feeling, by the way he said it, that the captain did not regard war—against the British Empire, anyway—as the worst of all possible things. But he did not say anything about it. Just: "We will be able to send messages to the Americans from Rivas."

Tim found himself working down in the hold as a general dogsbody and run-around-and-go-fetch boy working on the chief engineer's latest contraption. They'd used the one long-range tick-tock to spring the trap in the Bahamas; now they needed another. It had to be a louder and bigger one. They still had an inshore tick-tock, but the captain wanted lots of range and noise on this one. It was to be too big to launch from the escape hatch. Instead they had to make it in sections and haul these up from the hold, onto the deck, and then onto a raft under camouflage netting ready for bolting together. The whole thing had to be towed down to where the swamp channels met the sea.

The tick-tock itself was now inside a wood-and-canvas frame nearly as big as the *Cuttlefish*. Tim couldn't resist. He paraded up onto it. "I'm the captain of the *Cuttlefish Two*," he said giving a fair imitation of Captain Malkis pacing the deck. "Up periscope. Down snuiver!" Someone threw a lump of mud at him, and he took a step sideways and fell through the canvas.

The wetting and trouble he was in were worth it for the laugh, even if it was still getting colder, and the rain had started to come down. That afternoon the tick-tock was towed down, avoiding the struggling river-patrol boat, to the sea. The sea looked just like where one didn't want to be. The clouds were thick and heavy, and the ocean was gray and full of white horses racing shorewards.

The chief engineer's modified tick-tock set off into the teeth of the storm. There was only one vessel out there—yesterday there had been ten. But the smaller vessels and the dreadnought had all gone, the smaller vessels perhaps heading for safe anchorage, the dreadnought out to deeper water. Now only a lone armoured cruiser battled the swell, the smoke from its triple stacks barely visible in the rain squalls. Tim was one of the crew getting shivering wet, helping Lieutenant Ambrose and the chief get the mock submarine out into the sea.

"Have to aim just about at her. She might not hear the tick-tock otherwise," said Nicholl.

"Pity it doesn't hit her and sink her," said Tim, looking at the distant grey bulk of the three-smokestack cruiser.

"Then they'd chase us harder," said Nicholl.

Tim snorted. "You think? Harder than they are now?"

Nicholl gave him a cheerful swat on the head. "Well, they'd hunt the other subs. In a straight-out war we'd just lose. So we fight a slow war. We don't push them too hard, and they don't—usually— push us too hard."

Tim wasn't at all sure about this. It seemed to be a plan of letting your enemies decide when they wanted to fight. But he was just a cabin boy, so he said nothing more. He enjoyed getting back to the submarine, though, and getting warm and dry again. It seemed odd that two days ago they'd been too hot to want to breathe. A day later they sailed, unobserved at last, out into the Gulf of Mexico.

✳

After days of heat, the huge storm had cooled the air over the gulf—
for about half of their dash to Rivas. After that Tim found the air was
so hot and humid it was sticking his clothes to him. It was hardly
surprising no one lived in the tropical lowlands anymore if they
could help it. There were places where you couldn't sweat enough to
cool down, and the heat could kill you.

Except for the final leg, once they'd sighted the shore batteries
on the San Juan River, they'd been able to run with at least the
snorkel up, avoiding any ships. The San Juan was a short, very wide
and deep river. Going up it—especially the section of the turbu-
lences, which would have been rapids if it had been any shallower—
was slow. The electric motors simply weren't strong enough to push
them along, and they had to have the Stirling engines running. The
engine room was a sweatbox, and the engineers only did half-hour
shifts in it. And then the number two compressor broke down. . . .
They barely made it into the lake—nearly out of fuel, and with the
*Cuttlefish* in need of both repair work and some new parts.

"It's hard to believe this is not the sea," said Tim, looking
around as they paused after hauling the ropes on the sails that night.
It was choppy, and there was not a sign of land in the moonlight.

"Yeah, but closer to Rivas, you can see the volcanoes. And the
water is the wrong colour," said Tamworth, the sail-rating standing
next to him. "Besides being fresh. But you get sharks here, though."

"But it's fresh water!" The crew—or at least those who could
swim—had taken turns to have as near to a bath as they'd seen in
months, earlier, when the wind had been still.

Tamworth snorted. "Not after you filthy lot have been swimming in it."

"Huh. You were so clean. Are the volcanoes spouting smoke and
lava and stuff?"

"Why do yer think the water's so warm? Nah, they're just
pointy mountains sticking out of the water."

❖

Clara had been very jealous of them all getting to swim. But her mother and the captain had point-blank refused to allow her to join them—or even to swim on her own. "This is not Brighton, young lady," said the captain. "And with any luck you'll be enjoying a bath at the American Legation soon."

Her mother was too busy on what must have been her fifth attempt at a letter to the American Consul to say more than no. It put Clara in a filthy mood, even if the shower tank had been refilled with fresh water and would produce a lather with soap. She went back to the celestial navigation text, and did not even go out on deck to see the volcano islands of Concepción and Maderas in the dawn before they sailed on for a river mouth near the city of Rivas. Here, at last, they went ashore.

The local smuggler, Señor Omberto, who came to meet them, was also a wealthy farmer, and had a large villa next to the jetties down on the mouth of the river where he kept his netting barges . . . and a reason for him to have coal. The submarine would lie in the depths of the channel, just with a snorkel out, but Clara and her mother, four ratings, and Lieutenants Willis and Ambrose—in turns, while not on the submarine—could come up to the house. Part of the engine-room crew would be working on one of the compressors in the shed, but some would have to stay aboard and continue to work there.

Climbing the stair, Clara knew that the submarine was hot and stank of all its familiar stinks. She also knew that she would miss it terribly. The captain promised she'd get to say good-bye. There was a lump in her throat about leaving.

The villa had some lovely broad shade trees with strange roots that were almost like cathedral buttresses, and a huge aviary of exotic birds . . . and a fence and three guard dogs, and four or five men with guns wandering around, besides the crew that were there to watch over them.

"Rivas. It's a dangerous place if you have any money," explained Lieutenant Ambrose. "Someone is bound to try and take it from you."

Tim was quite pleased when he got called to the bridge. It beat working in the engine room. In fact anything beat working down in the engine room in that temperature.

"We need to send someone from the boat along to Rivas, to the American Legation, to drop a letter there. Señor Omberto says he'll provide a boy to guide them. The problem, however, is that there has been some trouble in the area with foreign sailors. The Nicaraguans and the Americans are trying to keep the canal they've been working on a secret, which means that they must be nearly finished—they're arresting anyone they're suspicious about, particularly men. So he suggested sending another boy or a couple of boys. So we're going to send you and Banks. We've got you some local clothes."

Tim groaned to himself. The other cabin boy had decided that he just didn't like Tim, even before their little fight. Now no matter what Tim did to try and keep the peace, Banks was always trying to make Tim's life a misery, without ending up in the brig. Banks was more experienced at life on a submarine, and bigger and heavier than Tim. He found ways to make that count. It had to be Banks! Still, it would be quite exciting to see this foreign city. "Yes, sir."

It was hot and sticky, although it was barely eight in the morning when they began their walk from the house in their borrowed clothes and bare feet. They'd given Banks a big hat, because he was too pale for a local. Tim had kept his breeches but had a local cotton shirt bright with coarse embroidery.

"Makes you stand out like a peacock in a coal scuttle, Darkie," said Banks, mockingly.

"Yeah? Well your white face makes you stand out like a bar of ivory soap in a coal scuttle," said Tim. "Hope we don't get caught because of it."

"Oh, it'll be a piece of cake. We get to go for a walk and look at all the pretty girls."

"Mr. Amos said that they'll shoot you for getting familiar with the women in the Spanish Americas," said Tim, anticipating trouble, but feeling like a bit of a killjoy and a prude. There wasn't any harm in looking, surely?

"Huh," said Banks, "you don't know nothing. Not even about that fancy Irish girlfriend of yours. Bet you haven't even made out with her, let alone got off with her properly, even though she's making sheep's eyes at you all the time."

Tim felt himself blush. He wanted to punch the fathead. "Captain Malkis warned us . . ."

"Aw, what does old Malky know. . . ."

"Shut up! There are some local people on the road," said Tim.

So Banks shut up. He didn't even greet the family and their geese, but Tim copied the boy showing them the way, and got a smile and a burst of a foreign language. Tim nearly panicked, but their guide rattled off an answer. The goose-herders laughed, and they all went on through a small huddle of houses, and on towards the town. It was a good four-mile walk, and hard on their bare feet. They worked barefoot a lot of the time, but there were no stones underfoot in the submarine.

Eventually they came to the outskirts of the town—it couldn't really be called a city, not by a boy who had seen London. The buildings were white—except for the bottoms, which were stained with the red dust from the road. In the market people were selling strings of beads, or trays of fruits and vegetables. Some of stuff he'd heard of, like corn, and those yellow curvy things that must be bananas. They seemed to come in green too, but much bigger. And other fruits—well they must be fruit, he thought—with strange smells and colours. The sacks of potatoes were at least familiar. There were stalls selling cooked food, with people yelling *"Gallo pinto!"* at them. It smelt of frying and beans, and as usual Tim was hungry. But food was not part of their plan.

The street was crowded. The crowds seemed to cluster around the sailors in uniform . . . who were speaking English to each other. Well, English that was sort of somewhere between proper English and Cookie's English. *"Americanos,"* said their guide, threading them past two sailors talking to a trio of dressed-up ladies. He didn't seem to find them worrying. Tim did. He also felt ghostly hands in his pocket at one stage, but seeing as the small envelope he had to deliver was in his hand, getting sweaty, and there wasn't anything in his pocket, that was just something he had to put up with.

They came to a triple-story white building, with pillars and a bit of a balcony . . . and with a heavy black iron fence, topped with spikes. Their guide pointed. *"Americano."*

Which made things rather difficult. Tim had expected to be able to slip the envelope into a mail slot and leave, hopefully without being seen.

There was indeed a mail slot in the big studded black door. Only it was fifteen yards away, on the other side of the gates. The gates had even more spikes than the fence had. One of the smaller gates was open . . . but a soldier in a blue uniform with gold buttons, wearing a white cap with a black peak, stood there in the guardhouse, with a bayonetted rifle.

"You distract him and I'll run in and post it," said Tim, measuring the distance.

"Not on your life!" said Banks. "He'll shoot us."

Tim looked it all over carefully again. And then decided that there was really only one thing to do. Gritting his teeth, he walked up to the guard.

The guard said, "Beat it, kid! Gowan. Vamoose!"

Tim held out the envelope, which wasn't quite as clean as when it had left the *Cuttlefish*. "Letter." He decided to try and play the local part. "Letter for you," he said, pointing at the door, doing his best to sound foreign. He didn't speak any Spanish! Actually he didn't speak anything but English. Aha! He remembered a word. "*Señor*," he said, bowing.

The soldier was about to take a poke at him with the bayonet . . . but paused. Looked at the neat handwriting on the envelope, and at the address. "Where'd ya get that from, kid?"

"Engleesh lady," said Tim. "Give for me. For here, *Americano*."

"Who?"

"Engleesh lady," repeated Tim. And trying to come up with anything that might sound like he was a local, said, "*Gallo pinto, señor.*"

The soldier shook his head. "Darn foreigners. Just go and put it in the slot. And don't try anything."

So Tim did. He walked back with his heart still hammering, but very pleased with himself. "Thank you, sir."

"You sound almost English, kid!" said the soldier.

Terrified, Tim shook his head, but somehow keeping a facade of calm he went on walking out of the spike-topped gates.

And then he nearly screamed.

Because Banks and his guide were nowhere to be seen.

He stared around frantically. Opened his mouth to yell. Somehow he managed to get a grip on himself. The guard was looking at him a little oddly, so he walked down the hot crowded street. All he had to do was get back. That couldn't be so hard, could it?

After a little while he realised it could be. He'd just followed the local boy on the way here. And trying to reverse that, he'd taken a wrong turning somewhere. He didn't recognise anything—none of the buildings on the street. He was sure he'd have remembered that big tree and the huge white church if they'd passed them. He had to breathe deeply, and turn back, trying to retrace his steps again. It took him quite a while to find his way to the American Legation and then, work out his way back to the noisy market street.

Only it wasn't quite so noisy or crowded now. The baking sun was high overhead, and the stalls were being packed up. But at least he was on the right route now. And with luck those two would have waited for him somewhere, or if he walked a bit faster, he'd catch them up.

Tim walked on determinedly. It did seem like he was the only one doing so. It was very very hot. Still he was at least going the right way, and he'd managed to do what had to be done. He was relatively pleased with himself. He whistled as he walked. He could do that here, without getting into trouble for making a racket on the submarine.

And then passing through the last little cluster of houses before the final home strait, everything went wrong.

A fat man sitting on the porch of one of the houses hailed him as he came closer. Tim didn't know what to say, as he couldn't understand a word of it, so he nodded politely and walked on. It was hot; he was desperately thirsty, and he was tired.

It was obviously not the right thing to have done. The fat man got to his feet and spoke quite sharply, stepping towards Tim. Tim did what maybe he should have done first: turned to run. Only he fell, headlong, over a skinny dog that had been sniffing at his heels.

And it all went downhill from there. Downhill from lying flat on his back, half winded.

Maybe trying the three words of Spanish he had used on the soldier at the legation was a mistake. Because after he said "*Señor Gallo Pinto*," the fat man got really, really angry, dragged him to his feet by the scruff of his neck, and marched him off to a cell. The cell had a barred window and a locked door, and a single straw pallet.

In case he got lonely, it also had fleas. And roaches almost the size of mice.

# CHAPTER 19

Clara knew that Tim and Banks had gone into the city. There really were very few secrets among a submarine crew. But she didn't realise that either of them were back until after the captain ordered all the shore crew and her and her mother back to the boat.

"Sorry, ma' am. We're going to have to move the vessel. If you can please go to your cabin." He was not going to explain right then, she could tell. She'd ask Cookie.

He was off duty. But she found a flushed-looking Banks gulping water in the mess.

"Hullo. You're back," she said neutrally. He was always quick to get a bit too familiar. He made her uncomfortable.

He nodded. "But Darkie got arrested. So we have to move."

"What!" She knew Banks and his friends called Tim "Darkie." She'd seen Tim didn't like it . . . but right now that seemed unimportant. "They can't just leave him here. Where did he get arrested?"

"He ran smack up to the marine on guard at the legation. He wanted me to distract him, and then he was going to make a run for the mail slot."

"So didn't you?" she asked.

Banks did a brief mouth-flap. Clara'd bet he didn't. "Yeah, but the guard was quick as lightning and caught him. Darkie cried like a baby and put his hands up. So we came back to warn the skipper."

"But we can't just leave him here!" exclaimed Clara again.

"Aw, we're just moving half a mile or so, upriver. The captain reckons if he plays dumb they may let him go. If he can find his way

161

back to the smuggler's villa, we'll get him again," said Banks. The idea plainly didn't appeal to him.

Clara made her way up to the bridge. Her mother had beaten her to it.

". . . the canal is now finished," said the captain. "That's obviously why security is so tight. It does present us with a unique opportunity. . . ." He looked at Clara. "Ah. Good afternoon, Miss Calland."

"Is it true that Tim got caught?" she asked directly.

The captain looked at her from under a frowning forehead. "It . . . would appear that stories spread throughout this submarine faster than water through a broken hatch. Yes, Miss Calland. If the other cabin boy is to be believed, Barnabas got arrested at the legation. They can't hold him indefinitely, but they might turn him over to the local police. We can't take a chance and remain in the same place. Unfortunately I don't speak any of the local Spanish, and our local contact has quite limited English, so I haven't really been able to find out much more. I only now worked out that he was telling us that the canal was actually finished and operational, and not just going to be, a little earlier."

"I speak fairly good Spanish," said Mother. "Although I speak the Spanish of Spain, of course, not the local Voseo variety."

"What?" said Captain Malkis.

"They say *vos* instead of *tú*. But I daresay I could still understand him, and him me. If you'd like me to speak to him?"

The captain nodded. "I'd be obliged, Dr. Calland. The Americans are unlikely to do the boy any harm, although they may try and get our location out of him. But he's a steady lad, which is why I used him as the actual bearer for the letter."

Clara had to wait several hours before the local smuggler and his messenger boy came paddling upriver in a canoe. She did listen in to her mother and Captain Malkis talking to him. There was no way she was not going to.

"So they don't really know what actually happened. The young boy walked up to the guard waving the letter, and the bigger boy ran away. He dragged my boy with him too. My boy got him to sit down behind some bushes, and went back, but the young boy was gone. He didn't know what to do, and it was getting late, towards siesta, so he brought the bigger one back."

"Ah, so he's just lost," said the captain. "Well, that's good. . . ."

The smuggler continued in his local Spanish, with hand gestures and, it appeared, incredulity.

Mother translated. "He has been arrested. He was apparently walking rather fast through the nearest little village to here, during siesta—the local afternoon sleep when it is too hot to work—and when the policeman asked him where he was off to in such a hurry, he called him a speckled chicken. The policeman thinks he is either crazy or a spy."

"I see. Can Señor Omberto get him bailed? Or let out?" asked the captain.

Mother translated.

No one had to translate the shake of the smuggler's head. "He says if they think he is mixing with spies they will shoot him," said her mother, grimly. "He says we should leave. And soon. His men will bring the parts you asked for, the compressor, and the coal late this afternoon."

Clara made her plans carefully. The first part had involved talking to that toad Banks. Being admiring. Huh. She got quite a lot of information out of him, even if it had meant putting up with having him put a hand on her knee. She'd slapped it off when he tried to move it, though. He really was a cockroach. The second had involved writing a letter to her mother, and making sure that it would not be found until she was well gone. The third involved organising a neat roll of clothes and the tools that she'd helped herself to from the engine room, and managing to have that and herself on deck in the leaf-shadowed twilight. She wore breeches and had tucked her hair into a cap. It was a problem having pale hair, but this hid it, and she had a lacy shawl of Mother's for later.

It was easier than she thought it would be, to jump down onto the stern of the barge, while they hefted coal off the front.

Then it was just a matter of hunching down in the deep shadows of some big floats and netting, pulling some of the netting over herself, and waiting while the little barge putted its way back down the river. She felt very alone, and very scared.

And very determined.

After what seemed like forever, the barge bumped gently up against a little jetty, and was tied up there. The crew got off and went on up to the house, through the big gates. Clara came out of her hiding place, and did not even get onto the jetty. Instead she climbed into a canoe, one of several tied up there. She'd never been in one before, and it rocked alarmingly. Still, there was a paddle, and she was able to clumsily row downstream a few dozen yards, to a track she'd seen some thirty yards from the edge of the fence. Getting the canoe up onto the bank made her a little wet and muddy, but there was water right there. She carefully did not think about crocodile-like caymans as she scooped water and washed her hands and face and feet as best as she could. And then she stole past the fence and down to the track. The dogs didn't bark . . . and no one challenged her.

In the deep shadow of some trees, next to where the rutted dirt track from the smuggler's house joined the bigger dirt road, she changed . . . into a dress. They might suspect a boy, she'd decided. With any luck, they wouldn't suspect a girl. And with a bit more luck, her mother would stop the submarine leaving without her. Without both of them.

Mother was going to be more than just angry. So was the captain.

She'd live with that.

She was not going to live with just leaving Tim behind. He didn't know anything but the submarine and the tunnels under London. He'd die here. A practical part of her mind said her experience of life in Fermoy and a trip to Dublin didn't make her much better off. That didn't stop her walking down the road. Banks had said that there were only about ten houses in the village when she'd picked his brains about it after they'd found out where Tim was, and thought it funny that Tim should get caught there—conveniently forgetting that he'd told her earlier that Tim had been caught at the American Legation. She had to be able to work out which of the ten houses was a jail, surely.

It was easier than she'd hoped, even if there were at least thirty houses. Tim was whistling. He often did while he was working on the submarine, and she recognised it at once. Of course working out exactly where it came from took a little longer. But soon she found the high barred window, and whispered, "Tim. Tim Barnabas."

In the cell, Tim had gone from bleak and absolute despair to gratitude for water and then, some food. Odd stuff, but food. And food helped his state of mind and not just his stomach.

What had happened next, didn't. By the light it was late afternoon . . . and a man spoke from outside the high window, in English. The English of England. "Young submariner. Would you like to get out of there?"

"Yes!" Relief flooded Tim.

"It can be arranged," said the voice coolly. "Of course, you'll have to do something for me. You'll be well rewarded for it. Manuel—the local policeman—is going to town shortly. He won't be back tonight, I gather. Now, do I have your cooperation?"

"Just what do you want?" asked Tim, suddenly doubtful. Who was this? How did this stranger know he came off a submarine?

"It's perfectly simple, really," said the stranger. "I believe there is a young woman from your submarine, now staying in the villa of Omberto Guerbata. I believe she's . . . shall we say, fond of you?"

"She's not! Where did you hear that from?" asked Tim, suspicious.

The voice paused. "I have my sources. It's worth, hmm . . . ten thousand pounds to you."

Tim snorted. "Ten thousand pounds. Are you mad or something?" That was a lifetime's money for an ordinary man.

For an answer the speaker held up a roll of notes to the window.

"This can be yours in return for a little help. You could have half up front. You could sail back to England and live the life of Riley. All we need is a little help."

Now Tim was thoroughly confused. And stunned by the idea of that kind of money. Ten thousand pounds! What his mam could do with ten thousand pounds. . . . "What are you talking about?" He couldn't help being interested. Suspicious, but interested.

"Your little girlfriend Clara Calland. Just tell her that you need to talk to her in private, when you get back, and bring her to me. I'll be about five hundred yards from the villa. Twenty pounds a yard. Just think of that," said the man, wheedlingly.

Betray her? As if! As it sunk in, Tim shook the bars. "If I could get out there I'd punch your daylights out!" he shouted angrily.

Someone said something in Spanish, and the cool-voiced man replied in the same tongue, not sounding quite so cool.

Tim shouted insults at him. He'd learned some fine swear words on the submarine. He pulled up on the bars to have a look at man.

But he had gone.

For a little while Tim just stared out at the alley, and then he lowered himself down and tried to work out just how to get out of his small prison. He knew he had to, and he had at least learned that his jailer had gone to town.

The rusty iron bars were not very thick. Still, even with his whole weight on them, they didn't break or even bend. So he set about trying to dig them out of the wall. The wall seemed to be nothing more than hard mud, and he had a spoon that had come with the bean-and-corn mush.

He hadn't meant to whistle while he worked, but he had been doing so. It was a habit he had been trying to break on the boat, but when he was doing something boring, it just happened.

And then, out of the darkness, she whispered his name.

"Clara?" he gasped, not quite believing his ears.

"Shh. I've come to help you break out. I've got a file and a hacksaw. Which do you want?" she asked.

"Um. Hacksaw, I think. What do you think you're doing here, you crazy girl? You'd better go!"

"I'm thinking I'm helping you escape, if you can stop talking and take the saw," she said.

So he did, and then put some spit on his fingers to try and keep the noise down. Fortunately the blade bit into the soft iron easily. She worked at the second bar with the file. It didn't take very long to cut through two bars and bend them out of the way. And then with a pull-up, a squeeze, a wiggle, and a tearing of his shirt, he was out.

And not, it would seem, a moment too soon. There were lights coming down the road . . . and a vehicle pulled up, partly blocking the alley that was their obvious exit to the road. A door slammed. "I think we should run now," whispered Clara.

Clara wished, now, that she hadn't changed into the long dress. It was a little too long for her, and would be impossible to run in. They rushed to the mouth of the alley . . . and quickly ducked back again. A second car had driven up, the lights bright in the dust of the first.

And someone was shouting from inside the jail in English with an accent straight out of an American biorama. "He's cut the bars!"

And then they realised that the other end of the smelly little alley wasn't going to help them escape either. It ended in a high wall. The beam from a powerful electric torch shone down the alley. Clara grabbed Tim and pinned him against the wall. Wrapped her shawl around both of them. The light shone around, and quite deliberately, she kissed him. Very noisily. Just like in the biorama. Not at all like her mother kissing her good night. She'd never kissed a boy before, and she was sure they weren't doing it quite right. But it was no time to get lessons first.

The light shone on them. "It's a couple of kids making out," said the American-accented voice, sounding amused. "Hey, *señorita*, your mama is going to be mad with you. You'd better get home."

Clara, to her pride, answered him with the Spanish phrase from the biorama that their teacher had been so horrified at the girls learning.

That made the uniformed man laugh . . . and shine his torch on the back wall, and leave. "He's not here," he said.

"He'll be long gone. We'd better get onto Commodore Watson."

"We should check out that road to the river quays. This road only goes there."

Moments later the two cars roared off. "You kissed me!" He sounded almost as if he didn't believe it.

"They'd have caught us, otherwise," she said, pushing him away.

"Uh. I suppose so," said Tim. "It was . . . just a bit of a surprise. . . . We'd better get out of here before they come back. What did you say to him?"

Even in the dark, she was sure he could see her blush. "I don't know."

"Worked better than my try," he said as they sloped off out of the alley. "The local bobby just got mad at me." The main street of

the hamlet was already anything but quiet. Everyone was coming
out to see what had happened. As they were all peering at the lights
disappearing into the dark down the track to the river, Tim and
Clara walked the other way—away from where they needed to go.
Just outside the village they followed a path that took them down to
some trees next to a field of corn. They crawled into one of the rows,
and sat down.

"Just what are you actually doing here?" asked Tim, now that
they could talk.

"I'd have thought that was obvious, then," said Clara, feeling
cross and underappreciated. "I've come to get you out of the jail.
They were just going to leave you there!"

"I'm . . . I'm really grateful to you," he said, awkwardly. "But I
really wish you hadn't come!"

That stunned her. "Is it back you'd like to go?" she said, even
more crossly. "I'm sure I can help you climb back into your cell."

"N-no . . . ," he stammered. "I'm really, really grateful, like I
said. It's just that you're in terrible danger. They offered me ten
thousand pounds to bring you out of the smuggler's house so that
they could catch you!"

"What!"

So Tim explained. "See, this man knew that I came off the submarine. He knew you're staying in the smuggler's house. He knew
his name and everything."

"The captain took us back aboard, and moved the sub," said
Clara.

"Good for the captain! At least the boat should be safe . . . or
safer, at least. He's a wily old bird, is Captain Malkis. But, but . . .
they must have someone on the boat spying."

The idea was really nasty. How could he even think that? "Why?
I mean it could be one of the smuggler's men. They looked a right
bunch of ruffians."

"Um. The man . . . knew you were a friend of mine. Um . . .

Well, how would a smuggler have known about that? We've got to get you back there, where it is safe, and tell the captain," said Tim.

"I don't think he's going to be terribly pleased with me," said Clara, in a small voice. Captain Malkis, she had a feeling, now that they were going back, was not a good person to make angry.

"We'll worry about that when we get to the sub," said Tim. "Hope he hasn't moved her again."

That idea hadn't occurred to her. It was terrifyingly likely. "Well, we'd better head back to the river. Um. I suppose we could always get hold of the smuggler guy. He must have a Marconi wireless set or something."

"We could just walk along the edge of the field here, rather than back on the road," said Tim, warily. "Those motorcars haven't come back yet."

"Wonder what they're doing?" asked Clara as they began picking their way along the field edge. The corn was nearly head high, so they were not very visible, but the moonlight did make it easy to find their way. They could see the little village lamps, and would have seen the motoring-cars, or at least their lights.

They walked on, over a stile and then along another muddy track, more or less parallel to the "road." "If I'm not in enough trouble with my mother, I'll be in more about this dress," said Clara, ruefully.

"She's very strict, your mother," said Tim.

For a moment Clara was actually quite affronted. "She's . . . well, my father always said she was just like my *oma*—my grandmother. She was from Prussia. But mother's not really. She was always a bit serious, though. It just got bad when my father got arrested. He . . . he could always make her laugh. He could make anyone laugh." Despite being in dire trouble, and sort of lost in the middle of a half-jungle place in Central America, it still made her choke up, every time she thought of him. "I've never understood why my mother divorced him," she said, to her own surprise. She never talked about it. Not to anyone. "She just . . . buried herself in her work after that. In her work and in me."

"My da got killed in the anti-foreigner riots," said Tim in the moonlit darkness, as they balanced over stepping stones across a small stream. "He came from Jamaica when he was about five years old. Lived in East London all his life. But they killed him because he was . . . foreign. Black. I know, it's not much help. But at least you knew your dad. I can't even remember mine."

"I miss him. I used to write to him every month. He won't even know what has happened to us. I . . . I used to dream of breaking him out of prison too." Only, she did not say, *I was ashamed of him. Ashamed because he was a rebel.* And suddenly she remembered: she wasn't anymore.

"What's that!?" A boom and a flare of flame lit up the sky ahead of them. There were shots too. Clara and Tim dived down and waited. There were no more explosions, at least. A few gunshots, though.

"It can't be the sub blowing up, surely?" Tim's voice sounded close to panic.

Clara peered toward where the noise came from. "I . . . don't think so. That was quite close. What . . . what should we do?"

"Well, I suppose the sensible thing would be to run away or just to find somewhere to lie low . . . but that won't get us back to the boat," said Tim, obviously gathering himself, managing not to slip into panic. "Suppose we walk so we cut down to the river a little upstream, instead of where they're shooting. It's not much of a river."

Clara turned her head, listening. "I suppose we have to. The shooting has stopped."

So they went on. Cautiously.

"I think all that shooting must have happened at the smuggler's place. Those Americans . . . Shh," hissed Clara. There was definitely someone coming.

"Quick, into the field," said Tim, pulling her.

They dived in among the stubby cornstalks. Lay still, listening.

And then Tim exhaled in relief. "Hello, *Cuttlefish*," he called out, recognising the gravelly voice of Thorne.

A shot whizzed over their heads just as Tim was about to stand up. He fell flat. "Hold your fire, you idiots," said Lieutenant Ambrose. "Who is that?"

"Us," said Clara.

"Ah. Our prodigal. You're in deep trouble, miss. We really didn't expect to find you. Who is that with you?"

"Barnabas, sir," said Tim. "Miss Calland got me out of jail."

"What!" His tone said to Clara that her running off had been very bad, but that actually having succeeded was worse. "Well," said the lieutenant, as Clara watched Tim getting slapped on the back by the men from the crew. "We set off for one prodigal and got two."

Thorne coughed. "Should we let the other parties know, sir?"

"Yes, and then we'll need to run. Are you two fit to run?"

"Yes, I think so," said Tim.

"Good," said the lieutenant. "Because there is trouble out there. Gunfire and an explosion."

"I think it was the Americans. They nearly caught us, sir," said Tim.

"Well, no matter what or who it was, we need to leg it. The flare will draw some unwanted attention." He drew a Very pistol from his belt and inserted a cartridge. "Green. Let them know that we've got you. Your mother will be very relieved, Miss Calland. She's with Lieutenant Willis's group."

*Just,* thought Clara, *when you thought it couldn't get much worse, it did.*

The run back to the submarine's inflatable cylinder-boat was quick and uneventful, even if the two of them ended up being carried. And then they were ferried across to the submarine, where Captain Malkis was waiting.

"I think, young lady," he said in a voice as cold as the Arctic ocean, "that you need to go to your cabin and remain there until I order you to leave it. You are lucky I don't confine you to the brig." Then he paused, seeing Tim. "Good gracious! Barnabas!"

"Miss Calland got me out, sir. Just in time, sir," said Tim, stoutly. "She's a heroine. At least to me, sir."

"She's a young woman in a lot of trouble," said the captain, but his tone moderated a great deal as he said it. "You seem to have lost some blood, and some clothing and got very muddy, Barnabas. Are you all right?"

"Just a scratch from the bars, Sir. I'm fine . . . just hungry, sir," said Tim.

The captain actually managed a twitch of smile. "You always are, I suspect. Right, get yourself washed, and go to the mess and get yourself some food before reporting to bridge. We're glad to have you back."

"I wouldn't be here without Miss Calland, sir," said Tim, sticking to his guns. "She's as brave as a lion."

"That may be. But—"

The captain was interrupted in his lecture about what he thought of lions that endangered his boat and his crew by the clattering descent of someone down the stairwell. Clara's mother, her face as white as chalk, burst in. She grabbed Clara, hugged her, and then started yelling at her.

The captain pushed the two of them along, gently. "To your cabin, ladies. Now."

Clara could think of nowhere she wanted less to go to, but she went.

Down the corridor, she could hear Tim whistling again.

# CHAPTER 20

"I think," mused Duke Malcolm, "that if we ever do catch this submarine captain alive, I should offer him the post of First Sea Lord in exchange for his loyalty. He's made a fool of your officers, my Lord Admiral."

"He's certainly out-thought them," said Lesseps. "Nicaragua, eh. The truth is, Your Grace, it would take a lot of force to take the forts on the St. Juan. We could, of course. But mining the channel should be reasonably effective, especially as it seems your target will be relying on the Americans for an escape route. If they take her overland, we have no chance of preventing it, my Lord Duke."

"It does put us on a different footing with the Americans, and the Canadian conflict," said Prince Albert. "We may as well throw our full might behind the Canadians."

Duke Malcolm nodded. "It's by no means certain that our agents won't get to her first, although the Americans, and what passes for a local government, are very busy trying to suppress information about their canal. If that fails, however, speed is of the essence. No matter what the importance of this method of Dr. Calland's, it will take a while to get it up to mass production. We need to be in as strong a position as possible."

"Excuse me, sir. There is a Marconi telegraph message from our operative in Nicaragua just arrived from decoding."

"I think we can trust the first lord of the Admiralty, Bowen," said Duke Malcolm, tapping his long cigarette holder and sending a cascade of ash to the Turkey carpets on his floor. "Read them."

"'Attempted to subvert submarine crew member. Information incorrect, was not receptive. Raid on smuggler compound with local operatives interrupted by US agents and marines. Presume C is now in US custody. Legation under surveillance. Advise next action.' Ends," said the aide, his voice deadpan.

Duke Malcolm, Prince Albert, and the Lord Admiral looked at each other in silence. "Begin drafting a letter of demand, Albert. We want into . . . and then out of this war as fast as possible," said Duke Malcolm. "Bowen. I'll want the St. Lawrence dossiers. They are too large to come up the message chute from records. See them brought up immediately. I need to check on certain aspects contained in them."

The aide saluted, and left them to their planning.

A little later he came back. "Pardon me interrupting, Your Grace, but there is another message in from our agent-in-chief in Rivas.

The duke nodded. "Read it."

"'Advise Americans do not have C. Full-scale search is under way. The target of raid was us, not her.'"

The duke turned to his half-brother, smiled savagely. "A good thing that you were being so fussy about the wording of that letter of demand, Albert. We will have to hold off on this war until we have some certainty of what is actually happening."

# CHAPTER 21

"What you've said about the nitrates seems fantastical to me, ma'am, but obviously not to the British Empire or, it would seem, the Americans," said Captain Malkis as they stood on the bridge. Tim felt very awkward being there, but it was at the captain's instruction. The captain gestured towards Tim. "Barnabas here confirms that the Americans were interested enough to send some of their marines and agents to fetch him. If they're taking it seriously, well, then I know I should be too, ma'am. I was not briefed as to your exact significance, before you and your daughter boarded the *Cuttlefish*. I was told only that you were the daughter of one of our founders, and the wife of one of the Irish Revolutionary leadership, and that you were a scientist."

Tim was a bit stunned by the "leadership" part. He'd bet no one had ever told Clara that. He grinned inwardly, trying to keep a straight face. He was going to enjoy telling her that! The part about the nitrates didn't mean much to him. Of course that was one of the things they transported with the submarine. He knew that much.

The captain took a brief turn about the floor while gathering himself to speak. "I'm afraid I didn't grasp all the implications, or why the Americans would be so eager to give you refuge. But it seems that they are very keen to get their hands on you. It makes sense of this frantically intensive pursuit we have suffered. I realised that there had to be more to it than I'd been told, but not that such a thing could change the world's power structures entirely. I honestly don't know what level of trust you can repose in the Americans.

177

They may be acting in good faith, but their shooting and the use of explosives does not inspire trust."

Dr. Calland looked as if the cares of the world were all on her shoulders. "My daughter is of the same opinion. She behaved extremely foolishly but—"

"She had no idea of the risks she took, or the dangers she faced, Dr. Calland," said the captain, gently. "She's an innocent young girl, unaware of the ways of the wider world, and of places like Rivas. She felt that she had a debt to repay. Unwise, but honourable, and with no real idea of the dangers to a young girl alone here."

Tim nearly said something in Clara's defence. He felt he ought to. But you didn't just interrupt the captain. Well. Not yet, anyway. He would if they didn't let him speak.

Clara's mother sighed. "She has ideas, but a great deal of foolishness and idealism too. She takes after her father."

The captain hid his mouth briefly by sliding his hand down his beard, to hide the smile. "Not like her mother, at all."

The idea seemed to almost startle Dr. Calland. "Oh, no. It'd be easier to stay angry with her if she was more like me. Anyway, to return to the Americans. It seems to me they voided any chance of my trusting them by trying to capture this young man," said Dr. Calland, waving a hand at Tim.

It made Tim feel very awkward. Clara had come to rescue him, and they hadn't. That brought back the memory of the very English-sounding man who had offered him money to capture Clara.

"And, by the lack of response to our Marconi wireless calls, and from our examination through binoculars, they've destroyed our smuggler contact's villa, if not him as well. I'm afraid, Dr. Calland, they have either decided to cooperate with the British Empire or they—"

"Can't be relied on to keep their word," finished Dr. Calland. "They offered me refuge, assistance to continue my work, and strictly no coercion or militarisation of that work. I asked for that, and they agreed. I should have been more suspicious, demanded some guarantees, but I was at a loss as to how to. I'm . . . still at a loss, Captain. If I could just broadcast my mother and Fritz's work—maybe even post the methods and results they achieved and the work I've done, to the whole world. That's what I was trying to do—to get it published in a paper on experimental chemistry. The two peers I consulted were Russian . . . and that's where it all started. And now I literally don't know where to go."

"Well, that's why I asked you to come up and talk to me, Dr. Calland. You see, I thought we might take advantage of their new canal before the Royal Navy attempts to put it out of use. The Americans have of course camouflaged it with netting, set up anti-airship guns, and set mine fields to protect it, but it's only a matter of time before spies get a very good idea of its route and airships are used to bomb it, and naval guns pound much of it. We have received coded shortwave instructions relayed from London, about our own course. We are to go and collect our cargo of caliche from Peru, and then head for Western Australia. We pick up the drogues at sea off the Galapagos, and Peru is probably not a safe country for you. But the Republic of Westralia would be. Besides the fact that they'd be, I would think, grateful for the knowledge you have, it's also a republic which resents the fact that it was abandoned by the British Empire and values its independence. The Big Dry has forced them to be a very clever and forward-looking people. When the Swan River dried up and the British governor-general ordered the territory abandoned . . . well, those who stayed had to learn fast."

Dr. Calland looked as if she might burst into tears. "We cannot impose further on you, Captain. But I am so very appreciative and grateful for what you've done, both for my daughter and for me. You and your crew have been wonderful. I am so sorry for the danger and the trouble we've brought to you. I would like to go to Westralia, of all things, but it is far too much to ask of you."

The Captain bowed. "Ma'am, that will now be our destination, and feeding two more people is no particular hardship." He smiled.

Tim did too. And while he managed to stop himself from cheering
—or even saying "Yes!"—by biting his lip, he couldn't help but nod.

The captain, unfortunately, noticed. So did Clara's mother. But
other than raising his eyebrow, Captain Malkis said nothing, just
continued as if he hadn't seen it. Tim knew that was worse. "I know
this as the cook—who is from Western Australia himself—took the
unusual step, for him, of coming to see me, and suggesting it. And
he wouldn't have done that if he didn't want to feed you. Besides,
your daughter did save all of us when we were trapped in the net in
the Wash. And she freed my young crewman. Of course"—and here
he looked directly at Tim—"we'll have to take steps to see that she
doesn't engage in any more madcap schemes."

At this point Clara's mother did start crying. The captain patted
her awkwardly. "Thank you so very much," she said, after a determined sniff. "It's such a relief. And I'll see that Clara stays out of any
more trouble. It . . . it isn't really like her."

The captain looked at Tim again. "Yes. I suspected so, ma'am.
Which is why I thought we needed to have a word with young
Master Barnabas here. I did make it clear to all the submariners that
. . . you were all to stay at arm's length from Miss Calland, did I not,
Master Barnabas?"

Tim felt himself blush. "Yes, sir. I have. Well, I've done my best
to, sir. Really." She'd kissed him. Not the other way around. He'd
never even touched her otherwise, except to stop her falling over or
washing away. And that kiss was only to stop them being caught,
really. No matter how he might like it to be otherwise. . . . "I've not
disobeyed your orders on the boat, sir." That was true. Questions
about what he'd done in an alley, in a village outside Rivas, were a
different matter. He'd decided that you might as well kiss back if
you were going to be caught. The tongue bit was a bit confusing.

"I believe him, Captain," said Clara's mother, although Tim felt
the glow from his face made him out to be a total liar. "I . . . um . . .
asked Clara the same sort of questions."

To Tim's surprise, Captain Malkis seemed happy to accept this. "Nonetheless, I think we need to see to it that the two of them interact as little as possible. For the sake of the smooth running of the boat," said the captain, "I think we'll have to see that Miss Calland is abed while Tim is at work, instead of having them awake on the same watch."

Tim's heart sank. Lieutenant Ambrose was all right, but Mate Werner frightened him a bit. "Um, sir . . ."

"I'm aware that you're a good lad, Barnabas," said the captain. "I believe you've kept to the rules, although you two are the youngest on the boat and have been in difficult circumstances together. I also understand just how Dr. Calland's daughter feels that she owes you a debt. That could lead to trouble, for her, for you, and in my crew."

"She doesn't owe me anything, sir. Never. She paid me back in spades. But sir, what I wanted to say is . . . we must have a spy on the boat. That's the only way all of this could have happened. That's how they're onto us all the time."

The captain shook his head. "Barnabas, any spy would be risking their own life. In the ports, yes, there are spies and informers. Almost certainly here in Rivas where everything is for sale, it seems. We're aware of that. That is why our destinations are secret. I'm entrusting you with a great deal, but you've proved yourself reliable."

"Well," said Tim, knowing it actually made it worse for both him and Clara, but knowing it had to be said. "Someone tried to bribe me while I was in that jail, sir. Someone who knew I was . . . friends with Miss Calland. That could only be known to someone on the boat, sir. They must be getting information from inside the crew."

"It's not possible," said the captain with finality. "Now get along with you, Barnabas. You'll have to swap duties and bunks with Standard. And young man, you'll have no further contact with Miss Calland. Understood?"

So Tim had to salute and leave, pack his kit and move. He had no part to play in the crew who were sent topside to strap piles of cut reeds and rushes onto the deck-brackets. He did have to listen to the mate complaining about how they affected the buoyancy later, though.

During his watch the submarine was under way, and soon the "all quiet" light came on. Then a little later, the light went off, but the engines did not restart. Tim—now on the same watch as Big Eddie, and doing dishes again, saw him when he came into the mess, demanding tea. "Water out there is like brown soup," he said cheerfully. "I hope I've got us under the right ship, and not a tramp steamer heading for Cuba."

"What?" asked Tim, puzzled.

"The sub is hanging like a leech underneath a gunboat about to go down the canal," said Big Eddie. "We've got magnetic grapples hooked to the catfish-feelers. The reeds and rushes on the deck act as buffers, and now all we have to do is hope the water is deep enough, and the mate can keep us lined up underneath, and next thing we'll be out in San Juan del Sur bay and no one any the wiser. Mind you, the water out there is so dirty, we hardly need a boat to hide under, except to get through the locks."

In the hot little cabin Clara was angry. Yes, she'd known there'd be trouble. It was just the kind of trouble that she'd not guessed at. She'd not even imagined it could happen this way! Huh. So now they were punishing Tim, who really hadn't done anything wrong. Because he was a boy. Honestly, her mother talked about women and equality, but didn't believe that if one of the two of them was keen on what mother called "initiating physical contact" in that tone, it was her. If there was one thing she liked more about Tim than any of the others, it was that he hadn't even tried to touch her. It was . . . rather why he was more interesting in that sort of way. Safer. And now, to add to that injustice, the captain didn't believe him, any more than her mother believed her, that somehow there must be a traitor on the submarine.

On the other hand, they had a long journey still, halfway around the world, on the submarine. She'd sort it all out. Somehow.

But it wasn't fair.

The air grew older and staler as the boat made its way down the canal under the American gunboat, a ship they'd deliberately chosen for its shallow draught. Tim was on messenger duty on the bridge, and like everyone else there, was watching the mate and the instruments. He had to admit, watching the big telltale dials from the catfish-feelers and the magnetic grapples, that the mate was a master at controlling the submarine. The ship was moving slowly and had to go up the locks and then down onto the Pacific side. It was an exercise in navigation too, as they had to know when they could break free. You could see the sweat bead the mate's forehead as the stress told . . . but they got there.

"We come out, ja. Prepare to dive," said the mate with obvious relief, reaching for the lever that channelled their battery power into the fore and aft electromagnetic grapples. There was a sharp click, and the *Cuttlefish* slipped free.

And then things went wrong.

The explosion nearly rattled them off their feet. It was the closest blast they'd experienced in all their brushes with the Royal Navy. Tim nearly panicked. But the mate stayed as cool as if it had not happened, pulling the dive levers, giving the twin screws of the *Cuttlefish* full thrust. Turning and corkscrewing away. "Damage reports, sectors," he snapped into the speaking tube.

One by one the sectors reported in. A minor leakage aft in upper steerage appeared to be all the damage there was. The "all quiet" light burned. There were no more explosions, and the mate began to adjust the dive levers. They were already at 220 feet. The *Cuttlefish* could not take much more, Tim knew. Three hundred feet was supposed to be her maximum dive depth.

Slowly, they began to rise again, still moving steadily away from the scene, still on dead quiet. By this time Captain Malkis had come up to the bridge too. There were no more sounds of the hydrophones, though, as the pressure gauge showed they were back to thirty feet, then twenty, and then ten feet—maximum periscope depth. They stopped there. "Raise the periscope," said the captain. Tim and the other rating on bridge duty wound the double cranks.

"Ah," said Captain Malkis. "It appears that the Americans were not as good at keeping the canal secret as they might have been. Their gunboat appears to be sinking. I would guess that the bay has been mined, probably by the Royal Navy. That was unlucky for them, and lucky for us that we did not strike it." He sighed. "We'd better see if we can render any assistance, and hope we do not strike a mine ourselves."

The *Cuttlefish* turned back towards the coast, coming slowly to the surface. "We'll need a deck party, Mr. Mate," said the captain. "By the looks of it there are a number of men in the water."

The submarine surfaced. . . .

But an explosion and a waterspout soon changed that.

"We're being fired on by the shore batteries, sir!" said the periscope man.

The mate swore. The captain took a deep breath. "It appears they don't want our help, gentlemen. It is time to turn and run."

So they did.

Tim was relieved to be going away, even if it meant that he now had to run for strong tea. Now all they had between them and Westralia was the vastness of the Pacific. They had an offshore rendezvous to

pick up a cargo of caliche drogues—which were like little submarines themselves, carefully weighed and air-buoyed to neither
sink nor float—that the *Cuttlefish* would tow underwater past the
blockades on Westralia's ports. But after they'd collected them,
attached them, well, then it would be just plain sailing across the
open sea, for months, in a small space, with a girl he was not supposed to speak to.

He should have guessed that she wasn't going to put up with
that. He was beginning to grasp some truths about Miss Clara
Calland.

"We can't just let him get away with it. We have to find out who
it is," she said quietly, on her way to the shower, just when he happened to be cleaning the brass fittings in the passage. She'd walked
past him as if he wasn't there. Now, without looking at him, she was
talking to him.

He looked around hastily. "Get away with what?" he asked,
nervously.

"Treachery, of course. There's a spy on this ship, and we're going
to have to catch him, because they won't believe us." And then she
walked on, as if she hadn't spoken to him, as Lieutenant Ambrose
walked down the passage.

It was all very well to talk of catching spies, thought Tim,
methodically rubbing the brass in small circles. The trouble with
boring jobs like this one is that they gave him a great deal too much
time to think. But how did one do it? And who could it be?

The problem for any spy was always going to be just how they
passed information on to Imperial Security. And of course just how
they didn't get killed too, as the attacks on the submarine had not
been anything but real. Still . . . the man back in Rivas had known
a great deal about who was on the boat and just who Clara's friend
was. Tim wondered if she would have trusted him enough to follow
him into a trap. . . . Not a good thought. He wished now he'd taken
the man's money and at least had that for evidence.

His suspicion lay with Sparks the Marconi operator. He could use the ship's wireless and its powerful shortwave transmitter. He told Clara this the next day when they just happened to encounter each other in the passage again. Purely by chance, Tim didn't believe.

"Good point," said Clara, wrinkling her high forehead. Then she shook her head. "But it couldn't be him. He knew that Mother and I were on board and not at the smuggler's house when that man was trying to bribe you. He could use the Marconi set to pass messages at any time without suspicion falling on him. And it seems as if they've been informed, but only sometimes. I know Sparks doesn't work all the time, and he just leaves the Marconi wireless set on the standard channel when he's off duty. There must be another radio hidden somewhere. You'll have to look for it. I'm not allowed into other people's cabins. Hmm. I wonder if I can make a crystal radio."

"A what?" asked Tim.

"A simple radio receiver," she explained. "We made one as part of our science class-work. Only that had some parts we put together. And an earphone. If someone else is using a radio, it must be when Sparks is off duty, or there would be a chance that he might pick up the messages. If I can make a crystal set, I could pick it up."

"Isn't that really hard to do?" asked Tim, doubtfully.

"Not really, no. Not if you're not inventing it. It's doing it for the first time that's hard."

Tim was actually the first one to spot the Galapagos Islands, by seeing the birds. He was on masthead watch, which having been ter-rified of once upon a time, he'd actually come to love. Deck watch was one of the few times one got to be truly alone on the submarine, and out in the Pacific, the decks themselves, extended with spars and nets, were used by the crew for a bit of extra space and, of course, for sail handling. Out here in midocean away from the sea lanes, only the big gossamer sails were used to propel the *Cuttlefish*, as she rode on her hydrofoil outriggers. The sails were just fairly transparent from close up, but from a few miles off looked rather like a slight blur to any observer. From up in the crow's nest Tim was above the sails that hid the deck, and, as there was only room for two people in the crow's nest if they got very close together indeed, he was alone. It was a good place for quiet, a good place for thinking. That could distract a lookout. It had taken Tim a little while to realise that that might be Volcan Wolf, beyond the birds, and that that vast flock of birds might indicate the islet that he was supposed to be looking out for. He used the voice pipe to let the bridge know, and soon the deck crew were hauling down the sails, and the distant volcanoes were more visible on the horizon.

The *Cuttlefish*'s exhausts belched coal smoke, and the compressors started up. Up here, at the tip of the mast, the vibration from them was magnified. Down below the belt-chains were powered up and the submarine began to crank the outrigger-hydrofoils back into position to be the outer hull, shaping the submarine for travel on the surface, pushed by her screws. Underneath the boat itself the telescoping centre-board keel would be coming up. Tim could hear the sail-master's bellows as the sail crew folded and stowed the vast gossamer sails into the compartments inside the outer hull. Tim's task, however, was to keep watch until they had to take down and fold the mast, and strap it to the deck. For the dangerous port runs it was stashed inside the second hull, but they would, they hoped, be using it again in a day or so.

They were due to pick up the drogues here, if the local weather —the *garuas*—cooperated. By the looks of the cloud buildup to the west, Tim had been lucky to see the islands, and the drizzly rain of the *garua* would soon resume. It was ideal cover, even though it meant that the rendezvous would be tricky. Picking up cargo was always a dangerous business. The drogues would be left at a seamount, anchored to the bottom, for the submarine to pick up. It was hard for observers to spot them, but it was also a good place for a trap: the submarine had to arrive at the drogues, sooner or later. It also required that the drop-off was precise. A buoy on the surface was easier to find, but it could easily be found by the wrong people, so that method could not be used. But finding something on the bottom, without a marker, was near impossible. The system the submarines had evolved was quite simple—the spot was marked with a buoy . . . but the buoy was merely attached to a lobster trap, with the drogue anchor dropped within yards of the buoy. It could still, Tim had heard from Big Eddie, take forever to find.

Clara was on the bridge as Mate Werner took control of the submarine on the approach to the pickup point. She'd found that the mate was, since her Rivas exploits, actually easier to deal with than the captain. He let her up on the bridge, sometimes. He was a cautious commander. They crept in underwater, on the batteries, with only the periscope visible, and with heavy drizzle and fog cover overhead.

It was unnecessary, this time. They found the buoy, and the divers went out, hooked up the line, and took an air hose to the big torpedo-like tubes of caliche—nitrates for the mines in Westralia. They would be towed like barges behind the submarine. The divers pumped enough air into their buoy section to make them neutrally buoyant, so they hung like whales in the sea, as they were pulled along. They did slow the *Cuttlefish* down, acting like sea-anchors, despite their shape, but it meant she could transport many tons of extra cargo.

Late that afternoon, still in the misty rain, but thirty miles from the nearest island, the *Cuttlefish* came to the surface again. Tim was up on deck, working. "One to six, haul! Heave away!" And under the sail-master's instructions, Tim and the others hauled up the mast again. Even the little foremast was deployed. Tim could never get over just how quickly they could turn the *Cuttlefish* from a submarine into a sailboat, with the outriggers out and the rubber inner pontoons inflated, and sails beginning to go up. Behind them the divers worked on the drogues, deploying their rubber pontoons so that they too could travel with minimum resistance above the water. There were quick-releases to be rigged on the pontoons and towlines to be checked, and the crew worked into the dusk; but soon, towing her four drogues, the *Cuttlefish* was under way again, sailing out into the wide Pacific, far from land or sight of man, far from hostile eyes and ships.

# CHAPTER 22

It had been two weeks since Clara had told him what his job was.

Up on the bridge, Tim stood to attention, looking straight ahead, although he felt as if he might just faint at any minute. If only he could faint. Or even die.

"Barnabas," said Captain Malkis, his voice as heavy as lead and as cold as ice. "You were caught red-handed. We can't tolerate thievery on this boat. I'd like to put you off the *Cuttlefish* right now. Instead, however, I'll keep you aboard until we can put you off in someplace where you can do no further dishonour to yourself or the Free Submariners. But you will be confined to the brig from now on."

"I wasn't stealing, sir," said Tim, wishing his voice wouldn't crack.

"You were caught rummaging in a locked cabinet, by Lieutenant Ambrose. Are you calling him a liar, Barnabas? I will have you know I trust my officers."

"No sir. I . . . I was looking inside the cabinet. But I wasn't stealing. I was looking for a wireless transmitter. Not to take anything. I swear. And the key was in the lock," said Tim.

The captain sighed in exasperation. "You weren't aware, Barnabas, that after your last depredations, we'd set a trap, with Sparks's help, that rang a bell here in the bridge when that key was turned. We suspected it was one of you cabin boys."

"Depredations, sir?" Tim wasn't even sure what the word meant.

"We know that you stole ten pounds and a valuable ring from the cabinet, earlier," said the captain. "If you return them, I will be

191

inclined to be slightly more lenient. Put you off in Australia where you can reform, and make a life for yourself."

Tim swallowed and shook his head. "Search my gear, sir. Please. I haven't got any ring or any big money. I've got one pound and seven shillings and sixpence in my spare boots, that my mam gave me. I told her not to. But she said a boy had to have some money."

The captain nodded. "Willis. Take Northham and go and search his cabin and his gear."

So Tim stood waiting. At least he knew that they'd find nothing. And that proved to be the case. "Just precisely what he said he had, sir. Precisely where he said it would be," said Lieutenant Willis.

The captain sighed. "He'd be a fool to keep it with his gear. There are other hiding places. And whether he had the proceeds of the previous theft or not, Lieutenant, he was caught red-handed this time. Take him down to the brig, please. After some time in there, he may decide that he prefers being landed in Australia. I'm very, very disappointed in you, Barnabas. I thought you were one of the more promising young crewmen I've had for some while. You are no longer a part of the *Cuttlefish*'s crew."

And that had hurt Tim far more than the idea of being put ashore on some island had. This was his family now.

Clara gaped at her mother when she was told. And then she found her voice. "But he really was looking for a spy. For a wireless transmitting set."

"How do you know, Clara?" asked her mother.

"Because . . . because we talked about it," said Clara, knowing she was admitting to doing precisely what she'd been told not to. "We tried to tell you and you wouldn't *listen*. So we had to try and find the transmitter. Tim wouldn't steal anything!"

DAVE FREER

"I know he once saved your life, dear, but how do you know how honest he is?" said her mother, repressively. "I hope Captain Malkis will relent. I'll ask, once he has calmed down. But for heaven's sake Clara, don't make things any worse, either for yourself or for him. You were expressly forbidden to talk to each other. He'd be in trouble about that too, and the captain might just go through with his threat of just casting him adrift if there was even one more point of evidence against him."

Clara was furious. And silenced. The only way to help Tim now would be to actually present the captain with hard evidence that the transmitter existed. That someone was signalling to their enemies. So she took a deep breath and sat down to stare blindly at a chemistry textbook. No matter how angry she was, it wasn't going to help to rush in, so she waited.

The next day she asked her mother if by any chance she had any galena in her trunk of chemicals and books.

"Galena? Why?" asked her mother.

"We made a crystal radio in class with a vacuum diode. I asked you why they were called crystal radios, remember. And you said they used to work with a real crystal. Seeing as I am supposed to get back to my formal studies, and not just submariners studies, I thought I might try to make one."

Her mother sighed. "The only radio signal you'll get out here is from Sparks. You're not going to find your imaginary transmitter. Well, you may pick up occasional shortwave or AM transmissions at night. But it will do you no harm, I suppose. It might turn your mind to other things. Yes, I have a small number of galena crystals. It was, oddly enough, one of the substances Fritz thought might be a catalyst."

Clara knew it wouldn't turn her mind from what was obsessing it in the least, but she had to do something. And it gave her a reason to visit the engine room's tiny electrical workshop . . . which was next to the brig. In fact, they shared a drain, down which one could

talk. Making the wire whisker and tuning coil had been a demanding and time-consuming exercise, even without the talking.

She really did hope that it wouldn't turn out to be Sparks who
was informing. She'd had to ask him for various things for the
project, like fine wire, and an earphone. He'd been delighted to find
out she was making a crystal set. It was all she could do to stop him
"helping" her, which would have put a stop to her talking with Tim.
He did make her a buzzer to test the device, but she was firm. It was
her project, and she'd show it to him when it was done.

Clara felt she had to talk to Tim. At first it was a duty, as it was
mostly her fault he was there, even if it was awkward talking to him.
But she got so used to conversation that it was no chore after a few
days. They talked of everything from tunnels to Fermoy and families
and food. . . . They talked far more than she ever had to anyone. She
was fairly sure Thorne and Sparks knew about it, because they always
coughed or whistled before opening the door.

And she was amazed to find her crystal set actually worked.
Sparks was very impressed.

Now she just had to find the wavelength the spy was using, and
be on it at the right time. That was going to be even more difficult.

"Look, we've only got Sparks, and Nicholl is his trainee, but the
radio's not manned 24/7. Sparks has his set times to check and send
messages. So if it is someone else, it'll be when Sparks is not on duty,
because they wouldn't want him picking up a strong signal by acci-
dent," said Tim down the pipe. He had it easy. He could lie on the
shelf and talk to her.

She had to bend nearly double to talk into the piece of tubing
she'd "extended" the drain outlet with. "And it's probably not a very
strong transmitter. More likely to be used when we're close to land,
or to the Royal Navy ships."

"We're due to pick up coal in American Samoa. That's close
enough to Prussian Samoa for the Royal Navy, I think. All you'll
have to do is work out when Sparks is going to be on . . . and listen

the rest of the time. I guess I am going to be short of company," he said, mournfully. "They'll put me ashore there, I think."

Clara was glad he could not see her face. "No!" she said, firmly. "We'll catch him first. I'm sure it's Lieutenant Ambrose. He's second in command and responsible for the forward sector, with the escape hatch. He'd use that if we were bombed."

"The officer in charge is supposed to be last out." Tim sighed down the pipe. "Do you think you could get me a navigation book or something? You could just push it through the bars quickly and go away. I'm so bored, when you're not here. I can hide it easily enough."

"Of course." Clara did not say that she thought Lieutenant Ambrose would desert his post and escape. But that was what she thought. She'd taken a violent dislike to him since they'd locked Tim up. She could barely greet him now. She'd got the whole story, bald and unedited, from Lieutenant Willis. "Once the old man settles down, he's likely to agree to let the boy off somewhere decent. But he won't have a thief on his boat, miss. He's as straight as a die, is Captain Malkis. Reasonable about most things, but not that."

"Tim's not a thief," said Clara.

The lieutenant tugged his moustache. "Unfortunately, he got caught with his hands where they shouldn't be, miss. And he was very guilty-looking when they marched him into the mast."

"He was guilty-looking because he'd been looking where he shouldn't have. Not because he had taken anything. He was looking for a transmitter," Clara said, firmly.

"Not what the captain thinks, miss," said Lieutenant Willis, without asking how she knew.

As they neared the secret coaling base on the American Possession of Samoa, Clara put in every possible hour that Sparks was off, scanning the radio frequencies. She got very excited at first, because she picked up a weak, regular signal. But it seemed just to be a kind of noise, not a message of any kind. She got her mother to listen to it, and then Sparks, seeing as he was off-duty and sitting in the mess, and she could ask innocently. "Aha! It's junk. They're charging the batteries. The brushes in the generator make sparks, which make radio signals. Fortunately for me, the frequencies are quite high, because they clutter up the airwaves. We use lower frequencies. You can barely pick those up beyond line-of-sight."

She got weak signals and even music from New Zealand. She sat there, for hours on end, looking at a nav text, sliding the bar on the tuning coil, tiny bit by tiny bit. Over and over and over. Nothing. Just that weak interference at the top end of the slide.

And then she hit the jackpot.

Clear, loud, and in Morse code.

Which she had no idea how to turn into something she understood. The only Morse code she knew was SOS. Three shorts, three longs, three shorts. This wasn't that.

"Mother! Mother, you have to listen to this!"

Her mother looked up from her notepad with the unfocussed gaze that Clara knew meant her mind was wholly absorbed in what she was busy doing. "Not now, dear. I've nearly got it."

"You must!" said Clara, thrusting the earphone at her.

"I don't have time for music right now, dear," said her mother, not taking it.

"It's not music! It's Morse code! And it's coming from the sub."

With a long-suffering sigh her mother took the earphone and listened.

"Not hearing anything, I am afraid," she said, after a while.

She handed the earphone back to Clara, who hastily plugged it into her own ear. To hear . . . nothing. And Mother had already gone back to scribbling equations, her face intent.

Clara took a deep breath, got up from her bunk, took her little crystal set and walked to the bridge. She didn't walk very fast because she was still very wary of the captain, after Rivas. But it had to be done.

"Captain Malkis," said Clara, very tentatively. "Can I talk to you, please, sir?"

He raised his eyebrows at her. "In a few minutes, Miss Calland. I am preparing to hand over the watch. Wait."

She stood, quiet as a mouse, just watching from the doorway.

Eventually he closed his chart-case with a snap. "Right Miss Calland. What is it?"

"It's my crystal set, sir," said Clara humbly, holding it out.

"Ah." By his expression that appeared to be a more welcome topic than the one he'd thought she'd ask about. "Better ask Sparks. I have no knowledge of such things. He'll be on in half an hour with the new watch. He does a spell then."

"Well, sir, it's just that I picked up a very clear signal. That means it's very close, in Morse code."

He nodded thoughtfully. "I'll tell the lookouts. Thank you. Did you get the message down?"

She shook her head. "I don't know Morse code, except for SOS, and I wasn't really expecting it. The thing is, sir, if there is no other ship in sight, it must have come from the submarine."

The captain raised his eyes to heaven and shook his head. "Now I see where this is going. No, Miss Calland. Just no. I appreciate that he behaved with considerable courage and saved your life—"

"And the submarine!" Clara thrust in.

The captain nodded his acceptance of this point. "And the submarine. But there is no wireless transmitter on the ship besides this one here. I'm—"

Clara surprised herself by starting to cry. "I did hear it. I know you don't believe me, or Tim, but I did hear it."

He was obviously trying to be patient and gentle, but he was looking angry at the same time. "It's possible that you heard something. The range on those devices is very variable, and I believe you can occasionally get atmospheric conditions that will let you receive a signal from many miles off. Now, I am sorry, Miss Calland, but we have to hand over in fifteen minutes. Please go."

So Clara went, dragging her feet down the steel narrow compan-

ionway, and along the gangway toward the officers' quarters. She felt
that she'd just made matters worse. She was not ready to go back to
their cabin. She was even less ready to make her way down to the
workshop and tell Tim. She was so despairing that she almost
bumped into the mate without seeing him.

"What is wrong?" asked Mate Werner.

"I picked up wireless transmissions from the spy and told the
captain, and he won't believe me," she said bitterly. "He just thinks
I'm lying to help Tim."

The mate was silent for a moment, looking at her. "I have
thought the captain was a little harsh on the young man," he said,
slowly, at last.

"Harsh! It was just unfair," said Clara furiously, letting it all
burst out. "Tim would never take anything! Never. He was just
looking for a wireless, which I told him to do. And he was right
about where he was looking. It must be Lieutenant . . . Um." She
suddenly realised who she was talking to.

"But you picked up a signal, ja?" asked the mate.

"Yes. I made this crystal set. But the signal was in Morse code.
I don't understand it," said Clara. "And the captain, and my mother,
they both wouldn't believe me."

The mate smiled. "But I know the Morse code. So too does the
skipper." He nodded slowly to himself. "Ja, well. I do not think you
are making this up. Say nothing of this, because we do not know
who we can trust. But it is likely you will get another signal, maybe.
You must write the pattern down. Or when I come off duty, I will
borrow your little crystal set, and see if I can hear anything. If it is
true, we will catch them. And you do not worry about the *junge*, the
young man. I have spoken with the captain. I will speak again. Not
until we reach Australia will he be put off. And now I must go. I am
on duty."

Clara felt as if all the cares of the world had been lifted from her
shoulders. "Thank you!"

He nodded. "But keep it to yourself, miss. Not even your mother must you tell."

"She doesn't believe me anyway," said Clara.

She walked on down the passage with a spring in her step, past the mess. Cookie waved at her. "You're looking a bit more chipper, missy."

She nearly told him why. And then swallowed it and waved, and went on down to the little electrical workshop. Soon she was telling Tim. He was, after all, the one person on the ship she could tell. And she could tell him that the mate would speak to the captain about him. That he was safe until Australia.

# CHAPTER 23

Clara had listened through the night, setting the little travelling chronometer to wake her when Sparks had finished his session. She'd picked up fragments of news and foreign languages, all faint. So she took the crystal set with her, when the mate had finished his watch, to his cabin in the bow area. Knocked.

He opened the door, smiled to see the crystal set. "Good. You have told no one?"

Clara could hardly say that she'd told Tim without having to explain. So she shook her head. It was a lie, but it was not going to hurt anyone.

"Ja. Well, you can leave the set with me. I will listen. I know wireless well. I have thought about it on my watch. They will most likely use a regular time. So what time was it when you heard the Morse transmission?"

"Um. Three quarters of an hour before changeover," said Clara, thinking.

The mate nodded. "Good. You will come back then. Maybe quarter of an hour earlier. We will see if we can catch them at it."

Clara did some serious catching up on her sleep that day, to the point that her mother noticed, and asked if she was well.

"Fine. Just tired," said Clara airily. "I was listening to the crystal set late."

"You've had it glued to your ear for days," said her mother with a wry smile. "Have you finally had enough of it? I see you haven't got it here now."

"I lent it to the mate." Clara looked at the chronometer. "I think I'll go to the mess. I have been through this book too often."

"Maybe you should offer to wash dishes," said Mother. It was the job Mother had always been keen on volunteering her or her father to do. Mother didn't like doing it herself, Clara knew. Well, there were times when to have to wash dishes was fair, but this wasn't one of them.

"I did, but Cookie said I'd chip the plates," said Clara, hastening out of the door. She went forward, not to the mess, but to the mate.

He had the crystal set set up, with the aerial wire spanned and had the earphone plugged into his ear. He opened the door with one hand, and beckoned her in, putting a finger to his lips. "Getting it. Hush."

Clara wanted to listen too. But then she could not have dealt with the Morse. He nodded, held up a finger, tapped the small shel-lacked desk several times. And then took the earphone out of his ear. "Transmission ends. You were right, miss. And they were not even using code."

"Good! We can go and tell the captain," said Clara, the huge relief making her want to dance, and laugh and yell.

He shook his head, very slowly. "I am afraid the captain himself he may be implicated, ja."

Clara gasped. "But he can't be. He's the captain. I mean . . . he could just have let us go or be caught a lot of times."

"I am not sure. But there is more than one person on this *Unterseeboot* they referred to. They did not identify themselves. And it seems Captain Malkis did not wish to let you leave, when you could have left safely with the Americans in Rivas. He got a wireless message saying that they agreed to all of your mother's conditions. I was there," said the mate.

Clara bit her lip. "And he wouldn't believe us about the spy. . . . No. But I still don't think it can be him, Mr. Mate."

The mate shrugged. "We cannot tell. We still do not know who they are, and the captain, he will not authorise a full search. I tried, because if they find the ring of Lieutenant Ambrose's mother, they would find the thief, not your boy. But we will set a trap for them. We lie off Tutuila in the daytime, ja. They have said they will signal the precise position with a mirror at ten hundred hours. So we will go up the deck well, and they will be trapped. Caught red-handed. It is on my watch, so it will be easy to organise. I have my *Pistool*. I will meet you at the hatch door to the deck well."

"And then, finally it will be over," said Clara, clasping her hands together and biting her lip.

The mate nodded. "Ja. Do not tip our hand, though. We do not know who it is, so we must be quiet, quiet like mice."

Clara knew she had four and a half hours to wait. She could hardly bear it. She ate almost nothing, to the extent that Cookie asked her if she was well. She just nodded, not trusting herself to speak. She waited until after changeover, then stole down to the electrical workshop. Inevitably she ran into Thorne, but all the artificer did was to smile at her. Knowingly. He looked a little worried. She had to wonder why. She hoped it wasn't him. She liked his mutton-chop whiskers, and he was kind to her.

Still, he did nothing to stop her going into the little electrical workshop and closing the door.

Tim, in the brig, had got quite expert at telling just who was walking down the passage. He recognised Clara, easily. Thorne had just stopped at the cell, and quickly handed him something through the bars. A little wash-leather bag. "Put it in your pockets, sonny," he said quietly. "Some fish hooks, some line, some copper wire. Some brass beads I've made with workshop scrap. You can at least feed yourself and trade with the natives. The skipper's going to leave you on Tau." Then, before Tim could say anything, he'd walked off. That was the sixth visit Tim had had, including one from a very pale-faced

Artificer McConnell, still on a crutch, doing his longest walk yet from the sick bay. Tim's pockets bulged with chocolate and even Big Eddie's precious clasp knife. The oddest visits by far were from a few people that he thought wouldn't care, or that he didn't like or he thought didn't like him. Submariner Jonas had brought him an envelope. "We had a secret whip round for you, Darkie. A little money will go a long way out here, when you can find some people. Slip it in your underdaks, on a piece o' string, to stop it falling out. They won't find it there."

"By half past ten, you should be out of there," said Clara, down the pipe. "We caught them at it again early this morning, the mate and I. We've got a trap set for them at ten o'clock, when they'll be signalling their friends on the shore. I can't stay. Thorne was looking very suspiciously at me." She paused. "The mate thinks . . . the captain may even be involved."

"That's impossible." Tim might be bitter about the fact that the captain didn't believe him, but he was the captain. Straight in his dealings and . . . well, the captain.

"Indeed, that's what he said about the transmitter and the traitor," said Clara. "Impossible. I'll be seeing you later, Tim. Got to run, or Mother will be asking questions."

And Tim was left alone to wait.

Clara went back to their cabin and tried to be a dutiful daughter and not kick her heels against the bulkheads. She watched the time carefully, hoping her mother would turn in. But Mother was, as usual, working. So, at three minutes to ten, Clara got up and announced that she was off to the heads, hoping Mother would not notice she was wearing her breeches under her dressing gown. And, once out, she walked very fast, to the deck shaft door. The mate was waiting there. "Good girl," he said. "I have my *Pistool*. Let us go."

He opened the door for her. If they were on the surface—as they must be to open the door—there should have been a watchman in the cowling if the mast was not up. But there wasn't.

There was just bright sunlight, and something suddenly pressed hard across her mouth and nose.

Dizziness. And that was all she remembered.

Tim sat and waited. And then he lay and waited. And then he tried to read the nav textbook again. Then he looked at the contents of the wash-leather bag Thorne had given him. Hooks, wire, beads, a spool of linen line . . . just what you'd need to survive being dumped on an island. He'd just put them away when hasty footsteps came down the passage.

It was not someone he was pleased to see: Lieutenant Ambrose, and with him Gordon—one of the senior ratings.

Tim wasn't pleased to see Lieutenant Ambrose. But Lieutenant Ambrose was utterly amazed to see him. "What are you doing here, Barnabas?" he demanded.

"Lying on my back looking at the bulkhead. Which I'd rather look at than you." Tim didn't feel he had to be polite.

"But . . . but you've run away!" exclaimed the lieutenant.

Tim snorted. "The door is locked and I'm in a submarine in the middle of the ocean. I can't run anywhere. Is that the next lie you'll tell about me?"

The lieutenant swallowed. "Gordon. Stay here. I am going to fetch the captain."

"What's going on?" asked Tim, beginning to get worried now, as Lieutenant Ambrose left at a sprint.

Gordon shrugged his shoulders. "They thought you done a runner. We came down to see what damage had been done."

Next thing the captain and Clara's mother arrived, also at the run. Both of them appeared stunned to see him. "Where is Clara?" asked her mother, as if she couldn't see that the little cell didn't have much in the way of hiding places for a mouse, let alone another person.

Tim felt his stomach sink. "She went with the first mate, to catch the spy with the transmitter." He pointed at the captain. "He said he thought it must be you."

Captain Malkis took a deep breath. Turned to the lieutenant. "Where is First Mate Werner?"

"I couldn't find him, sir," said Lieutenant Ambrose. "That's why I called you when the hatch-watchman reported finding Miss Calland's dressing gown on the hatch stairs."

It got through to Tim first. "He's kidnapped her," yelled Tim. "And I *told* you there was a spy. You wouldn't *listen* to me!"

"Ambrose, Nicholl. Check the mate's cabin," said the captain, ignoring Tim. "Search it thoroughly. And I want the hatch-watch to report to me on the bridge. Now."

"She said she'd lent her crystal set to the mate," said Clara's mother, wringing her hands.

"We'll get to the bottom of this," said the captain. "I will speak to you shortly, Barnabas."

And they went away, and Tim was left standing holding onto the bars, shaking them in frustration and fury.

A very little while later Lieutenant Willis came down, with the key to the brig. "You've been sprung, boy," he said as he unlocked the door. "Captain wants you on the bridge."

"What's happened?" asked Tim, trying to be rational, not angry and afraid for Clara. He was not succeeding too well.

Obviously the lieutenant understood. He put a hand on Tim's shoulder. "Cool down, son. Let the old man tell you. But basically Ambrose and Nicholl found a wireless transmitter in the mate's cabin. There's a small life raft missing. The mate ordered the deck watch in. He said the sub was going to dive."

Tim let the breath hiss between his teeth. "It was in the little shellacked desk of his, wasn't it? It was always locked. Not like Ambrose, who left the key in the lock either."

Lieutenant Willis nodded. "Nicholl broke it open."

"I should have done that," said Tim savagely, beating himself up for what he could not undo. "What worse could have happened to me?"

They arrived at the crowded little bridge. The submarine was under way, submerged, with a rating peering through the periscope.

Out of habit Tim saluted the captain. He didn't have to anymore. He wasn't part of the crew, after all. The captain, however, saluted him. "Barnabas," he said. "I owe you an apology. We have found the wireless transmitter in Werner's cabin. I should have listened to you, boy. I should have listened to my instincts too. I didn't think you were a thief, which is why I was so angry and disappointed when Lieutenant Ambrose caught you."

Tim swallowed. "I didn't want to believe Clara when she said that the mate thought you were the traitor either, sir."

"What?" The Captain shook his head incredulously.

"Only she said you were so busy denying the obvious that you had to be, see. But I didn't think it was possible. I didn't want to believe it. But it looked like it, didn't it? I told you there was a spy with inside information, and you told me there couldn't be, even though it was as plain as the nose on your face. You'd rather believe what you wanted to believe than me." Tim knew this was a pointless fight. But he was still wanting to have it, to say it.

"Tim-boy," said Lieutenant Willis. "How do you know what Miss Calland thought about this?" He turned to the captain. "Sir, with your permission, I'd like to ask Barnabas to give us the whole story. And I think it's only fair to ask that nothing further be held against him."

The captain nodded. "I think he's been punished enough. And he did say there was a spy aboard, and Miss Calland did try and tell me about the wireless transmissions. All truths, I am afraid. Please tell what you can, Barnabas. We need to try and get Miss Calland back."

That took the wind right out of Tim's sails. Because getting her back was the most important thing. "Um. Sir, fair enough, I was searching Lieutenant Ambrose's gear for the transmitter. But I wasn't stealing anything. I swear I never took anything."

"For which you deserved a clip around the ear, because I bet you searched mine too," said Lieutenant Willis cheerfully.

Tim nodded. "Yessir. I'd searched every room I cleaned. But not the captain's, sir. Or in the mate's locked desk. But he still had the knife that I found in the brig . . . after we had those Winged Hussars there."

They looked at him in puzzlement. "He said he was going to tell you, sir. Told me not to tell anyone else. He told Clara not to tell anyone else about the wireless signal too."

"But she told you? How?" asked Lieutenant Ambrose, picking up on the details. He was good at that.

Tim took a deep breath, told himself that he'd been wrong, and it hadn't been Lieutenant Ambrose, and there was no point in not answering his questions, and Clara could hardly get in more trouble. "Um. The electrical workshop is next to the brig. They share a drain to the bilges, sir. She came and talked to me most days. Kept me sane, sir. So she told me about the mate. . . ."

"Captain, Sir," interrupted the man on the periscope. "There is something flashing up the mountainside in the jungle. Looks like it might be someone trying to do SOS.

Clara found the world going up and down. And upside down. And her head hurt and she was going to be sick.

She tried to put her hands to her head and discovered that she could not move them. So she was sick anyway.

She found herself dumped onto the ground to finish throwing up.

After her breakfast had joined the jungle leaf-mould, she managed to look at just who had dropped her off his shoulder onto the wet ground. It was not someone she knew. Not someone from the boat, but a suntanned man with a pockmarked face. Behind him stood the mate, and another man. "Finished?" asked the pockmarked man, unsympathetically.

Clara nodded, feeling too drained to do more.

"Good. You can walk, then. Cut her feet loose, Disco, and tie the rope onto her. We don't want her running away."

The third man did, and they walked on, upwards. It was hot, and Clara still felt terrible. The trail was steep, and rather overgrown. The man called Disco had to keep cutting bushes away. "Making an easy trail for them to follow," grumbled the pockmarked man.

"They will not know where we went into this forest," said the mate. "That is why we hide the life raft, ja. The HMS *Forrest* will be close by nightfall. They do not have time to search all of this jungle."

"Besides, we could hold an army off from the pillbox, I suppose," said Pockmarks.

Clara could only be relieved by their getting to the "pillbox." Her mouth tasted dry and sour, and her head was whirling. It was an odd flat-roofed round building made of green concrete, dug into the side of the mountain, with narrow slits instead of windows.

And it stank. The smell hit them like a wave as the first man opened the door.

"Phew!" said the pockmarked man. "Did something die in there?"

Disco nodded. "Pig go die in there."

"And you didn't clean it out, you lazy good-for-nothing!" he exclaimed crossly, cuffing Disco about the ear. "Well, get the wireless transmitter out, and put the girl in there. We can bar the door and stay out here under the trees in the old gun-emplacements. We can let the HMS *Forrest* know we've got the girl, and await instructions."

# CHAPTER 24

Duke Malcolm pointed at the map. "We missed our guess. We'd assumed that they'd make for Vanuatu, which is the normal coaling spot for their submarines heading for Wyndham in Western Australia. I know several vessels had been dispatched to the area. Now we have a message from our agent, saying they're going to American Samoa. It suggests that Captain Malkis was not making for Wyndham as we expected, but for one of the ports on the southern coast, via the Bass Strait. I do have an operative in place there, who reports on the shipping in and out of Pago Pago. Our agent on the submarine says he will be able to take the daughter as a hostage; he's tricked her into his confidence, and he will get her ashore. The question is, of course, just what naval support can you give us, Admiral? I've discussed this with Professor Browne, and he is of the opinion that this woman could, alive, give us a new monopoly position. Alive, if we can have her, or she must be dead before anyone else can be allowed to know what she has in her head."

The admiral sucked breath through his teeth. "I'll have to check, Your Grace. There might be a gunboat or two at Port Solf in Prussian Samoa . . . but the Americans keep several cruisers and a destroyer stationed in Pago Pago. Lieutenant Corbett . . ."

"Sir," said the aide. "I believe there is a Delphine-class armoured cruiser in Port Solf, undergoing repairs. The HMS *Forrest*. Shall I have the Marconi room make contact, and find out if she can put to sea?"

The admiral looked at Duke Malcolm, who nodded. The aide left at a run.

He returned a little later. "They say she should be ready to sail by midday tomorrow, Admiral. If they have their engineers work through the night."

"Tell them to make that three hours earlier," said Duke Malcolm.

The admiral shook his head. "That would have them arrive in daylight, Your Grace. The Delphine class are really obsolete. No match for American vessels. A night rendezvous off the North Coast would be more sensible. It doesn't sound like a combat situation, but more a case of needing secure transport. They can't even track the submarine, not being equipped with the radio-pulse detectors."

"That is true enough. Let us make it so," said Duke Malcolm. "I'll have my man in Prussian Samoa get himself aboard the vessel so we can relay my orders directly. Hopefully, finally, we can put this matter to rest. I've got enough problems with the Canadian rout on the West Coast, and the Caliche War hotting up. The Japanese are being far too pushy in Peru."

# CHAPTER 25

The smell in the pillbox was enough to make Clara gag again. She staggered through the drifts of leaves and rubbish to the slit-window, where at least she could breathe air from outside. From the narrow window she could see the jungle slope and the sea—she had an excellent view of it, all the way along the coast from the narrow cliff-spit of an island. She took a deep breath and walked to the other long slit, and realised the pillbox perched on the top of a cliff on a narrow cape, allowing her to see into a second bay. She could just make out the edge of a corrugated iron roof, dazzling in the bright sunlight there. Most of it was hidden, though, by the branches of a tree and thick foliage.

She went back to the first window. The sea was clean and clear, transparent.

And unless she was very much mistaken that was a dark shape moving out there, in it, trailed by four other dark shapes. There was just a hint of haze over the water, behind it.

If only she could tell them where she was. And then the glare of the sun off the roof and the mate's lie about signals to the shore came back to her. If only she had a mirror.

She hadn't.

But in among the leaf litter, next to where the radio transmitter had been taken from, someone had dropped a piece of silver foil off a cigarette carton. And there was another next to the window and a piece of stump. And another beyond that, along with several crumpled cartons, and cigarette stubs. This was plainly their smoking spot.

Clara's hands were tied tightly together, but at least they had tied them in front of her, so she could fold the pieces of bright foil together, and shape them into a parabolic mirror and reach her hands out into the hot sunlight.

At first she just worked on flashes. Then she decided on SOS.

She had no idea if they would see it, or what they could do to help. She just went right on trying.

Finally something in the situation did make her smile. At least they couldn't blame Tim for any of this.

"If that is Miss Calland signalling, we should land some men at once. But would she know an SOS?" said the captain.

Tim nodded. "She said it was all the Morse code she did know, sir."

The captain nodded. "Now that you mention that, I do think I remember her saying just that. Well, I'll need an armed party. . . ."

"It's likely they'll have some sort of lookout, sir," interrupted Lieutenant Ambrose. "They'd see us landing and move her."

The captain tugged his neat beard. "We could land men in Vatia Bay. But that is visible from the settlement. Someone would be bound to go across to Pago Pago and tell the American military."

"Also there is cliff and jungle that side," said Lieutenant Willis. "We could swim some men in, sir. Just next to it's steep shelving. We could creep in just to landward of those cockscomb-shaped rocks—that little cliff-island. The charts show that as deep to within fifty feet of the shore."

"I am receiving a message, Captain," said Sparks. "It's the first mate."

They all crowded around the Marconi man.

"He says to tell Dr. Calland that if she wants to see her daughter alive again, she needs to come ashore, alone," said Sparks, listening.

"He says there is a small sheltered bay three-quarters of a mile from Vatia Point. He will meet her there in an hour. If she is followed, his associates will deal with the girl."

"Somehow I'll have his guts for garters," said Captain Malkis, grimly.

Sparks continued. "And we'd better be quick about it because half the Royal Navy is on its way here."

"Can you get me there in time, Captain?" asked Clara's mother. "If . . . if you can take that trunk, my mother's trunk, to Westralia. Any competent team of chemists should be able to work out at least the basics of the process from there."

"Easily, ma'am. We could do it ten times over," said the captain. "I think you should go to your cabin and prepare as many notes as possible, in the time available, detailing your own thoughts. If you don't mind." He gestured to the door of the bridge.

She nodded. "Thank you. Thank you all for everything." She paused a moment. "And thank you especially, young man," she said to Tim. "Clara told me you were no thief. She told me so again when she picked up the radio message. I should have believed her. I wish I had. I wish to heaven I had!"

Tim swallowed. "Uh."

The captain put his finger to his lips before what Tim wanted to say could come out. "Go, Dr. Calland. We don't have that much time," he said.

As she walked away, he kept his finger to his lips.

As soon as Tim heard her on the companionway, he burst out in a low voice, "We can't just let him get away with this, sir!"

The captain's eyes were narrowed. "I have no intention of doing so. I just wanted the child's mother out of the way. Ambrose, I want the drogues dropped with a buoy, now. I want both divers, ten strong swimmers, and weapons in waterproof containers ready in ten minutes, gentlemen. Report to the bridge. We'll go with your plan, Lieutenant Willis."

"He's starting to repeat his message, Captain," said Sparks. "Shall I acknowledge?"

"Ah. Let him repeat again. Then tell him we are east of Vatia Point. We will attempt to be there on time. He knows us too well to allow us to play for time. But this will give us a little."

"Captain," said the watchman on periscope duty. It was Albert, the other diver. "Pardon me, sir. But if we're to go out the escape hatch, well, good swimmers won't do. We need to stay underwater with the hookah. Big Eddie and I can do it. Nicholl has done a bit of diving too sir. . . ."

"And me," said Tim.

Albert gave him a grin. "And him."

Tim saw the captain's look of doubt. "I've earned my place, sir. And anyway you threw me out of the crew. I'd best get ashore," he said with a little smile.

The humour of it was lost on the captain. "You have earned your place, Barnabas," said Captain Malkis. "And of course I want you back as part of my crew. I was wrong, and I make good on my mistakes. But you also need to learn some respect, young man."

"I never lost it for you, sir," said Tim stoutly. "Not even in the brig. I wouldn't believe Clara about it maybe being you. You treated me decently. You'd decided to at least drop me in Australia. And I'll always be a part of the *Cuttlefish* crew, no matter if I'm not with her. She's my home, and you're my family."

"I had not decided that," said the captain. "Although Ambrose, Willis, and a few of the senior ratings and the chief engineer, the cook, and Mr. Amos all tried to prevail on me to do so. The mate is one of the few people who never mentioned the subject."

"Oh. That was just another thing the Mate lied to Clara about," said Tim. "He told Clara he'd got you to agree to it. Well, can I go, sir? I can swim with a hookah, and I can keep my head, sir. And I will follow orders. Please, sir?"

For the first time since he'd been caught ferreting in Lieutenant

Ambrose's locker, Tim saw that hint of a smile on the captain's face. "I said you'd earned your place. I'm a man of my word. Get to Mr. Amos; fetch the gear you need, Barnabas. We shall get the feelers out and edge this boat as close inshore as possible. Lieutenants. Diver Venables. I need to speak with you."

Tim ran as fast as his legs would carry him. And he was back on the bridge in the allotted time. Someone motioned him to silence. The skipper was edging the submarine forward very slowly, which was always difficult because they lost steerage at low speeds. There was a faint scrape and a touch.

"We are forty feet below the surface. Just to the lee of a very large rock. Fortunately with the swell from the present direction, Vatia Point shelters us almost completely. Now I calculate we are within seventy feet of the shore. Lieutenant Willis will be leading the shore party. Divers Venables and Markis will take the men in, as you will have to share mouthpieces. You will need to keep calm. The revolvers will be sent to the surface in the waterproof buoy and be pulled ashore. Good luck, men," said the captain. He smiled. "And I am quite angry with my officers for refusing to allow me to lead this expedition."

"The *Cuttlefish* needs you, sir. We don't have Werner anymore, and neither Willis nor I have the experience," said Lieutenant Ambrose. "Although I wish you'd let me go instead of him, sir."

"He has militia experience, Lieutenant Ambrose. Right. Time is a-wasting. The engineer's men have some rough weight-belts of heavy chain waiting for you at the escape hatch."

There was barely room to breathe with four of them squashed into the escape hatch. The water was actually pleasant, as it flooded in on them. "Right. You both know to breathe out as you head up, if you have to swim up," said Albert.

Tim had been buddied to share a hookah mouthpiece with Big Eddie, and he was glad of it. Eddie was grinning. "I suppose my jackknife is still in your pocket, sprog."

"I found it in your locker. Didn't know you wanted it," said Tim, innocently, grinning too, as the seawater poured in.

"Salt water'll ruin it."

"Yeah. Not as bad as it'll do to the chocolate," said Tim. And then the water was up to their heads, and soon they were out and heading for the shore. It took huge self-control to take a breath of air from the hookah, and take the mouthpiece out and hand it back. But he did it, and they swam on, swapping the hookah mouthpiece. Soon Big Eddie gave him the rope to the watertight drum with the guns, and pointed at the surface. There was a huge rock edge there. Tim started to swim up. Realised he wasn't managing to go up. Nearly panicked. It was the weight-belt of heavy chain. He fumbled desperately at it. Not enough air! He was going to drown.

And Big Eddie pushed the mouthpiece back to him. Pulled him down as he took a greedy breath, and undid the chain. Now swimming up was easy. Tim breathed out as he went up, as he'd been told, and broke water gasping. He'd popped up among the seaweed and the foam fringe around the rock. Lieutenant Willis was out already. He hauled Tim up the barnacle-covered rock into a little gully . . . and Tim realised he'd let go of the rope, when he'd struggled with the chain around his waist. The rope end was floating on the surface in the swell. Tim jumped back into the sea again and swam a few yards to grab it before the current took it away. Tucked beneath the cliff edge it was unlikely they'd be seen, even on the surface, Tim rationalised, feeling stupid for letting go of it. They needed those weapons.

This time the lieutenant scraped half the skin off Tim's leg, hauling him out over the barnacles. "Chump," he said, shaking his head with a half a smile.

"Yessir," said Tim. "But I shouldn't have let go."

They hauled on the rope together, pulling it in. The lieutenant cracked the cask open, and checked the weapons. They were still dry.

Big Eddie and Albert brought the next two men ashore, Nicholl and Gordon.

"Captain's orders. We're not bringing more. No time," said Albert, hauling himself up.

There were just six of them. How many did the ex-mate of the *Cuttlefish* have with him? He'd said he had "associates," thought Tim.

The lieutenant issued weapons. "Move it up, lads. Time's a-wasting," he said, leading them at a running scramble through the rocks under the cliff edge, and over to the fringe of jungle.

"Into that, sir?" asked Tim.

"Yes. Sharpish now. We'll be out of sight in there." But it wasn't so easy. Creepers, ground-hugging trees, and thorny bushes fought for every last bit of space, and they had to try to get through them. It was like pushing into a thorny tide-race. As soon as anyone pushed forward, branches would snap back and hit the next person. They were springy and tangled with creeper. Cutting with a cutlass was slow, and noisy too. "You're making a racket," commented Tim, worriedly.

"No other way of doing it," said Albert, chopping at another branch.

"Enough," said Lieutenant Willis. "We haven't got more than ten yards into the jungle, and this is taking too long. Back to the beach."

Back on the rocky beach, the lieutenant tugged his small beard. Sighed. "I'd have guessed it was about a hundred and fifty yards of steep jungle," said Lieutenant Willis, "to where the mirror-flash came from. We have, by now, less than half an hour to find our way to it. It could take us hours to batter our way through this tangle, if we didn't get lost."

"Werner must have a trail. We could find that," said Tim anxiously.

"Exactly. We'll have to find a trail. And there's no time to waste," said the lieutenant. "We'll just have to hope Werner has gone already." So they moved along the spiky rocks, which were black and hot underfoot. Their wet clothes were no longer dripping, and Tim almost wished that his still were. It was tricky enough balancing on the rocks, and they moved in as much silence as they could.

The lieutenant, in the lead, motioned them all to go down. . . . They did, and he crawled back a little. "We'll have to do a little jungle bashing after all. There's Werner and another fellow walking along the beach. They came out of the trees just ahead. So a little way in and up and we should hit their path."

"Should we not go after the traitorous scum and deal with him, sir?" asked Nicholl. His tone said "deal with" meant "shoot" if the mate was lucky.

The lieutenant shook his head. "I'd like nothing more, but that would probably be the end of the girl. We owe it to her mother to see if we can rescue her first. If it is before Dr. Calland gets off the boat, we'll signal the captain. Werner will probably do a runner, but at least we'll be rid of him."

"Hard choices, Lieutenant," said Nicholl, regretfully, as they used their cutlasses to slash their way in. Fortunately, as they got a bit farther away from the coast the trees grew taller and the vegetation less dense. Tim spotted the answer. "There's a crawlway, Lieutenant."

"Animal track. Probably wild pig. Let's crawl, boys."

It was easier going for Tim than for the two big divers, or anyone else, but it was hard on the knees. He was very glad when they cut across the trail of the ex-mate and his companion. Cautiously, they walked up the steep slope. There were occasional jungle sounds, strange birds, rattling leaves, and breaking branches, all of which made them freeze. They were all false alarms, and probably just natural sounds of the tropical forest too, but everyone was nervous. At length they came to where the track ran along the base of a cliff. Here the trees were vast and there was space to walk away from the trail, which they did, cautiously, because it seemed likely they were near the brow of the ridge where the flashes had come from.

As it turned out their caution here too was a waste of time.

There was a lower cliff, almost entirely hidden in trees, which forced them back to the trail. And it didn't matter at all, because the trail led to a little bowl that had plainly been blasted out of the rock for a long-ago gun-emplacement. Big trees now shaded it, but there was a pillbox, an earthen berm, a concrete slab, and rusting rails for moving the gun. And, sitting against the pillbox's closed metal door, a guard slept with a rifle on his knees.

There was at least forty yards of open concrete covered in dry leaf litter between them and him. Impossible to cross quietly. The lieutenant motioned them back. "How's your tree-climbing, Barnabas?"

"Never climbed one, sir," admitted Tim. "They don't grow underground. But I can climb pipes. Can climb anything you need me to."

"Right," said Lieutenant Willis. "It looks like the trees below the little cliff, that this nest of theirs is perched on, have grown up to just below that pillbox. There is nothing to walk along to it but the treetop branches. I think the rest of us are too heavy. Do you think you can get across there, peep in the gun slit, and see if Miss Calland is alone in there, or not? If she is, see if she can stop the door being opened. If you can, give us a signal. Thumbs up for alone. Fingers for the number of guards. And if they see you, we'll just go in shooting. Try not to fall out of the trees."

Tim nodded and went along to the edge of the cliff. Sure enough, the big trees from below were crowding up and pressing against it. It wasn't that difficult to get into the nearest tree.

The hard part was that he had to get from one tree to the next. That meant climbing along a branch until it bent down and touched a branch from the next tree, and then transferring himself onto that. The new branch sagged and creaked suddenly, as it bent under his weight. Tim looked down and realised he was maybe seventy feet above the ground. He clung tightly, and then forced himself to move on.

※

Clara had watched in despair as the submarine—if that was her dark shadow—slipped out of sight. She still stared out of the slit-window, and eventually was rewarded by the sight of the submarine, a good half a mile to the west, coming up. It came up a long way from shore too. Three people came out, and a small life raft was taken from one of the deck hatches.

And one person began the long paddle into the shore.

It had to be her mother, Clara realised.

And then a tree branch swayed across her vision. She glared angrily at it. She felt, right now, as if she'd done just about everything wrong, and that anything she hadn't done wrong had gone wrong, and the stupid branch was just one final blow.

And then she realised that clinging to the branch, like a very clumsy monkey, was Tim Barnabas. It did look as if he might fall at any moment, but he got his balance again, and moved on. His eyes met hers, and his smile almost made up for her mother also being a captive now. He held a finger to his lips and climbed closer. But the last bit was not going to be possible. He couldn't quite get to her. "You alone?" he whispered.

She nodded.

"Can you bar the door from inside?" he whispered again.

That was a brilliant idea . . . now that she knew there was help outside. She peered into the dimness. It had a pair of very big bolts. "Yes." She nodded eagerly.

He began climbing back, and she braved the stink of rotting, maggot-crawling pig to go and struggle with the rusty bolts with her tied-together hands.

Tim climbed back and gave the thumbs-up to the watching Nicholl . . . and spotted a branch that led up and onto the roof of the pillbox. He climbed it as the other five *Cuttlefish* men advanced in a spread-out line, weapons in hand. Tim dropped onto the roof, and slithered on his belly across to above the guard, over the slight curve on the roof, drawing the cutlass from his belt, sliding along with it in one hand.

He was close to the edge when a dry round berry from under his elbow started to roll down the curve. Tim reached frantically for it, nearly dropping his cutlass instead. He caught it, and the cutlass. But something—perhaps a sound he'd made—woke the sleeper. The man lifted his head, suddenly.

The *Cuttlefish* men were out in the open, all of them. And the guard had a rifle. One shot and Werner would know something was wrong.

"Freeze," shouted the lieutenant. "Put the rifle down, and you'll stay alive."

There was a moment's pause while the man took in the pistols pointing at him. Tim waited, heart in his mouth. But the man slowly lowered his rifle. "Now stand up," said the lieutenant.

From above Tim could see the man trying to detach a hand grenade from his belt loops as he apparently was merely standing up. "Don't," said Tim, poking the fellow's ear with the cutlass.

The guard dropped it with a clatter and raised his hands.

The lieutenant and the rest of the men came running up. Lieutenant Willis grabbed the prisoner and had him flat on his own grenade before Tim could have said "Jack Robinson." "Tie his hands," he snapped. "Barnabas . . ."

Tim expected congratulations for his quick thinking. "Yessir!"

"You idiot boy. How could we shoot him without a good chance of shooting you?" growled the lieutenant.

"Um. Didn't think of that, sir," admitted Tim.

"Think next time." The lieutenant rapped sharply on the steel door. "Miss Calland. You can come out now," he said, lifting the bar as Tim scrambled off the roof.

With a clank of the door Clara came out, her hands still tied, smiling. Her face was dirty and tear-streaked, and there was what looked like vomit on her dress. Tim could still have hugged her. Would have, except there were four submariners in the way.

"Right," said Lieutenant Willis with a smile. "Someone cut her loose." He drew a Very pistol from his belt. "Now to let the captain know you are safe, so that your mother does not come ashore, miss."

"It's too late. She's already ashore. I could see her row in from inside the stink hole," said Clara.

"Oh." The lieutenant tugged his moustache. "How many of them are there, miss?"

"Including him"—Clara prodded the tied-up man with her toe—"three. The mate, his friend with the pockmarks, and this one. They called him Disco. He's some kind of servant, I think."

"A native of this place, I'd guess," said the lieutenant. "Well, let's see if we can turn the tables on them. Quick, boys. Take this one to the far side of those trees, gag him. Tie him to the tree. Now, has anyone got any thin string?"

"Fishing line, sir?" offered Tim, digging the wash-leather bag out of his breeches pocket.

"Perfect, if it is strong enough. Tie it to the inner handle. Take it through the slit-window and pass it to Gordon. Up onto the roof, Gordon. They won't be human if at least one of them doesn't go in there. We can rig the bar to drop. Then we only have one to deal with." The lieutenant picked up the grenade, attached it to his belt, and took the rifle. Worked the bolt. Examined the rifle. "It'll have to do."

Tim went through the pillbox and its gagging stench, and held the spool out to the reaching hand. He was glad to leave the pillbox again.

"Right. You, Barnabas, you take Miss Calland into that jungle patch up above the site. You've both caused enough chaos for now. When we come up there we'll sing out. Otherwise, stay hidden!"

Tim saluted. "Yessir."

※

Clara opened her mouth to protest. And then shut it again, partly because Tim kicked her shin. "Come on," he said.

So she went along. The thicket was on the upper edge of the bowl, and they positioned themselves so that from behind several huge twisted tree roots they could peer out at the trail.

"What do you mean, kicking me?" she asked, eyes narrow. She was still full of adrenaline and ready, right now, to take on any ten of the mate and his cronies.

"I meant that I know the lieutenant," said Tim. "I've worked with him in charge of me, remember. He was just that close to ordering Gordon or Nicholl to take you off to the coast, tied up and gagged if need be. This way, we get a small chance of actually doing something, and knowing what is going on."

"I suppose so," said Clara, reluctantly accepting this. "But it is my mother! Can I have a gun?"

"Hush. I heard something." Tim showed no sign of giving her his weapon.

"Gun," she said quietly, insistent.

"You don't know how to use it," he whispered back. "And I've got orders and training. Mr. Amos says you don't touch one without that."

It was true enough that she didn't know how to use it. But that didn't stop her wanting to. That was her mother coming along the trail. And it was her the mate had tricked, and all of her friends on the submarine he'd betrayed. She wanted to shoot him herself, right then.

They heard people come closer, panting up the slope. The mate came in sight first, then her mother, and then the man with the pockmarked face.

"Where is that man of yours?" asked the mate as they walked down across the bowl to the concrete slab.

"Probably sleeping. He's a lazy good-for-nothing. Disco!" shouted Pockmarks. "Hello! It looks like the door is open."

"That *verdomde* girl must have got away again," said the mate, running forward and into the pillbox.

The door swung shut behind him. And Clara saw her mother duck and head-butt the pockmarked man in the stomach. A shot rang out, the ricochet screaming off the pillbox. Pockmarks's rifle discharged too, as they fell in a struggling tangle. The men from the *Cuttlefish* arrived at a run, as did Tim and Clara.

Someone kicked the rifle away, and hauled them apart, just as the pockmarked man pulled a knife. Big Eddie hit him very hard, and he slumped and dropped the knife. Blood streamed from his head and down his face.

"Search him, and tie him up," ordered Lieutenant Willis brusquely, as Clara hugged her mother. "We need to move out before it turns out that they have friends."

"Sir. What about the mate?" asked Gordon.

"My job was to bring the hostage in, Gordon. Not to take revenge," said the lieutenant. "We'll leave him barricaded in there."

"Yessir. But he knows a lot about us, and he'll tell them we got away, if he gets out. If he doesn't, well, he'll starve," said Nicholl.

Gordon looked at the barred pillbox door. "And the old man would like to ask him some questions, sir."

The lieutenant nodded. "But getting him out without someone getting shot might be difficult. It's not worth it."

"I have with me a vial containing a powerful lachrymal," said Clara's mother. "Tear gas, you would call it. I brought it as a last resort to try and get us away again. Why don't you have someone drop it in the slit-window, Lieutenant? He'll be very glad to come out. And he won't be seeing well enough to shoot at anything."

"An excellent idea," said the lieutenant with a smirk of delight. "He's caused us all a few tears. It'll be his turn."

"Lieutenant, there is their wireless set. Its light is flashing. Does that mean anything?" asked Tim, pointing to it.

Albert the diver picked up the headphones. Listened. Took them off his ears. "There is someone from the HMS *Forrest* calling, sir."

Lieutenant Willis beamed. "Excellent. Let me talk to them. And then we can call Sparks on the ship. I know enough of our codes and frequencies to manage that much."

The lieutenant did a passable imitation of the mate. "Ja, we have the Dr. Calland. But the Americans, somehow they are chasing us. We hide the wireless now. There are four American ships patrolling, ja. We call at nineteen hundred to arrange pickup. The marines search for us. Out."

He fiddled the dials—got Sparks. "Willis. All fixed," was all he said. He then pointed to Big Eddie, Gordon, and Tim. "Get down to the beach with the Callands and wave. Take the other two prisoners with you. They'll be watching from the boat, you can be sure. We'll sit on the pillbox until we see you heading out to sea. With luck we should be down soon. Either the tear gas or the hand grenade will sort Werner out." It didn't sound as if he'd mind if it was the latter.

So they made haste down to the shore. Clara's mother held her hand very tightly. But right now, that was all right by her.

Tim was just incredibly glad to be going back to the submarine. He didn't really want to be that close to someone being shot or killed ever again. He had realised that the lieutenant planned to shoot Dr. Calland's captors. The man's life had barely been saved by Clara's mother attacking him. He had a bullet-creased scalp, which was bleeding freely, and was looking as terrified as his prisoner must have been once. Tim wondered if Clara's mum realised what had been intended, and how close it had been.

The sight of the sub surfacing again, close in, and the inflatable pontoon boat coming for them, was a welcome one. They'd be back on the *Cuttlefish*, alive and unhurt, soon. Still, Tim wanted all of the crew back. Alive and safe. He wouldn't stop worrying until they were.

It took another ten minutes before the others came down to the beach too, with the third prisoner. Ex First Mate Werner did not look very happy to be coming back to the ship, and that was without the fact that he was still racked with coughing and that his eyes were red and streaming.

He didn't get a lot of sympathy.

# CHAPTER 26

"We will go on to one of the uninhabited islands on the Tonga group," said the captain, "rather than take a chance that Werner told the Royal Navy about our coaling connection here. There is a small emergency coal supply hidden there. We can also leave our prisoners there. Well, possibly not together on one island. It appears that Disco was merely a local Samoan, and Avery's servant. Avery was the Imperial spy, who was here to watch Pago Pago. It's not much of a task, and he is a trader most of the time."

He smiled to Dr. Calland. "We learned a lesson from one of our previous prisoners, and have had someone listening in to the cell from the electrical workshop. They're fairly nasty bits of work, but very small players in the larger scheme of things. We'll drop the two of them where they will have a few months to wait before someone comes to harvest coconuts for copra. Where, and with what, we leave Werner will depend on what he tells us. In the meanwhile Sparks still has the Imperials believing that Dr. Calland is a captive, and that Werner is being hunted by the Americans, rather than being with us, and a full day's sail away and heading farther off."

Tim was waiting on table in the officers' mess. And eavesdropping shamelessly. He felt this was his business, now.

"The ex first mate . . . ," said Clara's mother, with a sigh. "What drove him to take such terrible chances? He could have been killed himself. I can't forgive him for what he was prepared to do, but I just can't understand how he could do it. It was insanity, with him in our midst, calling trouble onto the boat."

"It appears, ma'am, to have been loyalty," said Captain Malkis. "He is German, rather than Dutch, but he grew up in Holland, where he felt he was ostracised and persecuted. He grew up there, spoke the language fluently, and learned about the submarine trade out of Holland. But he felt a second-class citizen there. So he gave his loyalty to the people who he could identify with and he hoped would accept him. Duke Malcolm's men saw him as a potentially valuable spy and deployed him to join the Underpeople, and offer his experience."

She looked at him over the tops of her glasses. "So he was prepared to risk his own life to do their spying?"

The captain nodded. "I gather he considers himself a patriot and a hero, ma'am. He'll have plenty of time to think on this. I have decided that we'll leave him on Pylstaart Island, to the south of the Tonga group. It is uninhabited since it was raided by slavers for the Peruvian nitrate trade. It lacks permanent water or a harbour. It is very rarely visited. We considered it as a base, but landing there is difficult in some weathers. There are coconuts, shellfish, birds. He can live there for many years, and although it is very remote, I imagine one day he will be rescued. I will not keep him on the *Cuttlefish*, and I will not take the chance that he is able to reach civilization too soon and pass on information about us."

"It seems harsh."

"Execution is the alternative, ma'am. He is a traitor to his submariner oath, and a spy for our enemies. The British Empire would shoot him, were our roles reversed," said the captain, firmly.

"I suppose so," said Dr. Calland. "I have a lot of sympathy for prisoners. And I gather he did refuse to kill me."

"He'll be freer than any other prisoner, ma'am. The island is not unpleasant, just lonely."

Dr. Calland nodded. "And then?"

"And then onward," said the captain. "We have another twenty-five hundred miles to travel—a number of weeks, maybe even months, depending on the winds. Which brings me to raise the matter of Miss Calland with you, ma'am."

He looked at Clara, who was attempting to look as demure and innocent as possible. Tim knew, all too well by now, that that expression was as real as a lead sixpence. So, by the look on the captain's face, did he, by now. "We know, from experience, that crews need to be kept busy. We do this, quite honestly, with make-work tasks and of course with the submariners working towards their various certificates." He smiled. "The devil makes work for idle hands, Dr. Calland. We're not a vessel designed for passengers." He waved apologetically. "It has led to problems and good things too, ma' am. But I hope that is behind us now. We just have a long, slow voyage left."

Clara's mother wasn't fooled by the Miss Prisms-and-Prunes expression either. "I think you should put her to scrubbing floors, Captain. Or to washing dishes, along with the cabin boys," said her mother, with an answering smile, glancing up at Tim, who just happened to be clearing the plates at the next table. Very slowly.

The captain nodded. "That was my thought, yes. A little discipline, ma'am. A little hard work. And to keep her mind occupied, I'll allow her to return to studying with the cabin boys, and the junior ratings, under Mr. Amos. They need the skills to keep the submarine intact, and who knows, it may prove useful to her too. She seems a resourceful young lady. I hardly need to remind you that the rules of conduct will still apply, young lady. Certain areas are off limits, including the officers' quarters. And no physical contact with any of my crew," he said, waving a finger at Tim, who hastily took the soup tureen to the galley.

Which was how Clara ended up learning how to apply new layers of shellac to damaged French-polished mahogany. And how to put little cardboard cutouts around the various brass handles before applying Brasso, and how to polish in endless little figure-eight circles. And she got to sit the basic submariner ticket and elementary navigation examinations.

She passed them. She did well. Tim, however, did considerably better.

"I thought you couldn't do the maths?" she said. "You got ninety-eight percent for nav!"

Tim shrugged. He was adjusting to the new way things were, it seemed, quite cheerfully. "It was while I was sitting in the cell. All I could do was sit there and work out nav problems. I did all the calculations, too, over and over . . . and I sort of got it. It makes sense now. Anyway, you beat me at the electrical circuitry question."

"I can't believe you didn't get that one. It was so obvious," she said loftily, looking at him down her nose, which was quite a trick when you're sitting down.

Tim was used to being teased by now. "Yes, well, I couldn't believe you didn't get the water density question completely."

Clara sniffed. "I forgot about the difference between fresh and salt water. Anyone could do that."

They bickered amicably, while painting opposite edges of the cowling. The *Cuttlefish* had all her sails out, and was up on her hydrofoil hulls. Others of the crew were out in the sun, working on various tasks. Thinking back Clara found it hard to come to terms with the person she had been before, back in Fermoy. That girl would never have teased a boy, and would never have felt comfortable in breeches. It was as if that life had belonged to someone else.

"Did you ever talk to your mother about your dad?" asked Tim, cleaning his brush methodically.

"No. It's, well, I can't. But Mr. Amos told me a bit about the ICA, the Irish Citizens' Army. I think that was what my father was charged with supporting."

※

Tim found that he'd evolved from just being a cabin boy to something of a favourite of Clara's mother. So he found a time when he could speak to her without her daughter around, while Clara was carrying coffee to the deck watch, and he was running an errand for Lieutenant Ambrose, and then supposed to be cleaning the cabin next door. He knocked, feeling nervous about this, but determined.

Dr. Calland smiled at him when she opened her door. "Hello, Tim Barnabas," she said. "And what can I do for you?"

"Um. Can I have a word, ma'am?"

She looked a little perturbed. "Of course, Tim. Is Clara in trouble?"

Tim blinked. "Er. No. It's a bit awkward this, Dr. Calland. But we were talking . . . about our fathers. And well . . . Clara doesn't think you want to talk about her father. But she does want to know about him. She doesn't even really know why he was jailed. It . . . troubles her, a lot."

Clara's mother blinked. Looked at him over the top of her glasses. "It was something I couldn't talk about back in Ireland, Tim. And to be honest with you, young man, not something I find easy to talk about now. I miss Jack very badly, still."

"But I thought you were divorced?" asked Tim, feeling as if he was trespassing on private property, but was determined to press on.

She sighed. "On paper, yes. But paper really doesn't mean much, any more than being married on paper means much to some people. We'd agreed to divorce, for Clara's sake, if he ever got caught. And when things started to go awry, with Imperial security sniffing at his heels, we . . . we separated. It was safer for Clara. He made me promise to do it. . . . She always came first, for Jack, and for me. If I . . . if I had ever let on how I felt, or what I knew . . . well, Clara would have lost both parents. And I couldn't tell her, in case she accidentally gave it away. It was the hardest thing I have ever done."

"Oh. Well, I think you should tell her now," said Tim. "Because, you see, she thought that the piece of paper was important."

Clara's mother nodded. "I'll try. It's not that easy, Tim. She's very like her father."

"Like her mother too," said Tim with a grin. "You wouldn't always guess what she was up to."

"I can't tell her all of it," said Clara's mother, seriously. "We could still be caught."

"Well, ma'am, she loves her father. And you. It would mean a lot to her, I think," said Tim, wondering how he'd blundered into a world he didn't really belong in.

Clara listened incredulously. "You mean you lied to me?"

"Yes," said her mother. "It had to be done, Clara. To protect you, and to protect others."

Clara stared at her mother, who was wringing her hands, with that creased look on her forehead. And it all erupted like a volcano inside her. "I can't *believe* that you . . . you lied to me like that! I thought you hated Dad for what he'd done. I *told* people that." Clara knew she was shouting, and knew that in the submarine others could hear her. Didn't care.

Clara's mother covered her eyes. "I'm sorry. I'm so very sorry, darling. We had to, Clara. Your father and I agreed . . . if he ever got caught, this is what we would do. And, darling, you've got Jack's temper. The first time anyone said anything you'd have . . . well, shouted. Like you are now. We only did it because we love you very, very much."

Clara had been about to start shouting again. She'd thought of a few choice things to yell too. She pressed her lips hard together. Stood staring at her mother in silence. Resentful. Finally she said, "It hurt me so much, Mummy." She never called her mother that.

Her mother nodded slowly. "I know. Oh, I know. I can't tell you how it hurt me too. But we did what we believed was best."

"You were wrong," said Clara, gruffly. "Both of you."

"I know that too, now," said her mother, giving her a hug. "I know now how brave you can be. And how you can keep your own secrets. You've showed me while helping young Tim."

Clara absorbed both this, and the unfamiliar hug. Her father had been the one who would hug her, and tousle her hair, just because he was walking past. "I had to. There was no one else there for him."

"That was what worried us about you, dear. That, and who would feed you, and who would give you a home."

"Cookie feeds me, and I have a home here. So you can stop worrying now."

Her mother smiled. But it didn't seem to have eased her worry entirely. She stood looking at her daughter's face with hungry eyes. Clara realised she was seeing someone else there too. It was . . . disturbing. She missed her father. But well, she was coming to understand just how her mother must have felt about a man. Not just Clara's father. A man she'd loved. And that was just . . . weird.

Tim's stay in the brig had left him with another issue to deal with. When he'd got back to the submarine, and examined the contents of his breeches pockets, the salt water had done the clasp-knife and the chocolate no good. The knife was as good as new after a careful freshwater wash, a rubbing with some fine sandpaper, and a drop of oil. Nothing was ever going to revive the chocolate. It was a mess. "I owe you for that," said Tim, returning the knife.

"Worth it," said Big Eddie, slapping his back. "I was a bit doubtful at first about a bloke with a touch of the tar brush on board, but you're all right, Tim-boy."

It had never occurred to Tim that the big diver might see him like that. It hurt a bit. He said so, as they broke off pieces of salty chocolate and pulled the paper and pocket lint off it prior to sticking it in their mouths. You couldn't waste chocolate!

"Reckon it's a case of not knowing anyone else like that," said Big Eddie, thoughtfully. "Now it seems a bit different, because you're one of us."

That wasn't all Tim had to deal with, or give back. Hooks, wire, beads . . . and a problem. The wet envelope he'd got from Jonas. It had a five pound note and five one pound notes. The wire, beads, and hooks were easier to deal with. Thorne grinned at him. "You know, I thought you'd nicked the lieutenant's stuff."

"Uh. So why did you give me this?" asked Tim.

The big artificer shrugged. "Because long ago, when I was a cabin boy, I prigged ten shillings. And I got caught. But the captain that I was serving under settled for frightening me to death and punishing me with two dozen lashes and having to apologise and give it back. And giving me enough kitchen parade to put me off dirty dishes forever. I was lucky. I thought you weren't." He looked at the hooks. "I reckon I'll give these to the first mate. I didn't like him, can't stomach what he tried to do, but I won't see a man starve for want of a hook."

It made Tim's decision easier. It still wasn't easy. He found Lieutenant Ambrose. "Sir. Can I talk to you, sometime? Privately."

The lanky lieutenant looked startled. "What about?"

"I've got a problem, sir. I . . . I don't want to tell the captain. I think, maybe, you should deal with it."

Lieutenant Ambrose nodded. "Very well. Come to my cabin after I finish this watch."

So, nervously, Tim went to the lieutenant's cabin. He knocked. And was told to come in. He closed the door behind him.

"I haven't apologised to you properly, Barnabas," said the lieutenant. "And I feel I owe you that. So, what can I help you with? Only please don't say you've got that young girl into trouble. The old man has his red lines, and that is one of them." He was half-smiling as he said it. But there was a wary watchfulness behind his eyes.

Tim was quite insulted. Not that he hadn't thought about things like that, but . . . anyway that wasn't what he had come about. "No, sir. I've obeyed the captain's orders there. . . . And when I was searching your gear, I was doing something I shouldn't have been doing, sir."

"Under the circumstances I would have probably done the same, and it was just bad luck that you got caught," said the lieutenant. "So, what can I help you with?"

Tim took a deep breath. "Sir, the captain nearly put me off the ship, onto that island, marooned because he thought I was a thief. I know you asked him not to."

"So did a fair number of others, Barnabas," said the lieutenant, his eyes narrowing slightly.

"They hadn't had anything nicked from them, sir. Sir, could you tell me, that ten pounds you lost . . . was it a ten pound note?" asked Tim.

The lieutenant shook his head incredulously. "No. But don't tell me you found one in your ferreting, Barnabas. You'll get into trouble all over again. It wasn't a tenner. It was—"

"A five and a bunch of ones. And I swear I never stole them, sir, or dug them out of anyone else's gear. But," said Tim, pulling out the still-damp remains of the envelope from his shirt, "someone slipped this to me when I was in the brig. I think it's your money."

The lieutenant took the envelope. "It . . . seems to have been places," he said, looking slightly bemused.

"Er. I forgot about it, when I went diving after Clara. Uh. Miss Calland. I had it in my pocket. The brown is just chocolate, sir. I think the money is still good, sir."

The lieutenant sat down on his bunk edge. He looked thoughtfully at the battered envelope and then back at Tim. "You say someone gave it to you in the brig. Well, I know you didn't have it with you when you went into the brig. I searched you myself. And it does seem a bit daft to soak the money and cover it in chocolate for no reason. It's so unlikely, I have to think you're telling me the truth, Barnabas. Besides, we didn't believe you before, and it turned out we should have. I don't suppose you'd like to tell me which someone? I'd still like my mother's ring back. It means a lot to me. More than any amount of money. I'd hoped to give it to the girl I'm getting engaged to."

Tim stood there. Indecisive.

"I want the ring more than to punish anyone, Tim. If . . . if it was you, please just give it to me. Nothing more said."

Now indecision turned to anger. "I told you it wasn't me, sir! My mam wouldn't let me steal! I came to you to give you your own back as best I can. I'm not going to send someone else off to be dropped on an island and never get home. I know what that feels like."

Something about his anger must have got through to the lieutenant. "I'm sorry. I . . . you know, Barnabas, you're making me know what it feels like to be the skipper. I thought I wanted to be. I hadn't realised that it would involve making hard personal decisions." He took a deep breath. "Thank you for bringing the money to me. It's all said and done now, and the matter is closed."

And it might have been, if he had not looked rather sadly at the picture on his little desk. The girl with the dark wavy hair had a nice smile.

Tim sighed. "I'll try and get it back for you, sir."

"And get yourself into more trouble?" The lieutenant was quick at spotting things. "No, Barnabas. Tell me, and I'll try to work out a way of doing this that does not get you, or me, tossed off the boat."

Tim bit his lip. "Will you promise not to let the captain into this, sir? It was Jonas, sir. He told me some of his friends had had a secret whip around for me. I don't suppose he could tell me the truth, or anyone else, without getting chucked off the boat in my place. And he'd seen that that was what the captain would do. He felt bad enough to at least give me your money."

"Jonas . . . but he's one of my trainees," said Lieutenant Ambrose. "I . . . I suppose I have sent him down to fetch things from my cabin on a few occasions. I didn't think of that. I assumed it had to be one of you cabin boys."

"And probably me, 'cause I'm a darkie," said Tim.

The lieutenant blushed. But he nodded. "We all make mistakes."

"I'm beginning to get why the old first mate was so hooked up on being loyal to Imperial Security because they didn't treat him like a foreigner. I was born under London, Sir. And I didn't exactly choose my dad."

"All I can say is that I got it wrong," said the lieutenant. "I prejudged you, Tim Barnabas, and I kept doing so, for no fair reason. I didn't accept what my eyes and ears told me, that you were a good lad, because I didn't want to accept it. Well, I was wrong." He sucked through his teeth. "I don't know how I'm going to handle this. But thank you for trusting me." He stuck out his hand while looking at the picture of his girl. "If I get the ring back . . . or even if I don't, I'd like to ask you to come to the wedding. Sally's Australian, so I hope it will be this trip. I'd be honoured if you'd be there. You've taught me a lot about myself, about making judgements. And some more about command. I'm going to be acting as the mate. I was pretty pleased. Now I'm realising the joy of just being a lieutenant."

Tim took the offered hand awkwardly. "I guess you did try and speak up for me, sir. I'm sorry I thought it was you."

"And I am sorry I thought it was you. You're about as solid a crewman as the boat has got, youngster. You should try out for officer training."

Tim blinked. "I dunno, sir. I wanted to do the bridge hand ticket. I'm getting the nav. But, well, sir, to you, and to some of the crew . . . I am a darkie. Not to be trusted. There are no darkie officers on the submarines that I know of. Some people have a problem with it."

"Then it's about time they got over it," said the lieutenant, firmly. "I've decided that I have. Listen, I'm going to have to ask Mike Willis and maybe one of the senior ratings to give me a hand with the search. That all right by you?"

"Suppose he's going to know I split on him anyway," said Tim, gloomily. "Oh well. It's better than living on a desert island."

"We'll work it out, subtly. Not search any one person."

# CHAPTER 27

The young major clicked his heels, Prussian style, as he saluted Duke Malcolm. The duke was in consultation with Prince Albert. The Canadian Dominion border incident was turning into a disaster—a disaster that could cost them the West Coast. And then there was this. . . . "Your Grace, we sent two agents in on the tramp steamer. Not only were all the American vessels in port, not steaming towards Prussian Samoa, but the hills were not being combed by marines either." By the wary look, he was plainly expecting his commanding officer to explode. Or at the very least to shout and blame him.

Instead Duke Malcolm brushed an errant strand of his thinning hair off his forehead. "So: either Avery—and he is an American and merely a paid informer—has taken advantage of our Agent Werner, or Werner himself has turned."

The major coughed. "Our men could find no sign of Avery either. He's been reported missing by his business partner."

"Whatever the case, it would seem likely that the Americans have her," said Prince Albert, resignedly.

"I don't think so. No ships, or airships, have left the island in the last three days, since our agent said he had captured Dr. Calland," said Duke Malcolm. He hit the desk with the flat of his hand. "I think, Albert, the reality is that Werner must have been a double agent. He misled us, which is why we've failed to capture her, over and over again. That finally explains all the near-misses. I think this was just a red herring, while they fuelled up and left.

Well, we know where they're heading now. We have one last throw
of the dice. The submariners are unaware that their generators put
out a very high-frequency radio pulse. They have to pass through the
Bass Strait or around Tasmania. We already blockade all their ports.
We will focus our effort there."

"Yes, Your Grace. There are a fair number of resources deployed
in that area, already. We've had incidents of unrest and outlaw gangs
attacking our soldiery. We've got another four squadrons of marines
on their way down there now."

"It's the convict blood," said Duke Malcolm. "Tasmania got
some of the worst, and they got Irish rebels too. Transportation was
a mistake. They should have hanged the lot of them."

"The worst problems are in the north of the state, which was not
a convict-settled area," said Prince Albert dryly.

He always knew too much about everything, thought Duke Malcolm with irritation. "It's a contagion. It spreads. It needs to be cut out."

"It hasn't been helped by your heavy-handed attempts to do so,
Malcolm," said Prince Albert, irritably. "Anyway. Have you seen to
it that sufficient vessels are equipped to pick up the pulses? It's a pity
the range is so short."

"If it wasn't such short range, their Marconi operators would use
those frequencies. More of the units have been shipped to Australia
by airship from our manufactory in New Calcutta. Of course the real
danger is that they decide to go south of Tasmania and run for a
remote part of the Western Australian coastline. However, if they
aim for one of the ports, we'll get them, and if they come through
the Bass Strait, we'll pick them up."

"It's to be hoped that you are correct this time, Malcolm," said
Prince Albert. "We're no closer to just how, or what breakthrough
this woman made, with her work on nitrites? Have you had her ex-
husband questioned? It would seem to me, to judge by her flight,
that she may not have been as uninvolved in his activities as was pre-
viously thought."

"It was the Russians, not the Irish rebels that she was in cahoots with," said Duke Malcolm. "And yes, we have had him questioned. The fellow is either too clever for his own good, or too stupid. I suspect the latter. He may be a lever to get the young girl away from the mother, but he was very loud in his anger with Dr. Calland, apparently. Called her a false Jade, and claimed she'd set his arrest up just to get rid of him. He ranted in that vein for quite some time. It is not true, but we've encouraged him to believe it. It seems our Irish section was very thorough in checking his story out. They engaged the mother of one of the other girls in the child's class to sound her out. Apparently the girl was very upset at the breach between her parents. It was a clever piece of work by my men: adults might be effective liars, but a child lacks the skill. The girl wrote affectionate letters in the permitted once-a-month mail. The mother never sent a word. He receives no other letters."

"The problem, of course, is communicating with the girl at all," said Prince Albert, in his "drier than the Sahara" tone. "Or any of them. The Americans have made all sorts of approaches, since their muddle in Rivas. If you believe them, that was the overhasty action of a junior executive. That's what they've been telling the Underpeople, I gather."

Duke Malcolm noted carefully that his dear half-brother must have spies of his own. He shrugged. "I've arranged for Jack Calland to be shipped off to a prison in Queensland—just in case they do succeed. We have a number of agents in the so-called Republic of Westralia. If we can't keep this invention from them, we'll make sure they don't manage to keep it from us."

Prince Albert nodded gloomily. "It will probably lead to the gradual breakdown of the Empire, though."

Duke Malcolm said nothing. He rubbed his hands and looked out of his soot-streaked window. It was winter here in London. Not a winter like those of his childhood, from which he could remember snow in London. Well. Albert could point to the good aspect of the Great Melt: people no longer died of cold in London's streets.

*No, now they drowned in her canals,* he thought sourly to himself.
If Albert's scientist friends were correct, the soot from the coal that
kept the Empire alive had a lot to do with the Great Melt. Mind you,
Russia had lost nearly a quarter of its population with the vast
methane burst from the arctic seas. The scientists said the levels of
methane were declining, gradually. And through all this, the British
Empire endured. Through the flooding of East Pakistan, the starvation in Europe and China, the loss of ports and crops . . . it had been
necessary to have direct Imperial rule. Britannia had kept chaos from
overcoming them.

He would see that that continued to endure, no matter what it
took.

He had—hidden, and coded—the plans he'd made to deal with
King Ernest and Prince Albert and his sister Margot, if they ever
weakened.

It was nearly a week later that the duke received a message from
Australia. A submarine's very high-frequency radio noise had been
detected off Cape Howe, on the border between New South Wales
and Victoria. Ships were steaming toward the Bass Strait. More were
waiting in a detector-line off Eddystone Point to make sure that the
submarine did not fool them again and slip away to the south around
Tasmania.

# CHAPTER 28

"**Y**ou going to give that money back to me, Darkie?" asked Jonas, in the fore'ard gangway, as Tim returned from the gray tank. It was the officers' quarters up here—the quietest part of the ship at this time of day. Tim had never really understood why the gray tank for dirty slurry should be up near the nose, but that was the way it was set up.

Tim had been doing a fair amount of worrying about the outcome of his talk to Lieutenant Ambrose. A few days ago the lieutenant had spoken to him in this very piece of passageway. "We searched his kit—Willis, Nicholl, and I—during the fire drill. It's not there, I'm afraid. Any ideas where else he could have hidden it?"

Tim had none. He'd been wondering, since he had worked out where the money had come from, where Jonas might have hidden it. But it hadn't even occurred to him that Jonas might ask for the money back.

"You said you got it from a whip around with your mates?" he asked, thinking hard.

"Yep. Only seeing as you're not going to end up put off on an island, but you're the old man's golden little boy again, I figure you may as well give it back to me," said Jonas.

Tim nodded. "I should give it back to the people who chipped in. I owe them a thank you. Tell me who it was again?"

Jonas looked briefly as if he'd swallowed something nasty. "I'll do it for you. They wouldn't want it known about."

"Oh, don't worry. I won't tell a soul. Just tell me who they were.

That was a lot of money for ordinary submariners," said Tim, earnestly. "I was very grateful. I would have done something about it before, only it got very wet."

"What? How did you get my money wet?" said Jonas, grabbing Tim's shirt front.

"Oh, so it was yours, was it?" said Tim, getting angry himself now.

"Yep, but I didn't want to tell you that. Now give it back."

"I will. For a ring," said Tim.

Jonas's eyes went wide. Then he slammed Tim back against the wall. "I'll kill you, Darkie!" he hissed, pulling his fist back.

Tim kicked him, hard and below the belt. As the man doubled forward he hit him as hard as he could. And then they were at it, hammer and tongs, with punches flying. Fortunately for Tim, they were a noisy hammer and tongs, as Jonas was quite a bit bigger than he was.

The first on the scene was McConnell—they were just outside the sick bay, and seeing as Mac was still needing dressings on his wounds, and he was not up to deck work or the engine room yet, he'd been acting as the boat's trainee medic. He had no real ability at medicine. But he hit Jonas hard enough with his crutch to stop him strangling Tim, which cured one of Tim's problems, not being able to breathe.

And next on the scene was a sleepy-looking Lieutenant Ambrose himself, in pyjamas, as he was off duty. He grabbed the two of them and hauled them out of it, holding them apart. "What's going on here!?" he demanded.

"Barnabas fell over and I was helping him up, sir," said Jonas, blood dripping from his nose, looking at Tim. "Bit of a misunderstanding, sir. Nothing else."

It was a look that said "play along or you'll really get hurt." And suddenly Tim knew where the ring would be hidden. Jonas had told him to hide the money there. Tim turned his earnest gaze instead on the lieutenant. "We were having a fight, sir," he said, his voice gravelly from his throat having been squeezed. "Better send us both to the brig to cool off."

Lieutenant Ambrose blinked. This was not quite what he had expected, obviously. But Tim knew him for a very quick thinker and one who picked up on details. A third person had arrived on the scene, a senior rating, and then behind that, a fourth. It was Clara with a bucket of slops from the kitchen. Tim could have skipped her being there too.

"Marquard, get the sergeant-at-arms," snapped the lieutenant. "McConnell, back to the sick bay. Miss Calland, get along with you. There is nothing that need concern you here."

They all did as they were told. The lieutenant's tone was not one that brooked argument, although Clara looked almost ready to try it. She might have started, if Tim had not shaken his head at her. And winked. He had never felt less like winking, but he had to get her out of there. Tim would bet McConnell's ear was to the door, and that Clara had ducked into the forward stairwell . . . but there were no witnesses.

Lieutenant Ambrose proved that, in pyjamas or not, he was a quick thinker. "I'll come along to the brig and oversee the search of the two of you. Every inch of you. You'll both go in irons or you might hurt each other further.

Jonas turned ghost-pale at the mention of the word "search." His hand went instinctively to his crotch and just as hastily pulled away.

"I'd give it to the lieutenant now," said Tim quietly. "If they find it when they search they can't keep it quiet. Give it over now. Otherwise you will be put off the boat onto some island."

Jonas's face crumpled. He stuck his hand down into his trousers and pulled out a string tied around his waist, and with it, the ring. "I . . . I . . ."

Lieutenant Ambrose let go of Tim, took the ring, and snapped the string with a vicious wrench. "I'll have to have it well cleaned after that," he said grimly. "Jonas, you'll be up at a captain's mast . . .

explaining why you attacked this cabin boy. Without provocation and with intent to beat him senseless. It's that or be charged with theft, and you know how the captain feels about that. And you'd better work out how the captain, and I, feel about a crewman who'd let someone innocent take the fall for him. You'll be in the brig until we get to Westralia, I'd think, and you will be lucky to be on board at all."

"I didn't mean to let him get put off for me. It just happened," said Jonas.

"And you didn't have the courage to put it right," said Lieutenant Ambrose. "For someone who had stuck his neck out for you. Well, Barnabas. I think you're so badly hurt you'd better lie down in the sick bay. It's that, or put you in the brig until the mast, and I won't have that." He tapped on the sick bay door. "McConnell, you can stop listening at the door and open it. I think that you heard Barnabas being attacked, right? The boy was struck from behind and didn't raise a hand."

Tim stepped into the sick bay . . . just as a small blonde figure came dashing past and flung a bucket of kitchen slops. "You toad! You piece of filth! You scumbag," she yelled, as she hit Jonas with the empty bucket.

Lieutenant Ambrose pulled her back. He was smiling more broadly than Tim had ever seen him smile. "I see the sergeant-at-arms is on his way. I think you should see to the injured"—he jerked a thumb at Tim—"before you clean this up." Then he led Jonas away.

"What a piece of work," said Mac, sitting down. "You sit down too, missy. Good shot, though."

"So he stole that stuff!" Clara was fuming. "Well I hope the captain will leave him on an island to starve!"

"Not if I can help it," said Tim, feeling his throat. "I reckon he'll either learn a lesson, or not find a berth again."

"But he was going to let you be thrown out. Marooned on some island."

"Yep. But he did try and make up for it a bit," said Tim. "And then he got greedy again. And anyway, I once prigged something too. Sweets from a shop Under London. My mam caught me, and made me take them back. I thought I'd die doing that. I didn't, but I learned. Maybe he didn't get lucky enough to be caught."

"It's an interesting way of looking at it, Tim-boy," said Mac. "Happened to me too, sort of, as a wee kiddy."

"I still think you're far too nice," said Clara, stormily. "But it's you being it, I suppose."

At this point Lieutenant Ambrose came back. "Get to cleaning up, Miss Calland," he said firmly. "Even if I am grateful to you. The gangways need to be clean and safe." He looked at Tim. "Did you have to orchestrate that without giving me any warning?" He asked, taking out the ring, inspecting it.

"Um. Actually, sir, I didn't plan it at all. He just came and asked me for your money, right there. And then it kind of grew into a fight. And then I suddenly worked out where he must have it. But I am really glad you've got your mother's ring back."

Lieutenant Ambrose shook his head. "If I'd known that . . . well. I have my own back. And I'll get it professionally cleaned in Westralia. And I will be forever grateful to you for that, Barnabas. I haven't much left from my own family. The skipper will smell a rat, of course. But I think he'll back me up."

And so it was.

In a mysterious fashion, of course, quite a few of the crew seemed to know the real story.

But they weren't talking to the captain about it either.

Several days later Tim and Clara were in the mess, working, and Clara got to asking about where they were going. "What's it like?"

"Westralia!" said Cookie. "Well, yous know what the Americans say about Texas, missy?"

"Um. No," admitted Clara.

Cookie grinned in delight at having a joke that they hadn't heard before. "They say that all Texas needs is a few good people and more water to make it heaven. Which is all hell needs too. Well, we've got the people. But it's mighty dry. We're working on it, though. There are big desalination plants on the coast, and we've got water drip-feeds that deliver water just to each plant. The Royal Navy have shelled a few of the desalination plants, so they have big sand-walls—we've got lots of sand, and batteries of rockets to defend them."

"Big sandcastles," said Tim, busy peeling vegetables.

Cookie laughed. "Something like that, yes. The newer ones just pump seawater in through the caves on the Nullarbor, so they can be further from the sea, see. But we'll probably head for the big plant they made at Eucla, or even to the new one at Ceduna. Used to be in South Australia, but the British pulled everyone back from the Nullarbor and the Eyre Peninsula. You see, the east got wetter, but the west got drier, in the Great Melt. When the Australian Commonwealth Government collapsed in 1941, and the governor-general called for direct rule for the duration of the emergency, the British Empire ran the government. Then after the Big Dry from '40 to '48, they just evacuated everyone—well, everyone who would go—to east of the Yorke Peninsula . . . Eh. I can see it means nothing to yous. I'll show yer on the map, Missy. But it meant that only the real Ozzie battlers stayed on, see. And now blokes who don't like direct rule keep moving to Westralia. At this rate the east coast will be left with nothing but a lot of city-born bludgers."

"What's a bludger?" asked Clara.

"A scrounger, someone who don't like to work much," said Cookie, pointing with an elbow at the sink. His hands were full of knife and potato. "Someone who asks questions instead of doing the washing up."

So Clara scrubbed pots. Still, it was on her mind. They'd sighted Cape Howe, as well as a Royal Navy ship, yesterday, which was why they were running below the surface by day again. Australia, and the end of their journey, loomed close. Simply because of Cookie, Westralia didn't seem quite so unfamiliar and scary as America had. That country she'd only known from the bioramas. It still meant she would be parting from the crew, and the submarine, which felt more like home than anything she'd lived in since her father had been arrested. It was just, well, good but difficult.

She really didn't know quite how to go on with Tim, though. It would also mean saying good-bye to him, and she didn't want to think about it. Yes, her mother had given her a long lecture about the dangers of getting pregnant. She hadn't even thought of going anything like that far anyway. She would settle for working on the kissing part, right now. No matter what Mother or the captain said. Except . . . she wasn't going to get him into trouble again. But another part of her didn't want to even touch him. The part that knew that she was going to get off the submarine in Westralia, and that their lives would carry them apart, didn't want to let him or anyone else get too close. She knew she'd probably never ever see her father again. That hurt more than she could bear to think about. So also did the fact that Tim would stay with the submarine and be carried away . . . maybe never to come back. And there was nothing she could do about it. That hurt already.

"We make landfall tomorrow in the Cameron Lakes on Flinders Island," said Cookie, cheerfully, on her next watch, when Clara reported for duty at the sink. Tim was already working. "The old man likes to stock up with coal and give the engineers a proper chance to give the engines and compressors a once-over. The navy keep a bit of a blockade on the Westralia Ports—which is why the submarines are so welcome—so getting in is always a bit of cat-and-mouse game. The government of Westralia have a few subs of their own too. Anyway, yous will likely get to see a bit of Australia on Flinders. The Straitsmen like visitors, so long as it's not the law or someone trying to tell them what to do. Skipper'll tell you too, but don't make no comments about black fellas. Not that you'd be likely to, I reckon, Tim-o. Them Straitsmen is a bit touchy about it. Some of them are a mix of black-fella blood and the old sealers, and them that is take exception, and them that says they isn't take exception too. Half of 'em are related, so yer just don't say anything nasty about anyone else. And just be careful about the mutton you get offered."

"Why? Is it stolen?" asked Clara. "I've heard about the sheep thieves in Australia. They wrote about them in the newspapers back in Ireland."

Cookie chuckled. "Yer think we're all a bunch of Ned Kellys, don't yous? No, it's likely to be sea-mutton or mutton-bird."

"They have flying and swimming sheep?" asked Clara, sceptically. She'd been on the receiving end of Cookie's tall stories before.

"And drop bears," said Cookie, with his best attempt at a serious expression. "Have I told yous about the drop bears? You see that you ask the Straitsmen for a nice pointy hat to keep off the drop bears, before you go walking in the gum forests."

"He'll tell you about the Bunyip next," said Tim, grating a floppy carrot.

"He did," said Clara. "And drop bears. But it's the first time he's brought up mutton-birds and sea-mutton."

Tim looked critically at the carrot stub. "Dunno about sea-mutton, but we could use some fresh food. These carrots are ready to be ghosts too, Cookie."

"Not ghosts, it's a monster the Bunyip is, Tim-o. We'll get some food on Flinders. But I'm not cooking mutton-bird on this boat again. It's a kind of seabird, and the fat has a strong fishy smell to it when it cooks. A very strong smell. Not a good idea in a submarine. The sea-mutton is good though—that's what they call abalone."

"What's that?" asked Clara.

"Ah, it is like a giant flat sea snail. . . . Yer shouldn't pull such faces," said Cookie, laughing at them. "Your faces will set like that. It's very good, so long as it's been beaten properly, I tell yous."

The "all quiet" light came on, and the sound of the engines was stilled. It had been so long since it had happened that it was a shock to them.

The game of cat and mouse was on again. And the mouse had got fat and lazy out in the peaceful South Pacific.

"They're doing a very much better job of systematically tracking us, since we got rid of the traitor on board," said Lieutenant Ambrose, tiredly. "Every time we come up to breathe, well, there's two of them, within the hour. Always two of them. The skipper reckons they must have some new hydrophones or something. But this hunting in pairs is new too."

Clara's mother looked thoughtful. "It sounds to me like they are triangulating on us."

"That's the captain's idea too, ma'am. But they are managing to do it even when we run on the electric motors, with the boat all quiet. We lost them the last time by even stopping those. He thinks they must have something that picks up our screws, whereas before this they were relying on the noise from the compressors, really. The Stirling engines are quiet compared to most engines, but the compressors aren't. It's not a good feeling to have the ship adrift, without steerage. We need to be moving forward for the rudder and vanes to work. Dangerous waters, the Bass Strait. Still, we should creep into Cameron Inlet and the lakes tonight. We can sit there and recharge our batteries and check the engines for the last leg. It's as dangerous as in and out of London."

# CHAPTER 29

The eastern side of Flinders Island had been, since the Great Melt, a swampy wild place, fronted with drowned land and sandbars and a series of interlocking salty estuaries and lakes, tucked in between small forested granite mountains. It was from one of these lakes, hidden behind three granite outcrops, that an enormous flock of ducks rose in alarm when they saw a submarine pop up in the predawn light. Tim was on deck-watch, helping to guide the submarine down an ale-brown channel to the secret quay.

Their tie-up was plainly a well-used one, carefully hidden from the air by nets that were laced with vegetation—some plants were even grown in pots.

A figure detached itself from the tree it had been leaning against. "G'day. Been expecting yous," said the man in his green-checked shirt and elderly floppy hat.

"You have?" asked Tim, nearly dropping the monkey's fist on the rope he'd been about to throw. They'd even kept radio silence, knowing Werner would have betrayed their codes and calling frequencies.

"Well, it seemed obvious that yous were on yer way. They're looking about for yous. Got troops up on Walker's Lookout and ships hanging about. So yous must be coming." He grinned. "I've never seen a search anything like it," said the Straitsman, taking off his hat and scratching his curly black hair. "What sort of cargo yous got that's so important?"

"We've a few days in hand to try and just sit it out, and hope that they believe we have been and gone," said Captain Malkis. "I will be allowing the men a little shore leave, in shifts, in the company of several Straitsmen. Normally, we spend a few days here allowing the men to hunt with the locals, and to do a little fishing, while we prepare the boat for that last haul. I've had to ban shooting for fear of attracting too much attention, but the locals will bring us fresh meat and fish. The final sector is usually quite demanding, so it's well to let the crew get plenty of rest and some exercise. So ma'am, while I am not prepared to allow you and your daughter off alone, I would be happy to include you into one of the shore parties. There is a group walking up the third Patriarch this afternoon, if you'd like to join them." He smiled. "The cook and young Barnabas I believe are both going out with them."

Clara's mother looked at the green bushland. "I would like to, but well, we've come so far. Is it worth the risk, Captain?"

"In many places I'd say no," said the captain. "But in all honesty, I think there is a minimal risk here. To give you an example from your home in Ireland, the island is about the size of County Waterford, ma'am. It's mostly forest or swampland or mountain. There are a hundred and twenty grenadiers, and fifty Hussars here, looking for us. The Straitsmen know these wilds like the back of their hands, and the soldiers are fresh out from England, apparently. The Hussars' horses are sick and the grenadiers kept getting lost. And informers are usually a problem . . . but this is a very closed society. The Straitsmen don't like what they consider 'occupiers,' and the idea of leaving these islands is frightening to them. They need to trade to survive, but the Imperials are stopping them from fishing or shipping hides. We take cargoes for them and bring them things they need. They've accepted us, and have never betrayed us. Saved my groats a few years ago, and that meant almost every man on the island had to cooperate. I trust them. Besides, you'd be with a party of thirty armed men from the boat, as well as ten Straitsmen. I think you will be safe enough."

So they'd gone out, threading their way under the she-oaks and up into the gum forests, climbing up to where they could look out over the eastern coast, high up the hill. The air was clear and still cool. The sea, a mile distant, was azure.

"The ships out there are as thick as flies on a three-days-dead 'roo," said the Straitsman, as Clara, her mother, Cookie, Tim, and a few others sat under the gum trees on granite boulders, which the lichen spattered into orange patches. He pointed out across Babel Island, where the hundreds of thousands of birds drifted up like smoke, to the open water beyond. "At night we been counting lights from the lookout up on Strzelecki Mountain. There are 'nother two ships in the sounds. 'Nother off Vansittart Island. If we get a good blow there'll be rich pickings," he said with relish, "because they don't know our water. One nearly run aground on Potboil Shoal already. They won't go near there again," he said with some satisfaction. "The tide runs strong over it. Your skipper knows where to set his course, because I showed him. Mind you, he still got stuck on a bank off Lady Barron once and had to wait for the tide. The policeman had to be called away up to Memana in a hurry or he'd have seen her; most everyone else on the island did! But the policeman's a mainlander, only been here thirty years."

Clara could hear that he didn't think much of "mainlanders." Plainly one had to be born and bred here to be a Straitsman.

"I told yous they're all wreckers and half-pirates," said Cookie, cheerfully. "You reckon they got any chance of finding us?"

The Straitsman snorted. "Not while yous are in here. The island's more'n sixty mile long, and most of it is still bush. They tried one of them airships, and the roaring forties took it off toward New Zealand. They tried bombing something here a few years ago, and it took us a month to put the fires out—burned their camp to a crisp. Mind you, when they landed that bunch of redcoats, they been asking questions. Everybody is being very helpful. We told them if they started any fires it'd burn the lot of them, though. And we explained how the fire will move faster than a running man. Filled them with horror stories. Gave them a Port Jackson shark, some salmon that hadn't been bled, and a couple of bluehead parrot fish. They told us how good they was."

He and Cookie doubled up laughing.

"What's so funny?" asked Tim.

"They're trash fish," explained the Straitsman. "We use 'em for bait in the crayfish traps. Now if someone gives you a feed of flathead, he's a friend of yours."

"And if he offers you a couple of pike and tells you to keep 'em cool for a few days, before you eat them . . . ," said Cookie, digging an elbow into his Straitsman-mate's ribs.

"Some people like them like that," said the Straitsman, grinning.

"And some people like mutton-birds," said Cookie.

"Heh. Well yer might have to get used to them. The net they've set for yous around here is pretty tight," said the Straitsman.

"There might be worse places to be trapped," said Clara, looking out at the coast.

"Too right!" said the Straitsman. "There's no better place in the world, and plenty worse, like Westralia, eh, Cookie. We could use some new people, beside the policeman."

"And in thirty years you'd still be a foreigner," said Cookie.

"I'd put up with being a foreigner for this," said Clara's mother, dreamily. "It's a wonderful place. Well, if I could have Jack with me here, I'd stay forever, I think. But I can't at the moment, and so I need to change the world first. Maybe when we've done that."

It had never struck Clara that that was what her mother was hoping to do. It was quite an ambition: changing the world. Changing the whole world to get her dad free—that was something only her mother could decide to do. She smiled to herself, her eyes a little moist.

She noticed that Tim had got up and was walking onward to the ramp of rock that led to the actual summit, so she casually got up and wandered that way too. It probably didn't fool anyone, but even her mother seemed prepared to not notice for a few minutes. The Straitsmen had checked the whole area over. They were expert trackers and were sure that there were no problems here. Except for the ones that they had brought with them, of course.

She found Tim a little higher up, sitting looking out at the sea, his face a little troubled. "Penny for your thoughts," she said, lightly. He looked up startled. He was a very intense thinker. And now that she'd learned to read his complexion, he blushed easily. "I was thinking about you," he said gruffly.

She sat down next to him. "Snap."

"What?"

"I was thinking about you too. About . . . well all sort of things. Us." It was her turn to blush. How did you tell someone that you had followed them to be alone with them? You could never be really, truly, sure that they were alone together on the submarine, short of going somewhere together they'd be in all sorts of trouble if they were caught in, like the escape hatch or one of the officers' cabins. And by now, she knew they probably would be caught. She'd briefly held his hand under soapy water in the galley. Stood with her hip touching his while washing dishes. Compared to the stories the girls told back at school in Fermoy—what a lifetime ago that seemed—that wasn't much.

"Yes. Well, that's the problem, see. Look, I'm just a cabin boy. In about two weeks, maybe, we should have you, and your mother, safe in Westralia. And I'll be on my way in a few days. I may not be back for . . . years. And I'm just a cabin boy. I might not pass my tickets. If I lose my place on the *Cuttlefish*, I won't be able to come back to Australia. I . . . I think I love you. But I may never see you again."

Clara wasn't ready for this. She really, really wasn't. He was being all grown up and serious. In the back of her mind she'd known this herself. Life would sweep them apart. And the world was so big and . . . She swallowed. She'd come up here wanting to be kissed. Not to cry. And he made it worse by taking her hand. She looked at his earnest eyes, not with their normal twinkle of laughter or mischief in them at all, and did not know what to say. He wasn't even whistling.

She gave a little sigh. "Of course you'll pass your tickets. Lieutenant Ambrose said he'd asked the captain if he'd sponsor you signing up as a candidate officer. I'm jealous. Mother is already trying to plan me going back to school." She squeezed his hand, leaned her head against his shoulder. "I don't want you to go away. But you must. And I still hurt so much from losing my father forever. I'm . . . I'm not . . . I don't know. I don't want to get too involved with a friend I know I have to lose."

He nodded, letting go of her hand. "I guess I never should have asked. I'm just an Underperson, a darkie too . . ."

"That's not true. It doesn't matter! Not to me. And I get angry when you talk yourself down like that. I . . . I like you more than anyone else I've ever met. I just . . . don't want to hurt like my mother does. Now that I know, I see how she looks every time something reminds her of my dad."

She laughed awkwardly. "I sound like a fool, don't I, Tim?"

He shook his head. "Not to me. Not ever."

"Even when I was kissing you in Rivas?"

He grinned, looking more like his normal self. "I'm not sure about the tongue bit."

She snorted with laughter and embarrassment. "You think you're not sure? I had to make it up from what I had heard, and what I saw the Cashel girls doing. They used to practice on each other."

"I wouldn't mind being used for practice. While we're not on the boat," he said, tentatively.

Downslope, someone called. "Time to go, if yer going to get back for yer tea."

It was still a good practice, even if it was cut short.

"No shore leave today. There's word from the Straitsmen that the Royal Navy have put sailors out in lifeboats to come and search the swamps," said Lieutenant Ambrose, when Tim reported for duty. "We need everyone on board, ready to move or dive."

He looked particularly upset about something. Tim, who had got a lot more friendly with the lieutenant than he would have thought possible a few months ago, asked what was wrong, a little later, when he brought some maps to the lieutenant.

"If I can't trust you, Barnabas, I can't trust anyone," said the lieutenant. "It's just that one of the Straitsmen—press-ganged to be a pilot for a Royal Navy ship coming into Lady Barron—overheard the captain saying they'd picked up a signal from the east coast. So we must still have a spy and another transmitter . . . or some kind of signalling device on the boat. It's really upset the skipper. Me too, I suppose." He smiled. "Have you and your co-conspirator got any more clever ideas about what we should have spotted this time?"

"Um. I'll ask her," said Tim.

The lieutenant chuckled. "And heaven knows what sort of trouble that'll lead us into. Only this time tell me what you're doing, please. I'm not going to stop you. Well, probably not."

So Tim soon found a reason to go to the galley, where Clara was pulling faces as she helped Cookie turn several wallaby into dinner. Part of it included skinning the tails.

"They look like rats!"

Tim nodded. "Yes, tasty. But much bigger than tunnel rats."

Clara's look reminded him again of what different backgrounds they came from. He was about to tell her what Lieutenant Ambrose had said, when it occurred to him that he'd been trusted . . . and that meant not telling anyone but Clara. He understood then, why Lieutenant Ambrose had been looking so uncomfortable. Cookie . . .

Cookie was a friend. But this situation turned anyone into a possible enemy. "Um, Cookie. Clara's mother wanted to speak to her for a minute or two. Can you spare her?"

Cookie gave him a knowing smile. "Run along. Don't be long and don't be caught."

Tim felt his face glow. He was a terrible hand at lying. Clara, however, had washed her hands and was looking worried.

"What's wrong with my mother?" she asked quietly, as they got to the companionway.

"Nothing. She doesn't want to see you. I just made it up because I needed to talk to you privately."

"Oh, Tim! You'll get us into such trouble. I—"

"Lieutenant Ambrose and Skipper think there is another spy on the boat." Quickly and quietly Tim explained. "And you're not to do anything without telling the lieutenant. And your mother. And me."

"I'm not a baby! Don't you trust me?" she snapped, firing up.

"I'd trust you with my life," said Tim, earnestly. "Anytime, anywhere. I just know what you can do! And we'd better get back to work."

"Um. It's a confusing boy you are, Tim Barnabas," she said. "I thought you wanted to kiss me."

"Always. But I gave my word about that too."

She bit her lip. "I'd better think of a story for Cookie."

"Yep. But I bet he won't ask."

Tim was right. Cookie didn't ask. Clara thought over what Tim had told her, as she chopped and washed. There was something there, lurking on the edge of her memory that she felt was a clue. The Royal Navy were getting a signal. . . .

She nearly cut her own fingers off. "Cookie. I need to go and talk to my mother. Right now."

He looked a little worried. "And there I thought it was just that Tim-boy wanted to kiss you. Something wrong, missy?"

"No. I just think I have an answer."

"Go then. We've got an hour before first sitting," he said cheerfully. "If it was any closer I'd have said answers wait, but good food don't. And then you can tell me the answer too. I been looking for it."

"Not this one," said Clara as she ran off.

Her mother was checking rows of figures on a pad. "Hello, dear. What brings you here?" she asked, obviously determinedly pulling herself away from her work. "I hear we may have to move again."

"Yes. But I need your help."

"Oh. Well, I am at your disposal," said her mother, pushing the papers aside. "Better than you rushing off and doing it without me."

"Tim made me promise to tell you," said Clara, scowling a bit. "The sub has to move because the Royal Navy is following a signal. . . ."

Her mother closed her eyes briefly with an expression of pain. "I thought . . . I so hoped once Werner was gone, the spying would be over, but by the way they've followed us, I suppose I was wrong."

"Well, maybe not. That's what Tim and Lieutenant Ambrose and the captain thought too, that we must have another traitor. . . . But Mother, you remember when I just got the crystal radio going? When I got you to listen to that funny noise? And Sparks said it was junk, very high . . . whatchamacallit . . ."

"Frequency," said her mother. "I am a chemist, but I seem to recall that high frequency has a shorter range. I think you need your crystal radio, and we should talk to the captain."

Clara grinned. "Not until I've told Lieutenant Ambrose and Tim."

"What? Why? I mean . . . the captain needs to know as soon as possible."

"Yes, but I also need to prove that I don't always get into trouble," said Clara, impishly. "Let me pick up my crystal radio and go and find them."

"I think I am only getting a part of this," said Clara's mother, shaking her head. "But I will go along with that part."

Lieutenant Ambrose had just got up, preparing for the evening watch, and was embarrassed to have opened his door to two ladies when he was half-shaved with shaving foam on his face. "My apologies. I thought . . . well, I thought it was someone else. Let me just wash my face."

The smell of the foam, and the sight of it, brought a flood of memories back to Clara, of her father. "Um. We could go away. It's just that I think I may have some idea of how it is that we're being tracked."

"That's more important than shaving. Tell."

Clara explained. And before she'd even finished, the lieutenant, not worrying about his half-shaved state, took them up to the bridge. Captain Malkis blinked at him. "What's wrong, Ambrose?"

"Hopefully something is right, sir. My apologies coming to you like this, but the sooner we do something about it the better. I know you were going to run the compressors this afternoon, and maybe we'd better not."

"I like to keep the tanks full, Lieutenant. Explain."

"I'd better leave that to Miss Calland and her crystal radio, sir."

So Clara had to explain again. And the captain called Sparks over.

Sparks blinked. "Could be right, Captain. And it ties in with their Marconi chatter. I just . . . never thought of it. We only use the medium frequencies and long waves."

"If they have some kind of signal strength measure, they could triangulate on us, Captain," said Lieutenant Ambrose.

Captain Malkis tugged his beard. "We need to eliminate this, gentlemen, um and ladies. Find it and suppress it."

"We could do one better," said Clara. "We could let them follow it. . . ."

The lieutenant raised his eyebrows. "We're all out of tick-tocks, Captain."

"Let me talk to the chief engineer about that! Miss Calland, may I borrow your crystal radio? If this is correct, I may tell you, you've taken a weight off my mind."

Clara felt pleased with herself. And then she caught sight of the chronometer. "I've got to get back to Cookie! He's got first sitting in eighteen minutes." She thrust her radio at the captain. "Excuse me, sir."

He smiled as he took it. "Dismissed . . . Cadet! Run. Tell the cook my apologies for having kept you."

Clara had time while she ran to feel guilty about not having told Tim.

Tim was working in the engine room when the captain came down there. He recognized the crystal radio set in the captain's hand. What had she been up to now? He soon found out. "The aftermath of your radio hunting is still with us, Barnabas," said the captain with smile. "Miss Calland has, I think, found an answer to how they're following us, Chief." He explained. "I've brought Sparks down to see what can be done to hide it, or to change the output, at least. And to discuss making another decoy, Chief Engineer."

"Clockwork mechanism is a bit beyond our making in short order, sir," said the chief.

Captain Malkis looked thoughtful. "Yes. But how much calcium carbide do we have, Chief?"

"Maybe twenty pounds, sir."

"Enough to turn a drogue into a torpedo?

The chief beamed at the idea. "No sir. But if you wanted that, I suppose something could be devised. I've got a little thermite, and I've seen a fairly good rocket made with that and some water. Those mad Westralians do it with ice in their shore-defence rockets. Dangerous as hell, of course."

"So is living, Chief, so is living. Design me something that will move an empty drogue, putting out a nice radio transmission, and move it very fast."

The chief engineer enjoyed that sort of challenge. So did Tim. It was fun making a dangerous rocket-propelled decoy. And now that they knew what the Royal Navy were tracking, it was easy to give them some signals from forty miles away. That gave them some security to launch the small test decoy on the Cameron Lakes.

The chief's little party were all stripped off to their breeches, standing in the water, holding ropes to the welded tubular device. "Right. She needs a little speed to get going. On the count of three, we run," said the chief. "I'll shout when to let go."

They ran through the shallows hauling, Tim with the rest . . . and then suddenly the small torpedo took off with an express train roar. Tim, from hauling, found himself skiing along on his belly. He clung for dear life . . . and then realized maybe he shouldn't, and let go. The shore was a fair way back for Tim to swim. Fortunately most of the water was quite shallow and he could touch bottom for a rest.

The chief was standing with his hands on his hips when he got to the shallows. "And how long is it, Barnabas, since I last told you you were an idiot?"

"Um. Twenty minutes, sir," said Tim. The chief sometimes let it go that long.

"Right. You haven't changed in that time. Why didn't you let go, boy?"

"Didn't hear you shout, sir."

The chief engineer rolled his eyes. "I'll make up for that now," he bellowed. "You were supposed to tow it, not get towed by it."

Tim decided it was maybe not a good idea to tell the chief it had been a lot of fun, while it lasted.

The test torpedo travelled three miles along the lake before bursting into flames and sinking. Tim was glad that he hadn't hung on till the very end.

Shovelling the caliche out of one of the drogues was less fun. It smelled and burned his eyes and nose and throat. Tim also knew what this meant. The island idyll was over. So was his chance of sneaking a kiss on a walk.

The next night the Straitsmen would launch the drogue-decoy for them from some miles away, and they would run.

# CHAPTER 30

Tim was on the bridge, captain's messenger, and on periscope duty, when the *Cuttlefish* crept down the scoured channel to Stellar's Lagoon. "Your night-spotting has not passed unnoticed, Barnabas," Captain Malkis had told him when he reported to the bridge for duty. "We note in the log what ships have been spotted at night, and at what range, and by whom. You and Submariner Gordon have the best records, and so you're on periscope duty for this section. It's a black night out there."

It was a heavy responsibility. As soon as the "all quiet" light came on Tim's stomach knotted itself with tension.

He stared so hard into the blackness that he had a headache. But he saw no sign of a vessel out there. Taking a deep breath, and hoping he was not wrong, he signed "all clear" from the periscope.

The captain waved Gordon to the periscope instead, and held a note for Tim to carry to the engine room. They were taking no chances at all. Tim ran as quietly as he could down to the engine room. And then back up to the bridge, as they eased over the bar in the cover of a wave, and out to sea.

Running silent but not daring to run deeper than periscope depth, or too fast in these treacherous waters, they slipped south. Tim was again peering through the periscope into the dark when he saw something frightening enough to make him break silence. "Breakers! Waterspout!"

Captain Malkis nodded, put a finger on his lips, and came to look.

He adjusted course very slightly . . . and then, just as Tim had taken the periscope again, the submarine began to roll and shudder. In alarm Tim looked hastily back to the captain, who appeared completely calm even though the boat was now behaving like a restive horse. . . . The "all quiet" light was off.

"Potboil Shoal tide-race, Barnabas. They couldn't hear us above the water noise. If we have it right, we'll be fine," said the captain, as the submarine pitched and rolled. "If not, we're going to drown. Keep a good lookout, when possible. And hold tight. It will get worse.

He was, Tim realized, not joking about any of it. It was a noisy, bucketing, wild ride that had Tim clinging to the periscope handles as the water slapped and raced around the submarine. There was a brief grating touch against the sand, and then they were no longer being thrown about.

"Phew!" said Tim.

The captain tapped his shoulder. Pointed. The "all quiet" light burned again.

Slowly and silently, they crept west.

Eventually he was relieved on periscope duty, and just had to stand there and watch . . . and think. The atmosphere on the bridge was tense and quiet as they navigated through shallow, dangerous waters in the dark.

It was odd that he could be so scared and yet . . . so secure with his "family." Because this was home, and this was his family now. He loved the submarine, and he hadn't realized that he really hadn't had anyone but his mam before. It struck him as he stood there, silent, thinking, waiting, that being sentenced to be marooned and exiled from it had done one thing for him—he knew just who his friends really were, now: some who had spoken up for him with the captain, some who had brought him things to help him survive. And one who had never stopped working on getting him free. She was a confusing girl for a boy to have in his life.

※

Clara found it easiest to keep herself busy. She reported for duty every morning. After all, the captain had called her "cadet." So, she'd be one. Busy was best right now. Her head was a mixed-up place. The crew let her work, but not all the jobs were good at keeping her head occupied, even if her hands were working. She ended up polishing, or working in the mess often enough. She saw how the constant vigilance and stress were wearing all of the crew down, especially the captain.

He came into the mess days after they left Flinders, when he ought have been off for many hours. . . . Sat down, and yawned. "Pardon me, Miss Calland. We're just burning the candle at both ends at the moment. It is difficult managing—though I never thought I'd say this after his treachery—without Werner. He may have been a spy and a traitor, but he was also good at his job and very knowledgeable about these waters. My lieutenants are good men, but neither are very experienced as yet. So we're relying on good fortune. That always runs out, eventually."

"We're relying on a good captain," said Clara. It was meant to be encouraging. He was a good captain, after all.

He sighed. Sipped his coffee. Gave her a crooked half-smile. "It's a heavy weight to carry, miss. I'm a captain who has made mistakes in the past, as you have proved."

It was a shock to realize that he was admitting his own frailty. He'd always seemed . . . well, superhuman, about controlling the boat. "Yes, but you've never made mistakes about the sea."

He shook his head. "I wish that were true. But there is a fair amount of luck involved in our survival. We are stretching it thin."

※

Duke Malcolm put the self-congratulation of Admiral Lesseps down firmly. "We destroyed something, Admiral. Something . . . from which we have found no bodies. I want a watch maintained for another two weeks, or until we get some confirmation."

The *Cuttlefish*'s luck finally ran out just west of Cape Carnot.

The worst part of it, for Tim, was that it was so completely unexpected. The whole boat's crew had been nervous and vigilant right across the Bass Strait, and onward across the Spencer Gulf. They'd run on coal and not sail, staying hidden almost all of the way. The water was clear and clean, so they'd spent the days lurking as deep as was safe, or camouflaged. They'd only moved during the short summer nights, creeping westward, just below the surface at periscope depth, with the engine snuiver up, but invisible otherwise.

And Tim had found that he could only be terrified for just so long, and then . . . one got sort of used to it.

The first they knew of the airship was the explosion.

It actually rocked the submarine, and was deafening.

Tim knew they'd dived by the tilt and that the engines were still running by the vibration . . . but he couldn't hear any orders. Or anything. He'd been working in the engine room, and in the aftermath of the explosion . . . he'd got sprayed in the face by cold salty water. The Stirling engine relied on outside water as a heat sink, and a thin jet of pressurized seawater was spraying in from the spot where the cooling pipe penetrated the hull.

More drop-mine explosions shook and jarred the sub, and the spray had turned into a fire hose of water, as Tim's hearing recovered.

He had his tasks for this drilled into him. It kept him calm . . . well, kept him coping, kept him working.

The chief engineer, in the midst of the chaos, was already winding tape around the pipe. He was soaked to the skin, but he shouted, "Tell the bridge we need to reduce depth. Less pressure. The solder on the pipe has cracked."

The speaking tube brought the captain's voice. "Status report, engine room."

Thorne told the captain. In the meantime the chief engineer went on winding the tape wider and closer in, while being blasted by water, which was now being forced upwards.

Someone grabbed Tim. "Help me get the bilge pumps running."

There was a terrible sharp tearing sound, and hissing and clouds of steam filled the room. "The Stirling heat casing!" yelled someone. "It's cracked!"

The next few moments were pandemonium. The lights went out. Several more things went bang. The air was hot with steam, and thick with smoke, and there was water sloshing around underfoot. Tim didn't know what to do.

And then the emergency lights came on. Orders were yelled.

Tim found himself priming the standby bilge pump, as Thorne, bleeding from a nasty cut across his chest, cranked.

Other submariners were changing fuses and helping the injured. The proper lights came on. Water was still running down the bulkhead from where it had been spraying in before, but now it was not bucketing in.

"Damage report, engine room," said the captain through the speaker tube.

"The heat casing on three of the Stirlings have definitely gone," said the chief. "We need to check the rest. We've still got water coming in the solder around the cooling pipe. That can be repaired, Captain, but only on the surface. At the moment the Stirling engines are unusable."

Tim saw bent brass rods—that he'd been greasing a few moments before—and a broken casing in the steamy smoky atmosphere, as oily water sloshed around his feet. "And we've lost at least one compressor."

"Can we run on the electric, Chief?"

"I will check, Captain."

Clara had been in the mess, laying tables, when it had all happened. Now she was trying to clean up broken crockery. And Cookie, somehow, was making tea. She'd seen a couple of burned submariners helped up the passage. And Cookie was making tea. "If they're not dead, they'll want it. If they're dead, they won't mind. Mind you, we have no engines, by the sounds of it. And she feels very sluggish in the water."

Clara wondered how he could be so cool about it. But it calmed her too.

So she carried trays of tea. The engine room looked as if a bomb had hit it. It was ankle deep in water, and people, including Tim, were working frantically. "Just put it there, luv," said the chief—he had a rough bandage around his head and was soaked to the skin. "We'll get there, if and when we can."

Up on the bridge too they were replacing several gauges, and there was broken glass underfoot, but they at least had time to drink the tea, and take some heart from it. Clara was there to hear the chief say, "We're starting the electric motor, Skipper," and then to have the lights go out again. The emergency light came on again.

"Fuses," said the chief. "We must have water in somewhere. It's awash down here, Captain. But the pumps are winning for now."

Light was restored, obviously the fuse changed.

"Is there any hope of fixing it, Chief?" asked the captain, his voice carefully controlled.

The chief didn't sound so controlled. "Possibly. If the seal we've got on the leak can hold the inflow to what it is now, the pumps can cope. If we start taking in more water, Captain, we'll have to either sink or surface."

"The airship is still up there, Chief," said the captain. "We've got a wireless aerial up. They saw us in the moonlight. She's sending our position by wireless, and is playing searchlights on the water. They'll turn their Gatling gun on us if we surface. The oil from our bilges makes quite a trail," said the captain.

"It's pump or sink, Captain."

Clara would have liked to stay on the bridge and know what was happening, but the captain motioned her to go.

So she went back to the galley.

Scared.

It was a huge relief when, a little later, just after the lights dipped again but did not go out, the sub began moving again. "That chief is a wonder," said Cookie. "You nip down there and see if they want fresh tea now."

The scene in the engine room was less chaotic than earlier. There was, it was true, what looked like a small scrapyard along one wall. They were all still working furiously. But the level of water underfoot had gone down, and the smoke and steam had at least spread out into a general fug. The chief nodded at her. "Tell Cookie fifteen minutes, if nothing else goes wrong."

On the way back she bumped into Big Eddie the diver, plainly preparing to go out. He waved but looked very preoccupied, and didn't say anything.

A little later the *Cuttlefish* stopped moving. Clara's heart sank. "Engines?"

Cookie shook his head. "Probably sent the diver out to slap a glue-patch on it. The pressure will pull it into the leak and then it will set. It's not a permanent answer, but may stop it leaking so much. Then they can stop pumping, so the oil sheen won't be marking our trail. We can dive a bit deeper, then stop being followed and move away. Then later they can maybe silver-solder the pipe entry."

"Oh. I hope so. I really, really hope so. I thought we were going to die," admitted Clara.

"We've got a little way to go before we're home and dry yet," said Cookie. "But she's a good boat, with a good skipper and a good chief engineer."

Clara didn't remind him that he sometimes said that only the good died young.

Tim's fingers were cut, and he had a row of blisters on his shoulder—that would have been much worse if someone hadn't doused the burning fabric—and he felt as if every bit of his body that wasn't wet was covered in oil and soot. He'd briefly seen Clara's scared white face when she had brought in the tea. It hadn't been until now that they'd had a chance to gulp the cold brew. The captain himself had come down to see how things were going. Tim sat on some scrap and eavesdropped, glad enough to stop working and sit down.

"Yes, Captain. We can hold off on pumping, I think. It's a trickle now. If we go deeper and there is more pressure . . . I don't know," said the chief.

"They can see us underwater in the searchlights. There is a dreadnought and three destroyers en route to here. They should be here in three hours. Another two airships will be overhead with more drop-mines within forty minutes for the first, and an hour for the second. Before they get here we must be able to dive to at least beyond their visibility, and then run as fast as we can," said the captain.

"Give the glue ten more minutes, Captain," said the chief with a sigh. "But I must warn you the batteries are not fully charged. If we have more than eight hours' life in them, I'll be surprised.

"And we have a ten-hour run to the nearest Westralian port." The captain tugged his beard. "Ten minutes, Chief. And let's cut all other power usage to a minimum."

"Yessir. I might be able to get three or four of the Stirling engine sequence going, sir, but the compressors . . . well. No," said the Chief, grimacing. "So we just have to jury-rig a pipe direct to the snuiver, and settle for an old-fashioned coal fire. We can get it heated up with some naphtha . . ."

"Do what you can, Chief. We've got three hours to dawn. We'll need to lie up somewhere. Cover with camo and inshore on the bottom for the day."

Ten minutes later they dived, with almost no one in the engine room, for safety. But even outside the engine room Tim could hear water spraying onto the temporary sheet metal barrier they had put up. The glue wasn't holding out the water.

The boat moved, though.

A little later they went back into the wetness of the engine room. The submarine had risen to just under the surface, and the captain was making as much speed as possible. In shallower water the leak was back to a stream running down the wall.

Tim knew all too well from his lessons that with no compressors running the compressed air to raise the sub was limited to what they had already. Dive too often, and she'd never come up. He tried hard not to think about it. He settled in to work with Thorne and Matthews, on one of the Stirling engines. Others were busy on the other engines—there were fourteen of them, each with their own firebox and coal-dust pressure feed—and the chief himself was trying to see if any one of the three compressors could be salvaged.

In the distance Tim heard drop-mines.

"That's good," said Thorne.

"Why? That means the other airship must be here."

Thorne gave him a half-smile. "If they knew where we were, they'd save them to drop on us. They're probing. They've lost us."

Tim could only hope that that stayed true.

※

The interior of the submarine was dark except for the dim emergency lights, although they were under way. It made working in the galley difficult, and hot food for anyone out of the question. But Cookie broke out tins of ham, ship's biscuits, and tinned fruit for dessert, and fed people. "Outside a meal, life don't seem so bad, missy," he said. "Takes a brave man to face trouble, and they face it better with a full stomach. Work better too. I reckon feeding them is a good thing."

Clara did too, seeing the crew's faces in the dim light as they ate. She hadn't realized before just how important the people who merely made food and hot drinks were.

Then came a noise that was even more welcome than the easing that plates of food had given to the frightened faces. It was half-hearted . . . but it was an engine noise, not just the soft, near-silent hum of the electric motors.

Cookie beamed. "That chief could make an engine out of a dustbin lid. I've kept what bread I've got for the engine room sandwiches, and we've got biscuits too. See if the bridge can use some of those, or if they can come down to eat? Engine room lads get priority over officers right now."

So Clara ran up to the bridge.

"It doesn't seem to have occurred to them that we could be listening in," said Sparks to the captain. "Here are the coordinates, Captain, for the RAS *Calpurnia* and the RAS *Balmain*. The other airship is heading for Adelaide, as she's nearly out of fuel. The HMS *Portrush* is still half an hour from where they lost us."

"I assume they think we can't receive wireless signals from underwater, and the idea that we might have an aerial up on an aquaplaned float at low speeds has not occurred to them," said the captain. "Three degrees starboard, steersman. It's that or they are trying to deceive us, and it is a trap. Right now we need to take a chance, gentlemen. The *Portrush* will have hydrophones, and running on the Stirlings and whatever cobbling the chief has managed on a compressor now will allow us a little recharging time. We can also refill our purge tanks."

"Sighting breakers, sir," said the periscope man.

"Black Rocks. With any luck they'll think we've gone to ground at Coffin Island."

"Aren't we going to, sir?" asked Clara, forgetting she was merely supposed to be here on an errand.

"No. We'll make for the Halls Reefs," replied the captain. "We'll have three-quarters of an hour of running in daylight, but until the sun gets high enough, even the airships can't see very far into the water. It's a chance we'll have to take." Then he took in who he was speaking to. "Miss Calland. What do you want?"

"Please, sir, Cookie wants to know if he should send biscuits up, or whether the bridge crew can come to the mess to eat. We've fed the rest of the crew, sir, except the engine room. It's all cold, sir, but it's food," she said hastily.

The captain shook his head. "Tell him I'll send the men down in shifts. And he can use his burners again at the moment, while we're on the snuiver, just not the electrical equipment. He can send me tea and some biscuits up. And he's to send some food down to the chief and his men."

"He has kept the bread for them, sir," said Clara. "Just in case they needed sandwiches."

That actually managed to raise a smile from the captain and the bridge watch. "Then I think I will ask the chief engineer if he can let some of his men have some relief. We'll find more labour for the chief. Let them eat cold canned stew with the rest of crew."

"Um. It's ham, sir. Cookie said things weren't bad enough for stew." That actually got them to laugh.

Walking down to the mess again, Clara thought to herself how she had changed on this journey. When the Russians had kidnapped them, she'd been afraid, for herself and her mother. When they'd been trapped in the nets, and when she'd been stuck outside, she was afraid for herself again. In the Faroes, she had been afraid, afraid Tim might be hurt. In Rivas . . . she'd been afraid people might be angry, and afraid of being left behind. When Tim had been locked up, afraid for him again. When the mate had taken her prisoner, she hadn't been afraid, just angry, mostly with herself. Now . . . now she was afraid for everyone on the crew, and also for the boat. They were hers, and she was theirs.

Tim was glad to leave the engine room and the erratic clatter of the jury-rigged compressor for the mess. Just how long the compressor would survive was another matter. They were busy with a frantic rebuild of the second one. Tim was no artificer or engineer, but it looked hopeless to him. The chief had bullied and sworn one piece of equipment into working again, though; he might succeed again. They had to do it, Tim knew. They needed to be able to empty the ballast tanks if they dived, and, if they stayed down long, for their breathing while submerged below snuiver depth.

Tim had been told to eat and sleep—washing right now was out of the question, because it would take power—so he did. He was faintly aware of Big Eddie coming in. They'd stopped and the divers had been busy. Then when he woke again the "all quiet" light was burning, and the sound of drop-mines echoed eerily again. They weren't close, but even hearing them at all was too close.

When it was time to go on his watch again, Tim was glad to hear the sound of the compressor. It sounded, even to his ears, irregular. Then it stopped.

The chief, who looked like he hadn't slept at all, was standing and staring at it when Tim got down there.

"It's not going to go again. We'll strip it for parts for number two."

"Chief," said Lieutenant Ambrose's voice down the speaking

tube. "You'll need to douse the fires on the Stirling engines. We're going to have to dive below snuiver depth soon."

As they couldn't run off the big compressor tanks, the Stirlings were drawing their oxygen for the heat-chamber fire directly from the engine snuiver. The problem with that was that there was no buffer—the firebox drew air from the inside of the submarine too. So now Tim hastily joined the engineers and artificers taking shovels of hot coal out of the heat chambers, and dropping the coal into buckets of water—which of course generated much steam and hissing, but at least the fire wouldn't be sucking oxygen from the engine room.

It looked like hell, and it was pretty nearly as hot as that.

"Tongs and hot iron duty, lads," said the chief.

Tim grabbed the tongs from the rack and joined in hauling the bits of scrap iron from the fireboxes and pushing them into the unbolted heat casings of the Stirling heating chambers. It would let the engines continue, silently, for a little while. Then they would have to switch to the power in the battery banks.

"What charge have we got, Chief?" came the captain's tired voice down the speaker tube.

"If you keep it to four knots, Captain, we ought to have about three hours' running. If you go any faster, we'll lose some time," said the chief engineer.

"How is the new patch holding?"

"I think the pipe itself is fractured, Captain. There is still a bit of leakage coming through. We've got everything as dry as we can. It's only a seep at this depth. There's a chance it might be fine. It could also give in completely if we get any more shocks. The glue is not as flexible as the solder."

"I'll avoid sudden dives if possible. I can't guarantee them avoiding drop-mines," said the captain.

※

"Last bit now," said Cookie quietly.

He'd made himself and Clara both a mug of hot sweet tea, and then Clara's mother one too, when she had come out of their cabin to join them. Quietly, although the "all quiet" light did not burn yet, they sat together in the mess, with its solitary dim emergency light.

They waited.

Clara's mother reached out a hand to hold hers. Clara held it tight. It did not seem a childish thing to do now.

The amber "all quiet" lights in the Bakelite holders were not lit yet, but there were orders that the noise was to be kept to a minimum. Down in the engine room Tim knew that the *Cuttlefish* had been staying just below the surface so that they could use the remaining jury-rigged Stirling engines for as long as they dared. Looking at the engine he'd been working on, Tim knew that it had been more a case of which came first: the engines dying or them needing to dive.

They all looked up when the engine room door was opened. "Captain said to let you know, we're going to go down gradually," said Nicholl, quietly. "Wireless aerial is coming down. We have to sneak past a line of vessels blockading the passages to Ceduna. They're lying just out of reach of the Westralian batteries on St. Peter Island."

The submarine dived slowly. Tim—and everyone else—watched the leak.

"You greasers, watch your fingers. I'll watch the water," said the chief

The problem, when it came, was not from the leak, or the mines, or the nets, but from the batteries.

The chief looked at his dials worriedly. He touched Tim—who happened to be nearest—on the shoulder, as he waited to take his turn at the dangerous task of greasing the brass rods, and drew him away. "Go to the bridge, quick and quiet. Tell the skipper we've lost a set of batteries, and he's only got twelve minutes' power left."

So Tim ran, on his toes, to the bridge, where he delivered the message. He came back into the engine room to see red warning lights on the panels. And then, suddenly, came the boom of a drop-mine.

And another.

Not too close, but still shaking the boat.

And then . . . a cracking noise.

Water began running down the wall from the patch.

"Out. She's going to blow!" yelled the chief.

Tim joined the scramble for the engine room door.

Water was pouring into the engine room as he helped to close it and haul down the sealing bars with a loud clank.

Tim knew the hydrophones on the ships above them could not have missed picking up that crack or clank and the yells. Now they were crowded into the narrow gangway, wondering what would happen next.

The skipper must have heard the noise too, and reached his own decisions.

The *Cuttlefish* accelerated.

For a full three minutes the boat continued at top speed, despite the engine room being flooded. Tim, moving to his emergency station, heard the sound of more drop-mines. But there was nothing he could do—just regret that he was here, and that Clara was somewhere else on the submarine. It was all that he could do to stay where he was supposed to stay, and not go looking.

And then . . . all was still.

The only sound Tim could hear was his own heartbeat.

It was dark, and then the emergency lights came on, dimly. Their batteries were not in with the rest, but they too were low.

And then there was a torch coming down the gangway. It was the captain. The chief engineer saluted him. "Not sure what died first, sir. The batteries or the motor."

"We'll need to manually purge the ballast tanks, Chief," said Captain Malkis, his voice emotionless. "We'll wait until the hydrophones give us the best window. We should be in sight of St. Peter's Island now."

"It's to be hoped we've enough air to purge with the engine room full, sir," said the chief.

Tim did not need to hear that.

Clara couldn't take the waiting in the dimness, as the emergency light grew weaker, for one more minute. The air felt old and stale. Then she heard a party of submariners coming along. "Let's go with them, Mother?"

Her mother shook her head. "I am going back to my cabin. I am going to seal as many of my notes as I can in these bottles I have got from Cookie. Maybe . . . maybe they'll wash ashore, if we don't make it." She kissed Clara. "Go."

So Clara went. The smell of coal smoke more than anything else told Clara the submariners came from the engine room. To her delight and relief, Tim squeezed her shoulder. "Clara," he said, quietly.

She'd only recognized him by the voice. "What's happening?" she whispered back.

His answer wasn't encouraging. "Going to see if we can surface. Engine room is flooded. We're a hundred and fifty feet down, and slowly sinking."

They arrived at the manual purge wheels for the forward ballast tank. The big brass wheels that Tim and Clara had both polished in happier times gleamed in the light of the torch Thorne held. "Put the bar in, Barnabas. You've had the devil's own luck. Maybe it'll rub off on that."

Tim threaded the pipe bar, and they heaved in unison. "Two . . . six, pull!" said Thorne. "Again. Two . . . six!" and it turned. Clara wondered what was so magical about two and six . . . and why everyone was listening.

"Again," said Thorne, his voice a little high.

And this time they were rewarded by the hiss of compressed air being forced into the ballast tanks, forcing the water out. "We just don't have much compressed air," muttered Tim to Clara, holding her shoulder. She could feel he was shaking slightly.

Nothing happened.

And then, as they stood there, panic written on their faces . . .

The *Cuttlefish* began to move, terribly sluggishly, barely shifting.

"She's stuck down here!" said a panicky voice.

"Shut up," snapped Clara.

"Yes. Shut up," said Tim, backing her up, as always.

They waited for an eternity . . . of maybe thirty seconds.

The angle of the floor changed slightly in a sudden rocking movement. "Close it down," said Thorne, relief in his voice. "We don't want to come up too fast."

They heaved on the lever again, this time turning it the other way.

Now the submarine's floor began to tilt steeply. Her nose was rising.

"Second air-bleed wheel, gentlemen. And lady," said Thorne, his teeth white in the dim light. "And keep it quiet. Jump to it. Quickly."

They did. It was all Clara could do, though, not to cheer.

Gradually, the submarine rose slowly from her watery grave towards the light and air.

Lieutenant Willis came down. He pointed at the pressure gauge. "Stop at one-point-two bar, gentlemen."

"And lady," said Tim.

"And lady," said the young lieutenant with just a hint of a smile. "Your mother is on the bridge, miss. She's looking for you too. And the chief engineer wants all hands to the engine room, the rest of you. He's pumping it out, and the divers will be trying a patch, again.

Clara managed a squeeze of Tim's hand before following the lieutenant.

"Captain," said Clara's mother, when Clara got to the bridge and stood beside her. Her mother was pale and stood very erect. "I know that my daughter will support me in this. We'll give ourselves up if they will let you go. You know that they want me alive."

"I cannot ask that of you, ma'am," said the captain.

"I can," said her mother, with quiet firmness. "Get your wireless operator to contact them. Your ship and your crew deserve no less. And if you reach shore give my mother's trunk to the Westralians. Tell them that it is pressure that is the key to making ammonia— pressure and a catalyst."

Clara looked at her mother. Blinked back a tear from her eyes. Stood just as tall and straight, and nodded her head. She didn't trust herself to speak.

The wireless operator coughed. "Ma'am. Their orders are to sink the submarine and machine-gun any survivors in the water. Orders direct from Duke Malcolm."

Captain Malkis shook his head at the two of them. "Dr. Calland. If I let you and your daughter do this, my crew would hang me from the *Cuttlefish*'s mast, and I would tell them to do so. We've got less than a mile to go to St. Peter's Island. The hydrophones say that the nearest Royal Navy vessel is some distance off, and looking through the periscope, we think that they are at least another two and half miles offshore. The tide is carrying us back towards her, though. So, Lieutenants. Get our sail crews and every other man jack on this submarine ready. We'll surface, and see if we can get in under sail."

"They'll fire on us, sir," said Lieutenant Willis.

"Then it's a pity we can't return fire," said the captain. "Get to it, gentlemen."

"Me too," said Clara. "And please don't stop me, Mother. Captain."

"I wouldn't dream of stopping you," said her mother. "Seeing as I will be up there too."

It was bright sunlight outside, and the sky was cloudless and blue—
except for the haze of coal smoke on the seaward horizon. The shoreline seemed so close now, but still far too far to swim. The *Cuttlefish*'s
crew worked like frantic ants. Her masts went up faster than they
ever had before, and the outrigger hydrofoil pontoons were deployed
speedily. "They've seen us," yelled the lookout.

"Up sails," yelled Lieutenant Ambrose, ignoring the lookout.
"Haul men! Haul!"

The first gossamer sail rose and billowed, as they pulled desperately on the ropes.

A waterspout exploded some three hundred yards away, as, ever
so slowly, the *Cuttlefish* began to move forward. Clara hauled at the
next rope along with the others, sending the big gossamer sail
belling upwards.

They could hear the echo of the heavy ships' guns in the
distance.

And a shell blew right through the sail. Ripping it from one
side to the other,

"Well," said Tim, standing next to her. She hadn't even known
he was there, but he was, and that was how it ought to be. "It's been
good knowing you." He put his arm around her shoulders.

She turned to face him, held on to him, pulled him closer. "If
we're going to die . . . I just want you to know that . . ."

He nodded. "Me too."

And then, as they stood there, the sky itself seemed to catch fire.
Roaring like a thousand lions.

A sheet of fire and smoke leapt up off the sea a mile beyond the
*Cuttlefish.*

Smoke billowed and wreathed up around the Royal Navy
vessels.

Something exploded out there. Something loud enough to shiver the air and send a plume of steam above the smoke haze.

The crew stood staring.

"Shore rockets!" yelled Lieutenant Willis, his moustache nearly lost in his beaming smile. "The Westralians can and do shoot back! Get to it, you lazy scuts. Come on. Move! Move! Move! Let's get some more sail up! That means you too, you two!" he said, pointing at Tim and Clara hugging. "You're not going to die, so stop fraternizing, or I'll toss you both in the brig!"

"We've beaten them," yelled Clara, smiling into Tim's face, ignoring the lieutenant. There were times to think of the future, to worry about distances and parting. But those were for tomorrow, if there was one. "And I love you," she said so quietly that only he could hear it.

"Somehow, the *Cuttlefish* has done it, dears," said her mother, standing next to them, smiling too, looking at the shoreline. "Australia is close enough now. They'll not stop us."

And another wave of rockets sped overhead as the *Cuttlefish* crew cheered and hauled sails, and the sweet breeze took them inshore, toward safety. Already several small craft were setting out to help them, under the cover of a third massive flight of shore rockets.

There were no more shells exploding near them. The noise in Tim's head was just his heart, beating like a drum.

# APPENDICES

## GLOSSARY OF TERMS

**Bridge**: The control room of the submarine, where the periscope is, and where the officer in charge of the bridge (usually the captain or mate or senior lieutenant) controls the course and speed of the boat. This is where the instruments measuring pressure, speed, and other variables have their gauges, where navigation is done, and where the Marconi wireless and hydrophones are.

**Catfish-feelers**: The submarine has to travel in the dark through very murky water. It can push out long thin metal "feelers" with pressure sensors on the ends that can tell the bridge they're about to hit something.

**Companionway**: A steep metal stair between decks inside the submarine.

**Cowling**: A streamlined, somewhat raised covering over the main hatch.

**Crow's nest**: A wicker "basket" at the top of the mainmast—the highest lookout point on the *Cuttlefish*.

**Deck watch**: Lookouts posted fore and aft and in the crow's nest.

**Draught**: The depth of water that a boat needs to float. So a vessel with a shallow draught can operate in shallower water.

**Electromagnetic grapple**: A powerful electromagnet on the end of a cable. These enable the *Cuttlefish* to behave like a leech under a steel-hulled vessel.

**Gangway**: A narrow passage inside the submarine.

**Hydrofoil:** A "wing" (like an aerofoil) designed to lift the *Cuttlefish* so that most of the vessel is above the water, thereby increasing her speed, as there is less drag.

**Hydrophone:** Underwater sound receiver.

**Marconi wireless:** A radio transmitter and receiver.

**Monkey's fist:** A round knot tied around a small weight on the line thrown to the shore for docking.

**Outriggers:** Stabilizing extra hulls, making the *Cuttlefish*—under sail and hydroplaning—effectively a trimaran.

**Periscope:** A tubular device that uses prisms and mirrors to allow the observer on the bridge to see up out of the water, even when the submarine is just below the surface.

**Ratlines:** The horizontal ropes on the shrouds (ropes holding the mast up), that make a kind of rope-ladder up the mast.

**Shrouds:** The ropes that keep the mast up.

**Two . . . six pull:** From the days of whale boats, where the coxswain would call the stroke. Like the "left, right, left, left, left" of calling step for marching, the call "Oarsmen two to six, pull" gradually got shortened. So, no, it's not that sailors can't count.

**Snuiver:** A Dutch word for snorkel (which was a German word), which was used at one time to describe the pipe that drew air for engines from the surface.

**Stirling engine:** An *external* combustion engine. It is much more efficient than a steam engine, and merely needs a cooling area and a place for applying heat. It's been around since 1816, and has been used in submarines.


## ON THE WAY THE *CUTTLEFISH* WORKS

I've always preferred science fiction that could possibly work. The science of the *Cuttlefish* universe is supposed to be just that—science that took a different turning. The problem with coal-burning steam-powered submarines is that burning coal (or diesel, or gasoline, or sticks) consumes oxygen. This was a real problem for all submarines, up until the nuclear era. Submarines ran on the surface on diesel, and used their batteries to run on electrical power when fully submerged. There really have been Stirling-engine-powered submarines; they just didn't burn coal. They're very efficient and very silent.

Submarines got around the problem of needing to run on the surface—and thus being visible—by using snorkels or snuivers. The downside of this is that the fuel burn actually uses a lot of oxygen, to the extent that if a wave (or sudden dive) cuts off the outside air, the change in pressure (from the oxygen consumption by the motors) could burst eardrums. The *Cuttlefish* has a complex system allowing the Stirlings to run (briefly) off compressed air, or to run the air through a compressor buffer, or to draw directly from the surface, risking those eardrums. She has large banks of batteries allowing her to run off those, when submerged. (Lead/acid batteries are actually old technology.)

There are two problems that nonnuclear submarines face: First, the best shape for running on the surface (with a V-shaped hull) is not the strongest shape for diving. They must be as strong as possible, because diving is the most dangerous part of what a submarine does. And vice versa—the best shape for diving (shaped like a torpedo) is not good for surface running. And surface running is actually what a submarine does most of.

The second problem that submarines have always faced is that they are relatively small. They simply can't carry fuel for very long journeys, which means secret fuel supply depots and refuelling vessels are needed. This is an even worse problem with coal. (You need more coal for the same amount of power.)

What the *Cuttlefish* and her sister submarines do to deal with both of these problems is to take the same solution as diesel submarines in our timeline did, and take it further. They have a double hull: a thin outer one, to shape the submarine to travel on the surface; and an inner, torpedo-shaped hull, designed to resist pressure. But, as they have to travel farther with less fuel than our submarines, they are also intended to be able to travel under sail. To do this effectively, the outer hull is extended on rails, becoming outriggers (for stability), which then push out "wings" to make a hydrofoil, which allows the vessel to lift up in the water so that much less of her hull is submerged. (Water keeps the boat afloat, but it also provides drag.)

A wider "deck" is provided with nets and spars, making the submarine a hydrosailer.

A hydrosailer can achieve far higher speeds because the boat is effectively "flying" above the water, with just the hydroplane fins in the water. At low speeds, on its Stirling engines, the *Cuttlefish* would sail just like an ordinary ship.

The one piece of "impossiblium" used in the book is the gossamer sails. We of course have transparent sails, so it's not that impossible, but ours are the product of the plastics industry, and the plastics of the *Cuttlefish* world are not as advanced. Still, there are natural fibres that would do a good job.

*Cuttlefish* is a vessel, in other words, that can operate as a submarine, a surface coal-powered ship, and a hydrofoil under sail.

# A SHORT-SHORT HISTORY OF THE ALTERNATE TIMELINE FOR *CUTTLEFISH*.

Most alternate-history stories revolve around a battle coming out differently or a famous general dying—about military events changing the world. However, wars are not the only things that have changed or can change our world. Scientific discovery has done so far more often than wars. One chemical discovery in the early 1900s changed our world in so many ways it is almost unrecognisable. That invention was the synthesis of ammonia. Almost all modern industry and commerce rests on this: from computers to farming, from explosives to the paint on fishing boats. These days the Haber-Bosch process is as ordinary as a coffeepot, but when the method was developed it involved working at pressures that had never been achieved by several orders of magnitude. And the leading expert of the day said it was impossible. This discovery changed wars forever, changed who controlled the world, prevented more than half the world's population from starving to death. No war, no general, no president ever had this much effect.

*Cuttlefish*'s history branches not with a general changing his mind or being killed, or a battle going differently, but with a simple premarital argument in 1898.

Dr. Clara Immerwahr (a brilliant chemist and a very unusual woman for her time; she was the first female doctorate from the University of Breslau) had an argument about the purpose of science with her intended, Dr. Fritz Haber (something that would happen in the marriage and result in her untimely death in our timeline). As a result, she broke off the engagement. In this alternate history, her family, one of the leading Jewish families in Breslau, felt this a disgrace and sent her off to visit relations in England. In our timeline, Clara Immerwahr married Fritz Haber, remained in Germany, and her contribution to the synthesis of ammonia is unknown, although we do know she translated her husband's papers into English. We know it was an unhappy marriage, as Fritz expected this brilliant woman just to stay home and be a housewife, and the two of them disagreed about science and what it should be used for. Clara believed strongly that the purpose of science was to make the world a better place, and not for war. Fritz was a German nationalist and wanted science to help Germany, the Kaiser, and the German military might. In the end, during World War One, Fritz was the driving force behind German poison-gas warfare. His wife found this abhorrent, and they argued. Her death was recorded as suicide, with his service revolver. It is notable that Fritz's chemistry thereafter did not show the genius displayed in the synthesis of ammonia. In the *Cuttlefish* timeline, Clara Immerwahr never returned to Germany, married happily in Cambridge, had a daughter in 1907, and took a different direction within chemistry, working on fabric dyes. (Cloth dyeing, then, was an enormously important part of British industry, with huge fabric mills exporting across the world. Many dyes, like indigo, were very expensive, and had to be collected from natural sources.)

Fritz Haber never recovered from this blow. He began drinking too much, and changed his direction from working on the synthesis of ammonia to the extraction of gold from seawater (a direction he took anyway, after the apparent suicide—well, death—of Clara). While other continental scientists were working on ammonia synthesis, they were somewhat behind Haber, and whereas the Haber-Bosch process was up and running by 1911, and able to supply the German war machine with feedstock for the manufacture of nitrates, this was not true in this timeline. The British Empire controlled access to the main natural supply of nitrates in the world (the Chilean caliche deposits), and World War One was a very short damp squib (as it would have been without artificial ammonia synthesis). Despite their use of the Birkeland-Eyde process (a way of making artificial nitrates), the Central Powers, having badly hurt Russia, began to run out of munitions after four months—at which point it became a race between the Austria-Hungarian Empire, the Ottoman Empire, and Germans to see who could reach a peace treaty first, knowing that would be to their advantage. In our timeline World War One dragged on until 1918 with terrible loss of life and much hatred. The cost of reparations for it—a huge bill handed to the losers, especially Germany—planted the seeds for the rise of Adolf Hitler and World War Two.

In *Cuttlefish*'s timeline Austria-Hungary won that race, and suffered a minor breakup of their territory. The Turks found the cave-in fraught with uprisings and lost much of their empire to the French and English, or to the rise of independent states.

Germany . . . The British Empire was determined to see it did
not threaten them again. This meant breaking it up into states
again, and getting rid of Kaiser Wilhelm II. The "agreement" was to
allow him to have a mental breakdown, which would allow him to
"retire" gracefully. However, his abdication would have made his
sons rulers, and the British Empire was having no more of that. So
the remaining German states were placed under the regency of Adolf
Schaumburg-Lippe. This minor German prince, with his vivacious
very pro-British wife Viktoria (a granddaughter of Queen Victoria)
were so adroit at reconciliation and in dealing with the German
High Command that a Royalist uprising by Wilhelm II's sons was
successfully put down. France, however, seized the moment to
invade a small German principality.

Thanks to Prince Adolf—and especially to his wife—the British
Empire intervened on the side of their historic ally, Germany, in the
process mending many fences. The result of this was an arranged
marriage between Edward VIII of the United Kingdom (who in our
timeline married Wallis Simpson in 1937, and had to abdicate to do
so) and the daughter of Prince Adolf and Princess Viktoria (in our
timeline their only child was stillborn), Princess Alexandria, in
1916. And thus a new Imperial line was founded, in which the
German Empire and British Empire largely became one. Russia still
had something of a revolution—but the Mensheviks won. France,
having alienated Britain, found itself mired in colonial wars.

And the world had no synthetic ammonia, and the British
Empire, dominant in coal, saw to it that coal, not these newfangled
oil-derived fuels, stayed dominant. The Windsor-Schaumburg-Lippe
family controlled vast coalfields—and had the means to slap puni-
tive taxes on oil and control and tax the shipping of it.

Coal ran the Empire.

But coal is a very dirty burning fuel, and as Europe had neither
World War One nor the Spanish flu, it had many people and much
use. Emigration, particularly to Africa and Australia, went full

steam ahead. Colonialism and racism flourished. So did the massive infrastructure of a steam-driven world.

By 1935, things began to go wrong environmentally, just as the British Empire began cracking under the strain of too many people and too little food, as synthetic ammonia was the basis of much of the fertilizer used in our timeline. The coal-based society was pouring out massive amounts of soot (particulate carbon), causing substantial ice melting in the Arctic, particularly in Russia.

And that led to a methane burst (where methane locked in by ice or pressure reaches a point where a lot of it is released) in the tundra.

Methane is a short-lived (breaking down in the atmosphere) but very effective (around seventy-two times as effective as carbon dioxide) greenhouse gas.

This caused real environmental catastrophe. Massive melting of ice, more outgassing methane, a warmer world. Over seven years average temperatures rose seven degrees.

It proved a disaster for Earth, but the saving of the Empire. Governments failed to cope as heat waves ruined agriculture and their coastal cities and plains were flooded. World weather conditions were very erratic, causing the collapse of already-overstretched agriculture, widespread starvation, wars, mass migration.

Elected governments in many countries failed. Government was suspended, martial law imposed, in the British Empire with authority returning to the royal family. Military intervention was largely brutal and self-serving—except that the British Empire, with more military might and infrastructure than any rival, did a generally better job of restoring order and seeing people at least got some help. More if you were white and British, of course. In India the suffering was terrible. But Commonwealth countries who tried to go it alone—Australia, Canada, South Africa—rapidly became chaotic, soon begging the Crown to intervene and restore direct rule. Which it did, and managed to stabilize things over the next few years (as the weather was resettling, at hotter levels). The Empire had its finest hour—along with some colossal failures, but these were lesser than the disaster's impact elsewhere.

Slowly (by about 1942) things began to return to a new form of normal. A normal where London is largely flooded, but not abandoned. Like Venice, her streets have become canals.

The British Imperial House was not ready to hand back the power it had been given or taken. The Canadian Dominions, with vast new arable lands and new settlements in Newfoundland and Greenland, was a major engine for the Empire. The restive factories of India provided goods for the Empire. In Australia, the western settlements had suffered withering drought and had been abandoned by the Empire, with forced resettlement to the east coast and Tasmania.

At home Ireland seethed. And coal, the driver of the Empire, began becoming more difficult to source and more expensive. In the tunnels and tubes under the drowned city, anti-imperialist republicans and Irish rebels, part of the Liberty—the people who would see a return to older values and free elections—eke out a strange existence. They are served by a fleet of Stirling-engined submarines. After the 1914–1915 War, submarines were outlawed by the Treaty of Lausanne, as the Kaiserliche Marine submarines had inflicted considerable damage on the Royal Navy, and were thus hated. But the revolutionaries, the Underpeople, operate a small clandestine fleet smuggling illegal goods—chocolate, teak, quinine.

The year is 1953. This is when *Cuttlefish* is set.

# ABOUT THE AUTHOR

Dave Freer is a former marine biologist (an ichthyologist) who now lives on an island off the coast of Australia. Besides writing books he is a diver and a rock-climber and perpetually has his nose in a book when he's not doing those three things. With his wife, Barbara, and his two sons, two dogs, three cats, three chickens, and other transient rescued wildlife, he has lived a sort of "chaotic self-sufficiency and adventures" life, sort of down the lines of the Swiss Family Robinson, only with many more disasters. A lot of Dave's time has been spent (and still is) in small boats, or in water that no one in their right mind would get into, full of everything (sometimes entirely too close) from hippopotami (in Africa) to sharks (he was the chief scientist working on the commercial shark fishery in the Western Cape, once upon a time) and lots of interesting creatures like the blue-ringed octopus and a poison-spined gurnard perch. He's written a slew of fantasy and science fiction novels, some with Eric Flint; being a scientist, he likes the strange creatures and machines he comes up with to work.

You can find out quite a lot more at http://davefreer.com/